SHALLOWS OF NIGHT

Second in the
SUNSET WARRIOR TRILOGY

...in which Ronin, Bladesman, sails a sea of ice with Borros, called Magic Man; discovers an exotic city on a continent undreamed of; and surrenders willingly to the temptress Kiri in his quest to decipher the scroll that is Man's last and only hope...

ERIC VAN LUSTBADER

The bestselling author of THE NINJA is unequalled as a creator of worlds dark with violence, bright with erotic possibility, and shimmering with magic and grandeur. This three volume series is the first paperback publication of his sensational SUNSET WARRIOR TRILOGY.

Berkley books by Eric van Lustbader

THE SUNSET WARRIOR TRILOGY

THE SUNSET WARRIOR
SHALLOWS OF NIGHT
DAI-SAN *

*Coming soon from Berkley

ERIC VAN LUSTBADER

SHALLOWS OF NIGHT

Second Volume of the
SUNSET WARRIOR TRILOGY

BERKLEY BOOKS, NEW YORK

All of the characters in the book
are fictitious, and any resemblance
to actual persons, living or dead,
is purely coincidental.

This Berkeley book contains the complete
text of the original hardcover edition.
It has been completely reset in a type face
designed for easy reading, and was printed
from new film.

SHALLOWS OF NIGHT

A Berkley Book / published by arrangement with
Doubleday & Company, Inc.

PRINTING HISTORY
Doubleday edition published 1978
Berkley edition / December 1980

ISBN: 0-425-04453-X

A BERKLEY BOOK ® TM 757,375
Berkley Books are published by Berkley Publishing Corporation,
200 Madison Avenue, New York, New York 10016.
PRINTED IN THE UNITED STATES OF AMERICA

For all the heroes

Contents

There is no journey's end.

—Bujun saying

ONE

·Ice·

Soaring through frigid mists and roiling clouds, he stretches fully his long wings upon the unpredictable currents. Streamers of silvered plumage, running bilaterally across his wings and cresting his majestic questing head, ripple and blur in the wind. He banks and dips. There is a moaning in his ears. His large liquid eyes stare unblinkingly ahead at the immense eye of the setting sun, its face a broad and flattened disk, wider at the sides as if caught in a vise of immeasurable proportions. Then thick ribbons of cloud of a metallic gray ride before it like the ghostly remnants of a once vast, victorious army, reaving it.

He banks again, deftly avoiding a treacherous downdraft, and turns his incurious gaze beneath him, through the layers of cloud and mist, to the painful twisting of the earth far below.

High peaks beaten by age and scraped by merciless weather, crowned in bitter frost, sealed in pearl and emerald ice, thrust their humped backs in snaking lines against the whipping winds which, forever swirling, gather layers of fine powdery snow from the mountains' slopes, turning them into rising sheets, hurling them forward, like giants striding across the barren land.

He floats over sheer gorges, frosted thickly in gleaming sheets of periwinkle ice, plumes of loose snow drifting along their flanks like smoke from a funeral pyre. His keen eyes trace the vertiginous descent from dancing ice crystaled green-turquoise-magenta in

11

the dying light to the violent violet of their yawning and uneasy depths: precipitous chasms sliced out of the land as cleanly as if by a cruel blade of immense size. Powerful wings flutter as out of these depths now is heard the agonized groaning of shifting rock. Ozone and sulpher fill the air as the earth shudders and trembles. Shards of ice shear off in the dense clusters with infinite slowness, hanging impossibly in mid-air, crumbling in layers until, with an abrupt and complete swiftness, they explode silently into vast spurts of hyalescent spray high in the sky that turn to rainbow arcs as they catch the last oblique rays of watery light.

He wheels in the colored, suddenly solid air, unperturbed.

Everywhere is ice and draperies of snow with only the occasional tired fist of granite or twisted schist rising like ancient tombstones in an alien desert, useless punctuation on a blank and crumbling page.

Against this inimical icescape nothing moves.

The bird banks and glides in the sky, his black-irised eyes scanning the dreadful sameness of the land. Into the setting sun he flies, his majestic plumage stained a dilute scarlet and, glancing once more earthward, he sees a dark and tiny shadow limned before the glare of the ice. Muscles respond to the brain's command and the wings dip, their silver plumage losing for a moment the scarlet wash, turning a rich lustrous gray, as he heads southward for a closer look.

Resolution of image comes far too swiftly, for the shadow is huge. Abruptly it moves and, startled, the bird wheels away from the edge of the steep precipice along which he has been flying and, flapping his wings in alarm, speeds westward, rising, gaining the high currents, diminishing into the light of the lowering sun.

Transfixed, Ronin stands at the verge of the high

ice ledge staring southward, oblivious to the receding speck in the sky.

Motionless, his body tall and muscular, he appears more a statue erected to the countless legions who, throughout the myriad ages, have fought across the changing faces of this land. For here once grew lush verdant forests of giant fern and slender willow spreading their fans of feathered leaves, building dense jungles of crowding greenery and thick tangles of vines through which cocoa warriors crept and crouched, sweating, listening methodically to the shrill cries of startlingly colored birds, readying the leap, an uncoiling blur, tan and brown shadow, flickering in the filtering light, the quick silent slash, the gout of bright blood beading the foliage, the dying body of the enemy. And in another age—earlier or later, one cannot be sure—here swelled and sucked fifteen fathoms of green water alive with the riotous growth of the sea. High-booted feet tramped the stained tarred decks of wide-beamed wooden ships, long oars extending from their high curving sides, beating through air and water in hypnotic rhythm. Hoarse shouts filled the sky heavy with brine and heat as helmed and bearded warriors prepared themselves for battle.

Layers of hard snow encrust the slippery ice of the precipice upon which he stands, feet apart and planted firmly in the frost. Unconsciously he clenches his left hand, which is covered by a strange scaled gauntlet, dull and unreflective. The wind gusts, screaming in his ears, and rushes by him, unheeded, sucked in by the crevices and piled hillocks of the plateau tumbling at his back. The air is dry and chill. The staggering sight at which he gazes longingly resonates in his mind with the supravivid impact of an ecstatic dream. And for this time, the event of the recent past mercifully dim.

For what lies before and below him, just past the

13

beetling lip of the high ledge, is a cyclopean sea of ice. Desolate. Limitless. Awesome and electrifying.

"An overwhelming sight," said the voice quite near and behind him. And he turned slowly, as if in a dream, to behold Borros, the Magic Man.

"The true wonder is that we have been denied this sight for all of our lives." A thin and weary smile curled Borros' lips.

Wind whipped loose snow against their legs as they stood atop the ice plateau, strange creatures garbed in the one-piece foil suits they had found on the highest Level of the Freehold before each, in his own time and his own way, breached the last metal defense of their subterranean world, cracking the outer hatch, buried in drifting snow. The suits were extremely light, skin tight along chest and arms, with filled pockets of hardware and food concentrates, vacuum-sealed, immune to the ravages of time, even a small supply of mineral-enriched fluid to refresh themselves. These pockets ran around the suits' waists and down the outside of each leg, somehow increasing the warmth of the garments.

Ronin stared at Borros, seeing him now as if for the first time, the focus of reality at last forced upon him, and all the raw hate that he had held in abeyance for these long moments flooded back on an inexorable tide. Caught in the slipstream of sewage; shook himself, as if the motion would somehow cleanse him. He knew that he carried now within his depths an anger and a sorrow, that thus was bound to him irrevocably a hideous strength.

The Magic Man had misunderstood the gesture and he grasped Ronin's shoulder.

"Surely you are not cold?"

His fingers moved along the foil to a fold at the back on Ronin's neck. "Look here." And he pulled gently upward, the metallic skin stretching to cover

14

Ronin's head, leaving only his eyes and mouth exposed. Borros wrestled his own hood into place.

Borros turned to stare behind them, peering across the rubble of the frozen waste to the hidden Freehold, the tiny access hatch leading down and down to the world inside, a world at war now, factions struggling for desperate power.

"Do not think me a fool," the Magic Man said urgently. "But we must flee from here at once."

Tears call to Ronin and the mountains melting as he ceases to feel the bite of the wind at his eyes and lips. The sky colorless and the earth with no substance. His feet leaden. His heart pounding as it hit him searingly like the aftershock of a deep wound, the rent cauterized but the nerves still in dysfunction. At first there was no feeling at all. Numb. The body protecting itself. But there is a limit. His consciousness narrowed because he was struggling against it now. All his loves, all his friends, all the people. Gone in a wink of an eye. Just a flutter of time, the space to pull two breaths and lives are snuffed like tapers at first Spell. K'reen and Stahlig and Nirren and G'fand and—the Salamander, the center of it all, still down there, alive, alive. . . .

"—now."

Slowly, it seemed to him, he became aware of a plucking at his sleeve.

"Ronin, please, we must be off." He heard the words as if from a great distance. They hung in front of him like lamps, separate and solid, one after another, turning on some unseen axis, their sheen . . .

"Chill take it! Ronin, we must go now! Before pursuit from below can be organized."

Then the meaning had penetrated and he started as if from a deep slumber.

"Yes," he said hoarsely, turned to look at Borros. "Yes, of course we must be off." His colorless eyes

15

were clear now, their gaze sharp and quick. "But which way?"

"There," said the Magic Man. And he lifted his arm in a sweeping gesture outward, over the lip of the precipice to the enormous expanse of the darkling ice sea.

There was nought but the crying of the freezing wind. The ancient rock at his face, rippling, studded with ice in pockets and rivulets, slipped away above him centimeter by centimeter. The sound was like the wailing of the damned. Striations made a constantly changing pattern that held his attention as he searched for foot and handholds. Following Borros down the immense face of the cliff toward the ice sea far, far below, he felt all too distinctly the void at his back. The magnitude of its emptiness beckoned to him, the wind its siren call, ululating hypnotically. Relax, let go, feel the gentle parting of warm flesh from cold stone, to fall backward, slowly, effortlessly onto the comforting cushion of the wind, turning, to be borne away, tumbling, into the void. . . .

An ending he did not wish.

"What, over the edge?" he had said.

A peculiar animation had come to the Magic Man's face, a keen anticipation. "Yes. Yes! Do you not see?" As if he had waited all his life for this kinetic moment. "It is the only way down to the ice sea. Our way lies south. South into the land of men."

And so Ronin had walked with Borros through the crusty snow and treacherous ice to the very edge, entirely free at last of the ties that bind every man at one time to home. Masterless but not directionless.

They went carefully along the lip for perhaps a thousand meters and then Borros slipped over the side. Without a backward glance Ronin too quit the plateau.

16

Ronin became aware that Borros had stopped below him. He called down but the fluting of the wind made communication impossible at this distance. Carefully he lowered himself to the other's side.

"The way below is blocked," Borros said in his ear.

Ronin peered down through the intermittent showers of snow. Indeed, directly below them a fresh fall of snow and ice crystals layered the cliff face and it was impossible to determine the nature of the footing. Suicidal to attempt the descent by touch alone, yet it was imperative that they move onward.

Ronin swung his gaze to their right where his peripheral vision has registered a dark area along the rock wall. Now, motioning with his head, he led the Magic Man toward its smudgy outline.

They inched along the narrow ledge upon which they had stopped their descent and soon the dark area took on definition. As Ronin had hoped, it was a cave of some considerable size and within its mouth they found a semblance of shelter from the wind and the cold.

Borros sighed deeply as he pulled off his hood. His hairless skull, faintly gleaming in the dim light, seemed peculiarly fitting for this foreign and forbidding place; its singular saffron color could almost have passed for the patina of age.

Ronin went away from the rough rock walls to the lip of the cave. Below him the cliff dropped precipitously. Beneath the heavy fall of new snow clinging to the rock with an almost sentient tenacity there must be a way down to the ice sea. He could just make out a sliver of its surface sparkling in the lowering light. But from what he could see, there was no way of knowing, therefore no practical way down. Laterally there was only the mean ledge along which they had come. Farther to the right it disappeared into the rock face only meters from where he stood. He kicked at

17

the snow, left plumes arcing out into the wind as he returned to the twilight of the cave.

Borros was agitated. "What are we to do?" he asked Ronin as he stalked back and forth. "We must continue the descent. Already men from the Freehold will be searching for us."

Ronin's mouth moved into the semblance of a brief, chill smile. "Do you really believe that they would allow anyone onto the Surface? They must think that we shall perish out here."

The Magic Man's eyes darted from the cave's opening to Ronin's face, back again. "You do not know Freidal. Or Security. My escape—" His eyes flicked back to the cave's mouth. "He will kill me if he catches me." His gaze passed across Ronin's face again like clouds across the face of the sun. "You also. If he finds me, he finds you."

"No one is after us," Ronin said flatly.

Borros pulled his hood up over his bald skull. "You are wrong but it makes no difference. Even if Freidal was not coming after us, we would still have no choice. We must descend to the ice sea. We cannot survive long here."

"Better to die on the way down than here in the cave," Ronin said sardonically.

Borros shrugged. "Are you coming?"

He did not answer immediately but walked away from the light, into the cave's dank interior, smelling the acrid odor of raw minerals and rock dust, hearing the whistling of the wind diminish. Yet there was sound.

Far back in the cave he dimly heard the Magic Man's strident call but he ignored it. He listened intently, moving purposefully, his pulse quickening. And now he was sure. Excitedly he put his arms out, hands floating through the blackness, feeling along the wall like a blind man's.

18

He heard Borros calling thinly again, a forlorn and lonely sound, and he went slowly forward so as not to miss it. As last he stopped, his fingers running over the metalwork he had been searching for and his heart soared because he knew now that there was after all a way down to the ice sea. He called out to Borros.

What he had thought was the soughing of the wind had in fact been the distant sound of rushing water. The wind had been in his ears for so long that it was not until he moved farther back into the cave that he had been able to pick up the subtle tonal alteration. Even so, had he not made the long descent from the Freehold to the City of Ten Thousand Paths—the flicker of G'fand's smiling face frozen in his mind's eye, dissolving into the bloody wreck of the Scholar's corpse flung along the dusty cobbles of the ancient street, eyes bulging, throat torn out by the nameless towering thing that Ronin had tried twice to kill and failed, inhuman eyes like crescent moons, a chill more deadly than a coffin of ice and a power—he never would have recognized the new sound as a torrent of water pitching headlong over smooth rock down and down in a frantic cascade. He and G'fand had encountered the immense waterfall on their way to the City of Ten Thousand Paths and its reverberations had been with them for many kilometers. It was the same sound now, merely muffled by distance.

"Borros," Ronin called again.

They were obviously far from the cataract yet the presence of the sound was a clear indication that this cave was perhaps more than just that. Ronin believed now that they were in the outermost reaches of a tunnel. He thought of Bonneduce the Last, the small, lame man, and his companion, Hynd, a creature that was more than an animal. He and G'fand had encountered the pair in the City of Ten Thousand Paths. Bonneduce the Last had assured them that he and

19

Hynd dwelled on the Surface but had given no indication of how they had come to the City. Could this have been his entrance and egress? Ronin was certain that it was. Given that, the cave must contain a means to descend to the ice sea.

His hand wrapped around the haft.

Borros came up then.

"I have found something," Ronin told him. "Do you have tinder?"

The Magic Man reached into one of his pockets, produced tinder and flint. Together they lit the torch.

The flame, tiny at first, sizzled pale yellow and smoked on the damp material so that they choked and, coughing, were forced to turn their heads away. The orange light leapt and quivered and, wiping the water from their eyes, they were for the first time able to see the rough and gritty walls, black ice gleaming like obsidian in the shadowed hollows, the surface streaked ocher and green silver and pink by the exposed minerals.

Everything they needed was there, hanging by the metalwork of the torch's niche. Long coils of rope of a peculiar material not thick but, as Ronin pulled on them, obviously more than strong enough. Beneath the ropes, small metal hammers with long heads and with these bags filled with metal spikes of unfamiliar manufacture, flattened and broader at the end through which was punched a circular hole large enough for the rope to pass through.

"And so," said Ronin, "we descend the cliff after all."

His head whipped up and his nostrils dilated as the smell came to him. They had worked hard, on their knees driving the spikes into the rock floor of the cave just inside the mouth. They had inserted the ropes and tied double knots, leaning back and pulling hard to test the fastness of their handiwork. The small bags they had tied to their suits; the hammers dangled from their wrists by short thongs. Wrapping the ropes about their waists, they had walked to the lip of the cave. Ronin let the rope drop and his fist went to the hilt of his sword.

Before, it had been a stench when the monstrous thing came for them from out of the black shadows through the dry dust and golden dimness, its fearsome visage dominated by the glowing eyes and the curved, wicked beak. His stomach heaved at the thought of its invulnerability, the desperation of his attack as G'fand lay mutilated. The smell was like a living thing then. Now it was far off but, he surmised, reachable; it was getting stronger. He let the anger and fear mingle within him until it became rage. Adrenalin rushed through his body and he clenched his hand within the gauntlet left for him by Bonneduce the Last, cunningly made from the giant claw of one of the hideous creatures. How many of them were there? he wondered fleetingly. He began to withdraw his sword.

And felt the hand on his shoulder, heard the voice crying urgently at his side, "What are you doing? You fool, we must go now! There is no time to lose!" His hand tightened on the sword hilt. "Ronin, we must reach the ice sea!"

Instinctively he knew that Borros was correct. Their survival must come first. His battle would have to wait. And perhaps that was for the best. He wanted to be able to pick the time and the place when he would next meet the creature. But more importantly he needed more information about it if he was to have a real chance of killing it and surviving.

He let go the sword and picked up the rope, securing it once more about his waist. He nodded wordlessly to the Magic Man and they crunched backward through the snow. On the ledge the wind bit into the exposed areas of their faces as they went over the edge.

He hung suspended, dangling, the rope biting cruelly into his ankle. Momentum, he thought as warily they circled him, knowing their advantage but fearing him still. He had no weapon and of course that was the point. Because, as he had once told G'fand, learning the art of Combat meant much more than being taught to wield a sword.

His body, near naked and slick with the sweat of exertion and heat, swung along its brief orbit. Keep the body relaxed, the Salamander had told him. Work within as small a space as you feel you can allow without sacrificing the momentum provided by the orbit of the swing. You understand, Ronin, that once inertia takes over you are finished because an opponent will gut you in the time it takes you to overcome it.

Other students in the special Combat class presided over by the Salamander had attempted the *cruol*, that length of rope suspended from the ceiling to which one was tied head down a meter off the floor. Four students attacked with wooden staffs the length of a man's body. No one had survived for long. However, none of the students had been trained by the Salamander as extensively as had Ronin. And none had his skill.

Because it was so terribly difficult, the *cruol* was now used almost exclusively for punishment. Yet up here on the Salamander's Level it had other uses.

He kept the momentum going, consciously feeding the adrenalin flowing through his body, knowing he would need all that he could produce in the coming moments. A staff came at him, whistling through the air. He twisted his shoulders and felt a burning down his back at the narrowness of the miss. The students

22

fanned out, swinging at him again and again. He used his forearms to block the staffs, while gradually increasing the length of his arcs. Less and less, they found the need to advance toward him in order to make contact; they were too intent on the attack to take notice.

He swung, waiting for a peak, and for a lateral cut. He saw one coming from the left and he knew that it would be close because he was just at the peak of his arc and the student's blow had to be fast or he would lose the advantage of the momentum. But the staff came at him with tremendous force and it was all right because now he was beginning to arc away from the oncoming staff, his momentum picking up, and now, instead of blocking the blow, he reached for the blurred weapon, his tightening fingers slipping along its length in the slick sweat running off him. Palms burning with the friction, a blow from another staff numbing the muscles along his back. Ignore the pain. Concentrate. He used his mounting momentum and, twisting his wrists at the last instant, wrenched the staff from the startled student.

He was moving to his right with great speed now and, taking advantage of the direction of his swing, slammed the staff into the collarbone of a student on that side. He crumpled to the floor as Ronin began to reverse his arc and caught a second adversary in the mid-section so that the student doubled over, retching and gagging.

There was only one now because the one Ronin had disarmed was forbidden to interfere once he had lost his weapon. This one was wary. He would not be trapped as his fellows had been. Ronin noted that he was concentrating on Ronin's weapon. Then he attacked, swinging at the base of Ronin's staff, seeking to bruise his hands. The blows were rapid-fire so that, for every one Ronin blocked, one slammed into his

23

knuckles. They soon turned red and the first spattering of blood appeared as the skin split and tore. The student pressed his advantage, moving in, the bright blood fascinating and irresistible. His concentration narrowed.

It was then that Ronin used his free leg, slamming the sole of his boot against the side of the student's head. The man staggered, off balance. The blow had not been hard enough to knock him down because Ronin lacked the leverage, but it was enough. The staff sang through the air, catching the student on the neck. He gasped hollowly, his face turning white and his mouth hinged open as he fell. There was only the sound of forced breathing then as Ronin dropped his staff, relaxing his body, turning slowly again in his brief orbit.

Suspended in whiteness, his breath fogging the frigid air, descending hand over hand, Borros slightly above him a meter away, Ronin recalled well the lesson of the *cruol*. But now the context had altered, small patterns interlaced with other patterns until, as one steps back to view the configuration, an overall image begins to emerge, different, unexpected.

"My dear boy, of course they hate you."

The voice was rich and vibrant but with more than a hint of effete coyness that was as disarming as it was spurious.

"It is quite understandable, really."

The Salamander, the Senseii, the Weaponsmaster of the Freehold, stood in the doorway of Ronin's spartan cubicle. Not much time had passed since they had cut Ronin down and told him to return to his room.

Ronin moved to stand up but a curt motion, a flash of the Salamander's wide wrist, stopped him.

"Sit, my dear boy, by all means. You have certainly

earned the privilege." The voice flowed thickly, honeyed the air.

The Salamander, an immense figure, was garbed informally in crimson shirt, hung in layers which cunningly concealed the extent of his true bulk, jet-black leggings and high boots of the same color polished to glossy perfection. His rich black hair was swept back along his skull like the wings of some awesome predatory bird. His thick brows and high cheekbones managed in some unfathomable fashion to accentuate the large onyx eyes, oval, and as hard and opaque as stone.

He moved into the room and it seemed to shrink in size, a diminishing and insignificant background in his presence. He stared unblinkingly at Ronin.

"You are not happy here, my dear boy." It was not a question. "Perhaps this is because you feel that you have no friends."

"Yes," Ronin said unknowingly. "All the students hate me."

The Salamander looked at Ronin with a veiled gaze and smiled without warmth.

"But of course that is true and that should please you greatly. It does me." Ronin's face was blank with surprise but the Salamander ignored that. "You are the best, my dear boy; without question the very best student that I have trained. And now no one can touch you, not student, not Bladesman. Oh yes"—he laughed at the expression on Ronin's face—"that is quite true. You are as far above them as I am above you." His laughter took on a manic quality.

Ronin was acutely aware of the compliment. It puzzled rather than delighted him. The reaction was quite inexplicable.

The Salamander's fist clenched and his rings caught the light in brief explosions of color. He bent forward slightly, his voice less oratorical now, more personal.

"They hate you, my dear boy, because you are better than they, you have the talent that they wish they possessed, and they will not rest until they best you in Combat." His laugh was a bark of emotion. "Good! For that too serves my purpose. My Bladesmen must be the best in the Freehold." He touched his chest, a dramatic gesture he nevertheless managed to imbue with a certain grandeur. "Am I not alone of all the Saardin, Senseii? It is honor. What do the other Saardin know of that?" His voice lowered in volume and gained in intensity. "They know only to bicker among themselves, vying for power." He threw his head back and his eyes squeezed shut, then flew open, impaling Ronin with their implacable gaze. "They do not understand the meaning of the word 'power.' " He stopped abruptly, realizing that he had revealed more than he had intended. "It is honor," he said then, "that must be upheld always." He stepped closer to Ronin. "You must understand this totally."

He came and sat on the thin bed.

"But you, my dear boy"—a heavy bejeweled hand stroked softly Ronin's arm—"you also serve my purpose. I have labored long and hard to make you a Badesman unmatched by any bound to the Saardin of the Freehold. Tomorrow you will enter the Square of Combat for the last time as a student." His voice held a quivering note of triumph which he did not bother to conceal. "You will stun the Instructors who will be there to judge you and then, when you have emerged from Combat a Bladesman, the Freehold's finest Bladesman, while the Instructors and the Saardin are still babbling to each other of your skill, then you will return here to be my Chondrin."

A stillness eddied in the room, as absolute as a vacuum. For a time it ruled and then, quite slowly, it seemed to Ronin, the tiny background sounds of the Level returned to his ears, drifting male voices, the comforting slap of boot soles against the wooden floor, the distant metal clangor of Combat practice, sounds which had comprised the environmental context of his life for so long. Changed now, these noises came to him as harsh and brittle and without meaning, as if, of a sudden, he found himself in an alien world, wondering just how long he had been there. And looking into the glittery, obsidian eyes so close to his, he saw nothing whatsoever.

They dropped silently into the void, from time to time using hammer and spike to gain footholds along the sheer face of the cliff, or to circumnavigate an otherwise impassable section. It seemed that they had descended for hours, through the mist and the small snowfalls like choking dust storms flung against them by fierce updrafts. They paused neither to rest nor to eat, gulping handfuls of snow occasionally to slake their thirst, to keep them going.

Borros' urgency had become infectious. For Ronin it was perhaps the stench of the monstrous creature, still crawling in his nostrils, which had finally severed the twanging chord of his grief, once as raw and painful as an exposed nerve, and which now allowed him to focus on the reason for this journey. He had gone to the City of Ten Thousand Paths on Borro's urgings. The Magic Man was convinced that a terrifying menace was threatening to engulf the world of man. Perhaps Ronin only half believed him when he first journeyed forth but after encountering Bonneduce the Last and Hynd, after the battles with the thing that killed G'fand, he felt within him a peculiar kind of personal confirmation of what Borros had told him. And the journey had been successful. The Magic Man had sent him on a quest for an ancient scroll, which Ronin had found in the house of dor-Sefrith, purportedly the most famed and feared sorcerer of the legendary isle of Ama-no-mori, now no more than mounds of cracked stone and masonry beneath some far-off sea, Ronin mused. Pity. But I have the scroll now and, as Borros has told me, it is the key to stopping this inhuman menace. He smiled to himself. Despite Freidal's efforts, despite the Salamander's attempted interference. Only I have the scroll. He glanced at the thin face, drawn and haggard with fatigue, the yellow tinge sickly in the failing light. I have yet to tell him. That should bring a smile. And when we find out what it says, we shall return.

Ronin indeed returned from the Square of Combat a Bladesman. He had, as the Salamander had correctly predicted, stunned the Instructors and the Saardin, who had never before seen his like in skill and speed in Combat. Their excited talk sickened him. Yet in one important decision the Salamander would be proven wrong.

Ronin returned Upshaft to the Senseii's Level not in the least elated. He had had no doubts as to his ability and therefore felt no trepidation when it came time for his Trial. On the contrary he felt that the Salamander had dawdled over him, procrastinating, postponing again and again his Trial date. In his own mind, he had been ready many sign ago. Now it seemed to him that the date itself meant more to the Salamander than the Trial itself.

The Salamander was waiting for him in the Hall of Combat. His enormous figure was draped in ceremonial robes of jet. His hair was newly coifed and oiled and the fan that he could wield as dexterously and as fatally as a sword or dagger protruded from his wide scarlet sash. He wore a sword on his left hip, sheathed in a formal scabbard of openwork silver with an ebon tip, intricately carved in the shape of a rampant lizard on a bed of black flame.

On either side of him, dwarfed by his bulk, stood two of his Bladesmen. One held the bands which went obliquely from left shoulder to right hip across the tunic of each Chondrin. These bands were differing colors to identify which Saardin the Chondrin was bound to. The Bladesmen held black on black bands, the Salamander's colors.

The moment Ronin saw the bands, his decision was made. He knew quite clearly what he should do, what he had after all been trained for. He stopped before the Salamander and bowed stiffly, his face a mask, thinking, I know too what I must do. There was a great sadness within him. The Salamander inclined his head solemnly. He was more to Ronin than Combat Instructor, Senseii, Saardin. Yet still Ronin would have no man his master; would have no one now impose his will upon him, that time was surely passed forever. Free at last, he would not enslave himself within the complex political labyrinth of the Freehold society. He had his strength and power; he required nothing more.

"Now you are Bladesman," the Salamander said formally. Was there a trace of pride in his voice? Oh, surely not from the Salamander. "You are henceforth my vassal. You obey my commands; are subject to my disciplines, my ordinances, and my will. No other may command your arm or your mind so long as I shall live. In return, you have my protection, the power of my office as Saardin and my power as Senseii of the Freehold. In honor I offer you the bands of the Salamander, Saardin, Senseii of the Freehold, as my Chondrin, to advise, to defend, to command my Bladesmen, to obey me."

The Bladesman holding the bands stepped forward.

"Do you accept the bands of Chondrin and by so doing pledge your arm and your mind to me?"

"Salamander," said Ronin hoarsely, "I cannot."

"Not much more to go," Borros said over the crying of the wind. Ronin looked down. The mist and snow had thinned enough for him to see that several hundred meters below them the cliff face ceased its precipitous plunge earthward and became a widening slope upon which they could likely walk downward the rest of the way to the ice sea.

The expanse was lit now by the wan silver light of the moon, its mottled face hanging large and hungry in a sky of trembling cloud. Ronin stared at the oval, then back again to the ice sea still far below them.

And still they descended, though weariness gripped them like a tightening vise.

In the end it would be his face that stood out in Ronin's memory. For just an instant, a sliver so brief that perhaps only Ronin could have caught it, the seemingly impenetrable façade of the decadent and rather bored Weaponsmaster, refined and honed for so many years, appeared to crack and, like the onrush of a spring waterfall, sending rainbows into the light, a score of emotions seemed to dart across his visage. So quickly were they covered that Ronin could not even be sure. Had he seen sadness, shock, anger, hurt? All of them, Ronin surmised. He had been too wrapped up in what he had to do to understand then the larger pattern.

"You cannot!" bellowed the Salamander. "Cannot? What are you saying, you cannot? You will! You must! It cannot be any other way!" Still impaling Ronin with his furious gaze, he reached out, clutched at the Chondrin's bands, waved them at Ronin. "You mock this trust! Just as you mock me!" His face was red and spittle flew from the glistening surfaces of his wet lips. He crumpled the bands and threw them in Ronin's face. Ronin felt unable to move or to speak.

The huge face quivered before him. "You cannot?

You do not even understand the meaning of those words." He raised a huge fist. "I saw in you what no one else could, what you yourself were blind to. It was *my* vision which created you, *my* ideas which molded you into the Freehold's finest Bladesman." His voice had risen in volume and force; now his entire frame shook as if within him a fierce storm raged. "I trained you, accepted you, offer you the highest honor!" He advanced on Ronin. "And you spit in my face!" The voice was a shriek now, echoing off the high walls. Abruptly he swiped with the back of his hand, the motion so swift that Ronin could not have reacted if he had wanted to. But he had not wanted to; he knew with a chilling finality that if he moved at all he was a dead man.

The blow caught him full on the face, the rings scouring his cheek. It was a gesture of disdain and that hurt him more than the enormous force of the blow, more than the cuts opening up the skin of his face. Those would heal eventually.

"You do not understand. You know nothing of honor!" The Salamander hurled the words out as if they were somehow tainted. Then he hit Ronin again, and a third time with his hand now a clenched fist, crying out in rage because Ronin would not fall, would not retreat, would not retaliate. "How dare you! How dare you!" A litany of humiliation. Pounding at Ronin. Now his Bladesmen attempted to restrain him. He shook them off like droplets of water.

"Get away from me!" he screamed. "Get out of here! Get out!" And they scrambled obediently from his presence.

Still he beat Ronin, howling "Aaahhh!" beyond coherent speech now, staggering, irrational, inhuman.

He reached thick fingers into his sash, grasped the fan, about to draw it forth, spread its lethal edge, a supple guillotine. Then he stopped, his breathing hard and irregular.

"No," he gasped. "No. That would be too easy." His hand came away empty and, turning, he lurched out the door.

Ronin stood in the center of the Hall of Combat, hearing the susurration of his harsh breathing like the pounding of wild surf upon a desolate shore, his head and torso aflame with throbbing pain he only dimly felt, and thought, Now we are both shamed.

"What now?" Borros called to him.

They twisted in the air. Some twenty meters below them beckoned the lower slopes of the cliff. But they were, literally, at the end of their ropes.

"We are short," said the Magic Man. He kicked at the rock face to stop his twisting; it only made it worse.

"Quit that," Ronin said. "Relax your body."

"I have no strength left," Borros called pitifully, "I am exhausted."

"Then save your breath," Ronin said reasonably. He peered down again. In the uncertain light, as dense clouds rode across the moon's pale face, he could just make out the blanket of new snow covering the upper slope. But how deep was it? he asked himself. He took the small hammer off his wrist and let it go. It hit the snow and disappeared. He unhooked the bag of spikes and dropped that too. It hit the snow near the spot where the hammer went in and disappeared. Only one thing left to do, he thought. And let go the rope.

He heard a scream and it confused him momentarily and then he was into it, under it, its weight upon him, and he could not breathe and the blackness was a suffocating mass around him, above him but he pushed up, straining and clawing, and broke the surface, inhaling the chilled air in great lungfuls. He felt ice and rock beneath his feet.

The scream came again and he knew that it was Borros.

"All right, Borros," he shouted, cupping his hands by his mouth. "I am in the snow below you. Can you hear me?"

The sobbing of the wind.

"Yes."

"Let yourself drop. The snow will cushion your fall."

"I am afraid."

"Close your eyes and let go the rope."

"Ronin—"

"Chill take you! Do it!"

He heard the crunch against the crisp top layer of snow and was already moving, using sound as well as sight, as fast as he could to the spot. But the deep snow pulled at him and he panted, thinking of the Magic Man's exhaustion, knowing that he would have to pull him free very quickly or he would suffocate.

The undulating expanse of snow was albescent in the moonlight. He waded through it, tired himself, and stumbled, face in the snow, and instinctively pushed up with his hands, sinking deeper into it. Then his brain began to function again and he pushed this time with his feet and knees against the ice and then he was up. He located the darkness of the hole, went to it and dug down hard, shoveling desperately with his fingers, feeling at last the body like a dead weight, and hauled upward now with all his strength, hauling at a weight that seemed inordinately heavy, feeling time slip away beneath him, willing his fingers not to slip.

Borros came up slowly, like an ancient galleon buried beneath a sea reluctant to part with its prize, and as soon as his head came into the open Ronin slapped it. The Magic Man coughed and sputtered and half-melted ice drooled from his slowly working lips. Ronin picked him up.

"All right," Borros whispered, so softly that it could have been the moaning of the wind. "I am"—he choked, caught himself, then inhaled his first deep breath—"quite all right."

Ronin shoveled snow with his arms, making a shallow depression along the lee of the slope just below the sheer face of the cliff, an implacable wall lifting black shadows, it seemed, into the reaches of the tremulous sky. Deep enough for them to huddle, taking respite from the constant bite of wind and frost while they rested. Borros attempted to rake out several small packets from within his suit but his hands were shaking badly and Ronin had to lift them out, feed Borros as he fed himself.

Across the trackless slope they went dazedly, down, ever down, the wind blowing the drifting snow into their faces mingled with sharp-edged ice crystals as the temperature plummeted. Their lips were frosted and their eyebrows and lashes rimed with ice. Beneath their hoods, their cheeks were already numb. Still they moved painfully onward and when Borros fell Ronin bent and lifted him, the weight as nothing now. He half dragged him, stumbling, along the downward slope, through the drag of the heavy snow, deaf from the wind and then blind in the night, animal instinct alone lifting one foot after another onward, onward. . . .

His first thought was the warmth and he recalled a fire leaping and logs crackling and the cheery orange glow. He tried to move closer to the warmth and could not budge. Through a thick haze he understood that something was wrong. One side of his face was warm and—— With a start he realized where he was, that he was face down in the snow. With infinite slowness he lifted himself centimeter by centimeter until he was sitting up. He touched the side of his face eventually and discovered that it was numb.

Even then, when it occurred to him within the context of reality that they might die, he would not give in to it. He went to his hands and knees, saw Borros lying beside him. He was facing the way they had come, away in the distance the solid rock of the awesome, towering cliff down which they had made their descent.

He tried to stand and slipped, sliding downward along his belly. It took him several moments to realize. Then he looked down, oblivious suddenly to the freezing cold and the harsh bite of the wind. He reached out with his hands, felt the ground.

Smooth.

"Borros," he called in a cracked and dry voice.

Smooth and flat and hard.

"Borros!"

And he turned his face, then his body, until he was facing southward and he beheld the enormous glowing expanse of the ice sea.

"We are here!"

Heat fled up his arms from his finger tips into his shoulders. The image of the flame, dancing lazily from behind the small grating, was hypnotic. The gentle bumping, the soft creaking, a soporific. Across from him, Borros was already asleep, his utter fatigue taking him. Ronin felt the swift motion under him, knew sleep was almost here. Almost.

They had lurched, insensate, down the final series of low slopes, to the very edge of the ice sea, without knowing it. There at its banks they had collapsed.

At first Ronin had believed Borros delirious when he had revived him and the Magic Man had told him

35

at last the secret of survival upon the ice sea. Impossible. But already Ronin was learning to ignore that word, for he had been through so many seemingly impossible situations, seen so many startling sights, been forced to readjust to many of the concepts he had originally been taught, this was but a momentary reaction. And too it was their only hope of survival upon the world's forbidding surface; he lost no time in useless queries, he began the search.

It was easier than he could have imagined. Barely a thousand meters from where they had fallen, he found the small headland that Borros had assured him would be there. Mounded in snow many times higher than any area near it, it jutted out into the ice sea. And feverishly now he began to dig.

Moonlight, pale and glittery against the smooth surface of the platinum ice, revealed to him what Borros had told him he would unearth.

Even so it came as a shock, a current like lightning racing through his body momentarily thawing the chill. He began to dig harder now that the outlines had been uncovered and at last he was through and he turned and brought the Magic Man, a muscular arm across his back for support, so that they could both see it together.

The mist had risen, diffusing the monochrome light, but above the moon was riding free, its intermittent cloud cover racing westward. Of this fact they were oblivious as they stood, captivated by the image which loomed before them.

It was sleek. Long and curving, raised on slender runners.

"A felucca," Borros breathed almost reverently. "They did not lie." There were tears standing in the corners of his eyes. "For years I read and dreamed and, when I was sure, I promised myself that one day—" He shook his head and the tears flipped to the piled snow of the promontory. "But now I see that I was not so sure after all, a doubt remained. Until this moment. Oh, Ronin, look at it!"

It was a ship. An ice ship.

Slowly they went on board, explored the high prow and the sweep of its beam all the way to the low stern; they strode along the smooth deck, ran frozen fingers across the top of the low cabin aft rising just above the gunwale.

They went below, finding narrow berths with blankets along the hull, and a black metal oblong in the center of the cabin. Ronin took tinder and flint and, on Borros' instructions, opened the small hinged grate in the front and sparked a flame. The fire came instantly to the interior and Ronin, closing the grate, was too grateful for the warmth to inquire about the fuel source.

He put Borros on a bunk, listened to him talk for a short time, then went on deck. He took the mast from its storage rack along the port sheer-strake and set it in its place just astern of midships. He set the yard, low down on the mast. Then he went over the side and hacked at the metal chocks holding the runners in place. When they were freed, he went aboard and unfurled the high sweeping lateen sail.

Coming down the low slopes, the wind had been off the sea, into their faces. At some point it had turned and, picking up velocity, was now whipping almost due south. Ronin, setting the last of the rigging, thought, Now there is nothing more to do. Borros assures me that we need not stand lookout this night, that there is clear sailing. Does he really know, I wonder?

At that moment there came a powerful lurch and, as the sail caught the wind, the vessel, now standing clear on its runway of ice, was launched upon the ice sea.

Ronin, fatigued and unprepared, fell to the deck. Moving cautiously to the stern, he hauled hard on the wheel and lashed it tight as Borros had instructed him. They flew along the ice due south, the stiff wind billowing the sail, pushing them. He stared ahead for a moment, but the moon had disappeared behind racing clouds and new mist was settling in. Nothing more to do. With a final glance at the fastness of the rigging, he went below.

Sleep.

"Tomorrow night."

A small squat lamp hanging from a beam in the cabin's low ceiling had been lit. It swung with the ship's motion, shadows fleeing across the bulkheads.

"What?" he said thickly.

Through round crystal portals set in either bulkhead he saw that it was still dark out. It was warm and comfortable here and he closed his eyes, sighing.

"We slept through the night," said Borros from his berth across the cabin, "and all of the next day." He smiled wearily. "I got up once and it was near sunset, that is how I know. I went on deck and found that the wind had changed slightly. We were running more to the west than I wanted, as close as I could tell—the sun sets only roughly in the west—so I reset the wheel." He stood up carefully. He looked thin and gaunt. "Hungry?" Ronin opened his eyes.

They ate voraciously from the stores on ship; concentrates with unsatisfying flavors, but they filled the belly. Abruptly he remembered the frostbite of his face but, lifting a hand, he could feel no burn or discomfort.

"The ancients anticipated that possibility also," said the Magic Man. "You will find a packet of the unguent in one of the pockets of your suit. When I woke yesterday, I fixed us both up at the same time." He smiled almost apologetically. "I did not see the need to wake you." He lay back on his bunk, as if the talk had weakened him.

"Are you all right?" Ronin asked.

The Magic Man lifted a slender hand. "Only—it will take me somewhat more time than you to recover." His lips turned up again in a watery smile. "The disadvantages of age, you understand."

Ronin turned away. "I have a surprise for you," he said.

"Ah, good. But first you must tell me of your journey to the City of Ten Thousand Paths." Ronin looked back at him in time to see the sorrow and regret in his eyes. He shook his head ruefully. "I am so sorry, Ronin. I sent you on a madman's quest, an impossible—"

"But—"

"They told me about G'fand—"

"Ah." His heart felt as cold as ice. "Did they?"

"Yes." He grimaced. "It was part of my treatment. Freidal had already subjected me to such prolonged physical torture"—unconsciously his thin fingers sought his forehead, where before Ronin had seen the terrifying marks of the Dehn spots—"in trying to pry out of me all that I knew of the Surface, that he felt it was time to change tactics. I knew all along that I had sent you down to the City of Ten Thousand Paths and he could have stopped you at any time—"

"He wanted to see what I would return with, since he could not break you."

But Borros was not listening; he was remembering. "He was so clever, Chill take him! He came in and told them to stop; gave me water and let me rest. Told me that I had been through it all and had not given in; that it was useless for him to try any more. He—he said that he admired me"—his voice turned to a tremulous fluting—"that as soon as I had recovered, I

39

was free to go." He passed a frail hand across his eyes as if the gesture would blot out the nightmare that played in his mind and which, compulsively now, spewed from his mouth.

" 'Oh, by the way,' he said, as if it were the last thing on his mind, 'we have taken Ronin into custody. He has just returned to the Freehold after making an unauthorized exit. We have asked him quite politely where he went, after all it is a Security matter. The safety of the Freehold is at stake; if he can egress, others may gain entrance. So you understand that we must find out where he went and why. It is a matter of utmost importance.' Freidal sighed. 'But so far he has been most reluctant to accommodate us. He refuses, Borros, to do his duty to the Freehold. You understand what must be done now.' I did indeed; he meant to use the Dehn on you. 'His disrespectful actions leave me no choice. Oh yes,' he said then, 'I almost forgot. The young man who accompanied him—a scholar, I believe—G'fand—was killed. Unfortunate, but scholars are hardly essential to the stability of the Freehold.' "

Borros shifted uncomfortably on his berth but found no surcease. His eyes were still turned inward. "Freidal was furious that I did not crumble then, as he had hoped, so he"—the Magic Man's thin frame shuddered—"he had Stahlig brought in. He had his daggam drag Stahlig in front of me. Someone held my head so that I could not turn away; they hit me when I tried to shut my eyes." He lifted his head, the narrow skull shining like ancient bone, his eyes lusterless. "When Stahlig looked at me—I have never seen such terror written upon the face of a human being." He let go a suspiration then, and it all came out. "Freidal said to him: 'What is it that you fear most, Stahlig? The loss of your feet? Would you care to crawl through the Freehold on your knees? Perhaps your eyes. Do you fear blindness? No? I could break your back then; leave you alive, alive and immobile.' And seeing the look in Stahlig's eyes, he continued: 'That would be most fitting, would it not? Your friend Ronin left my man Marcsh with a broken back. But you know that; you treated Marcsh. You will be totally helpless; to be fed and wiped like a baby.'"

The wind, muffled somewhat by the cabin's bulkheads, moaned mournfully, momentarily drowning out the soft scraping sounds of the runners gliding swiftly over the ice, as if it too was witness to the horror that the Magic Man had conjured.

Borris put his head in his hands. "In the end," he whispered so softly that it was like a ghost's breath, "Stahlig died of fright."

There was silence for a time save for the moaning and occasional creak of the fittings abovedecks. Ronin lay back on his berth and tried to think of nothing, but his brain was on fire and he got up and went silently up the short vertical companionway.

The small ship shot through the mists of night ever southward. Ronin, on deck, could see nought but the blurred shadows of the ribboning ice as it sped by beneath the vessel. It was a quarter wind which now propelled them and he busied himself learning the fundamentals of tacking into it, working hard at the rigging to keep them on course.

He went aft and freed the wheel, steering manually for a time, letting the vibrations flow from his hands into his body borne away on an imaginary tide. The endless gentle soughing of the runners peeling a thin film of ice below stood by him like a spectral companion.

The wind strained the sail. Already the weather was changing, the air wetter, denser than before and, because of it, the cold seemed fiercer, creeping beneath

41

the skin into flesh and bone. At length Ronin lashed the wheel to and, taking a last deep breath, went below.

Borros lay on his berth staring blankly upward.

"The surprise, Borros," Ronin said gently. "I have not told you what it is."

"Uhm."

"Do you remember why you sent me to the City of Ten Thousand Paths?"

"Of course, but—" He sat up so suddenly that he barely missed hitting his head on a beam. Color had returned to his yellow face. "You cannot mean—" At last there was a light kindling his eyes. "But Freidal had you and—"

"And the Salamander also; his men took me from Security." A wintry smile broke out on Ronin's face.

The Magic Man's mouth opened soundlessly.

"And?"

Ronin laughed then, for the first time in many cycles. "And? And? Freidal found nothing, though he was justifiably curious about this"—he lifted his strange gauntlet—"and the Salamander lacked the time to find anything—"

"Are you telling me that you actually found the scroll? Ronin, you have it?" Borros came excitedly across to him.

Ronin withdrew his sword, grasped the hilt, and twisted it three times. It came away in his hand. From within its hollowed-out recesses Ronin gently pulled forth the scroll of dor-Sefrith. He handed it to the Magic Man, who delicately opened it and stared, breathing, "You *have* found it. Oh, Ronin—!"

He gave Borros several moments before he said, "Now you must tell me what it says and why it is so important."

Borros looked up at him, the flame from the swinging lamp reflecting in his eyes, turning them colorless.

"But you see, Ronin," he said in a tired voice, "I do not know."

There was a time—he could actually force himself to remember that far back in the dim and cloudy past, though he rarely wished to—when Stahlig, the Medicine Man, was not a part of his life.

He had fallen down half a flight of stairs, choked with rubble and debris. Exploring. As he had come to a landing, something had shot across his path, tiny nails clicking industriously, and he had lost his balance, tumbling down the Stairwell.

He might not have been hurt at all if it had been clear. But he had fetched up against a fallen girder, twisted and red, his leg slamming into its side where it lay slashed through a rent in the outer wall. Perhaps he passed out from the pain. Eventually, he got to the Medicine Man on the next Level, limping and crawling because no one was about to help him.

His left leg was broken but he was young and strong and Stahlig knew his business. It was a clean break and with the white end protruding through the torn flesh appeared worse than it in fact was. The bones knit perfectly but that became secondary to him. Stahlig talked to him while he went about setting the leg. That was what interested him, intrigued him, what, ultimately, caused him to return to Stahlig's med rooms whenever he was able. The Medicine Man had no reason to treat Ronin in a special way, yet he did, recognizing somewhere within him a potential others would not.

The two became friends and the reason did not matter at all, at least to either of them. That did not mean that it did not go unnoticed in some quarters of the Freehold, noted, written down, filed away for future use.

We accepted each other, Ronin thought as the ship

rocked beneath him. And now you have joined so many others who have known me and because of it have died.

Outside, the wind was rising, plucking at the rigging in mournful melody.

"You do not know?" echoed Ronin without emotion. "What have you done to me?"

Borros put the scroll back into its hiding place in the hilt of Ronin's sword. He rubbed his eyes.

"Sit," he said, and put his hand on Ronin's shoulder. "Sit and I will tell you all that I *do* know."

In ancient times, when the world spun faster upon its axis and the sun burned with energy in the sky, when multitudes of people roamed the surface of all the planet and, beneath their feet, the land turned from dirt and high grass plains as they walked, to fields of rowed food plants green and golden in the sunshine, to arid deserts smeared with low-growing flowers of many hues, to steep windswept steppes and mountain ranges blue with haze, when high-prowed ships from many nations plied the seas in search of trade with new lands, then Ronin, then we were known by another name. We were scientists and then our work was highly empirical, our theorems coming almost exclusively from the forebrain. Are you familiar with the word 'empirical'? Ah, good. Methodology was our watchword, this strict catholicism a firm and supportive base for our work.

But times changed radically and the world of the ancients was disappearing. In that interim period, the world was seized by a progression of natural cataclysms. The continents broke apart and fell away to be replaced by others, rising steamily from beneath the boiling seas. As you may well imagine, many people died but, perhaps more importantly, at the same time the laws that had heretofore governed the world of the ancients were overthrown and destroyed. Others came into being.

The inconceivable had occurred; by what means it is impossible to say, nor is it entirely germane to this account. Still, whatever formal records of that time ever existed are lost now—what remains are but fragments pertaining to the world as it was before.

Naturally, among the living were numerous scientists, yet so tied were they to the bedrock of their empiricism that, though it was clear to many others that the world had irrevocably changed so that the old methodology now worked only sporadically, the scientists refused to listen.

Certain members of these others, born to the new order of things, were able to make, because they had not been trained in the traditional ways of man, the great leap forward in thinking. These then became great mages, as they explored new methods, discovering alchemical, then sorcerous pathways, shining like beacons in the night. So they grew in power, at length banishing the scientists whom they scorned and ridiculed as they threw them down. Then they took upon themselves the mantle of overlords and in so doing lost sight of the original goals of their creation. Irresponsibly, they began to vie with each other for territory and power.

The inevitable holocaust of their quarreling spread throughout the world. The destruction was ghastly; its extent blossoming to unthinkable heights. Many people went underground. The City of Ten Thousand Paths came into being in this way. It was an attempt to form a peaceful society composed of members of all the surviving nations.

But among the populace of the City of Ten Thousand Paths were both mages and scientists, and they were ever at war. It is said that of all the mages only dor-Sefrith of Ama-no-mori remained unmoved and uninvolved though both sides desperately sought his considerable power.

From the time of the holocaust onward, there was of course an attrition of knowledge and each succeeding generation learned less and, eventually, when even dor-Sefrith's long neutrality ceased to maintain the uneasy peace, factions broke away, tunneling upward through the mineral-rich rock to form our eventual home, the Freehold, only residues of each side's knowledge remained.

We became the Magic Men, not-scientists, not-mages, struggling with but scraps of the methodology of both, learning languages long dead, convoluted equations which we neither understood nor would likely work under our present laws. And even if we grasped the tatters of the ancient concepts, even if we were somehow able to piece together the scattered information to make a coherent whole, we lacked the resources—our Neers so ill-trained that they could not even repair the essential machinery of the Freehold, let alone building for us the machines we would require—to accomplish anything.

Most of the Magic Men languished until enterprising Saardin began to see that we had a limited usefulness in the Freehold's power struggle. Then, one by one, the Saardin sought us out for affiliation. It was the end for us. From noble beginnings, we had been reduced to the lowest level, devising projects for the Saardin to increase their power.

I turned my back on them and for many sign would not even step onto their Levels. I spent my time with the remnants of the scholars, on the twenty-seventh Level, studying as best I could the lore of the ancient world, so that I might regain for myself some semblance of my heritage.

But the more I read, the more convinced I became

46

that we were a dying race, strangling in our own mingled blood, indolent, inbred, incestuous.

"G'fand felt the same way," Borros concluded.

"You knew G'fand?" Ronin asked.

"Oh, yes. He helped me quite a bit in deciphering many of the ancient codices. There were revelations each cycle, but everything was in fragments and too often we were only tantalized by the pieces we had managed to decode, discovering afterwards that they were isolated passages, their beginnings and endings lost."

"I remember," said Ronin, "that when we arrived in the City he would stop at every corner to read the glyphs carved into the buildings."

The Magic Man nodded. "Yes. I can imagine his excitement. Such a storehouse of knowledge." He reached into a cupboard under his berth and pulled out food concentrates. He offered some to Ronin, who shook his head, then sat and munched thoughtfully for a time.

"One day," he said—his voice had a thin far-off quality now—"we came across a rent manuscript. It was frightfully old and so desiccated that it took us more than three cycles to carefully clean it enough so that we could begin to read the glyphs and restore the missing characters. Then G'fand set about deciphering it and I lost interest as I was involved in a project of my own at the time. Several cycles later he came to me saying that he could make no headway at all; the glyphs were totally alien to him; they bore no resemblance to any language he had studied.

"I laughed. 'Well, what can I do?' I said. 'You are a far better translator than I.' 'I do not know,' he said, 'but come take a look in any case.'

"The glyphs which were so baffling to him jumped out at me with such vividness that I had to conceal my surprise, and for once I was grateful for my peculiar

47

training. For this codex was written in one of the forgotten—and I had supposed useless—languages which I had learned as a child.

"The codex foretold of a drastic shift in the presumably immutable laws of our world. 'When the foundations of our science are thrown down, then will man tremble before the true power. Conceit is his undoing and he will not heed the coming of his doom until it crushes him. The Dolman, a sorcerous creature of terrifying power beyond man's ken, will come against mankind. The shifting of the laws presages his invasion. Indeed it is his invitation. First his legions, then the Makkon, then The Dolman himself will come to claim the world. With that, annihilation.' "

The wind outside had picked up in intensity, buffeting the ship as it sped across the ice sea. Yet the sound seemed remote to them, unreal, frozen in sticky time. Neither one said anything for a while. Then Borros roused himself and, listening for a moment, made a motion upward.

"The sail."

If they had left it up any longer it would likely have been torn to shreds. As it was, they managed to reef it just in time. The wind, blowing frantically out of the northwest quarter, tore at their faces, forcing them to gasp for breath and turn their heads from its might. They were blind in the pit of night and only by guesswork did they surmise their direction.

Below, they blew into their cupped hands and shoved them near the fire, trying to warm their faces. Ronin prepared food for himself and before he had eaten his fill Borros was already asleep on his berth. He stretched out and stared at the swinging lamp, thinking long about The Dolman.

He must have dozed, for when he next looked about the cabin the ports were illuminated by a thin milky glow.

"Dawn," breathed Borros, and sat up. "The sun rises. Soon we can unfurl the sail."

On deck they got their first real glimpse of the ice sea since setting sail. Ronin saw now why Borros had not been concerned about keeping watch at night. In all directions the ice flew away from them flat and seamless and dark. No high ridges, no steep protrusions marred its surface. And there was a limitless horizon which in all directions held no sight of land.

In the east, the gray clouds had taken on a pale saffron color as the sun began its quotidian trek across the heavens. The wind came in gusts and Borros was obliged to go aft to reset their course.

Ronin stared southward, watching the shredded clouds pile and tumble, blown across the sky by the high winds aloft. Are there really people out there? he asked himself. Would they look like Bonneduce the Last? He shrugged and busied himself with the rigging, tightening knots which had loosened during the night.

The air became heavier still, leaden despite the strength of the wind, and there was a slight pressure in his ears. He took special care, moving along the rocking deck, remembering his slip the first night and, peering into the wind, he spied the purple and black thunderheads massed just above the horizon on the northwest quadrant that heralded the coming storm.

A shout twisted his head aft, but he could see nothing amiss. He made his way toward Borros, who was already pointing northward.

"What is it?"Ronin asked, coming up to him.

"A ship." Borros clutched at the wheel. "Following us."

Ronin peered aft but could still discern nothing on the expanse of the ice sea.

"Obscured now by the mist."

"Borros, are you certain—"

49

"This ship's sister," the Magic Man hissed. "Yes, Chill take it! I did see it."

Ronin turned away, twisted Borros with him. He stared hard into the old man's face and tried to ignore the terror squirming like a serpent there.

"Forget it," he said reasonably. "You are still fatigued. You saw what your imagination wished for you to see. You have been through so much but it is over now. Freidal cannot threaten you now. You are free."

Borros glanced briefly sternward, into the building mist.

"Let us pray so."

All the day the wind strengthened, a gale now whose great gusts shifted from one quarter to another, hurling them southward at ever increasing speed. It seemed to Ronin, as he worked the rigging, that their runners barely touched the ice, so swiftly did they fly across the frozen wastes. From time to time he caught Borros gazing aft, but he said nothing, keeping his thoughts to himself.

He marveled at the workmanship of the craft. He watched the small storm sail which they had unfurled when they came on deck at first light. Buffeted by the strong winds, stretched to its limit, it yet would not tear. It was constructed of a different fabric than the woven canvas of the main, lighter, more supple.

For much of the time the pair did not speak. It was essential that the wheel and the sail be manned at all times now because of the sudden unpredictability of the winds. Ronin worked the sail because that took more strength. He spent most of the time hauling on the rigging and staring ahead, one arm about the wooden mast, feeling it tremble, listening to the rhythmic creaking of the fittings, the soughing of the runners against the ice, the desolate call of the wind.

He thought then of nothing; the future would be as

it would be. But a peculiar warmth stole over him in those solitary moments against the varnished wood, counterbalancing the pull of the ropes, and he absorbed the transmission of their quivering strength, their pliancy the key to survival upon the ice sea. A bond was slowly forming of which he was not yet perhaps fully aware, as it had inevitably with many men, throughout many ages, on seas too numerous to count. It was an instinct rooted perhaps in some ancestral memories, if such things indeed existed on that world and in that time. It was what allowed him to feel the changing of the wind on his face and pull or slacken the rope immediately so that they continually maintained their course. It was what caused him to pick up a thousand different subtleties of sailing in so short a time.

Just past midday the winds ceased their gusting and steadied enough for the pair to decide to lash wheel and storm sail long enough to go below for food and rest.

While they ate, he told Borros the details of the events which had transpired in the City of Ten Thousand Paths. When he recounted the creature's attack, the Magic Man exclaimed, the sound exploding through his lips. He coughed and swallowed convulsively. Then he had Ronin describe the creature again as best he could.

"The Makkon," he said then, his face drained of color and looking more than ever like a skull. "The creatures that are not animal, the four Reavers of The Dolman." He quivered involuntarily. "If that is truly what you encountered, then The Dolman is closer than I had suspected." His eyes closed. "Is there still time? Oh, Chill, there must be! *There must be!*" He looked up. "Ronin, we must make all haste southward. Nothing must stop us, nothing, do you understand?"

"Calm yourself, Borros," Ronin said gently. "Nothing shall stop us."

Late in the afternoon the day darkened prematurely and the violent storm which they had been attempting to outrun began to overtake them with an inexorable fury.

The wind shrilled in the rigging like the screams at the gates of the damned and Ronin went to reef the storm sail.

"No!" bellowed Borros, the gale causing his voice to sound muffled. "Leave it up! We must make all speed no matter the risk!"

Ronin looked to the sky. The racing purple-black clouds, thick now and lowering menacingly from the west, were gathering themselves. Within them, the storm.

"We may turn over if it does not come down!" He yelled into the wind, the words blown from his mouth like crisp leaves.

Borros' face was mottled in fear.

"I have seen the sister ship again! She is closer! Ronin, she stalks us!" His eyes bulged. "I will not be caught!"

Ronin began to reef the storm sail.

"You have only seen what you want to see; no one is following us. I want to survive this storm!"

Moments later, slender fingers grasped his arm, tugging feebly. He turned and looked into Borros' rolling eyes, saw the line of sweat freezing along the Magic Man's forehead.

"Please. Please. The ship comes after us. If we slow, it will surely overtake us." Borros' voice came out in puffs of steam on the chill, dense air. "Do you see? I cannot go back. I can take no more. Freidal had done what—"

Ronin touched him gently. "Return to the wheel

and guide us," he said softly. "The storm sail will stay up."

Gratefully Borros went again aft and Ronin retied the knots, vowing to reef the storm sail at the first sign of the gale's full force.

So they raced onward, riding before the gathering wind.

TWO

·Aegir·

He has turned from the west, away from the murder of the sun at the grasping hands of the ice plateaus. Frightened now, he flees before the turmoil of the vast sky. He feels, just behind him, the intense excitation of the storm as it bursts open and he is engulfed now by the fierce bite of the high winds, the pressure of the roiling banks of dark cloud, the kinetic scrape of leaping lightning.

Of these elements he is not afraid as he soars upward in a futile attempt to fly above the storm. He had ridden out many a gale, safe on the shifting wind currents, the whirling flurries of snow, the hard pellets of ice affecting him not at all.

The fear is of another kind and he is frantic to escape. His silver plumage a blur, he dips now, the air this high too thin for even his avian lungs, and desperately he tries to find a swift current to take him away from the feel of the living thing behind him, its frozen breath on his spread tail feathers, a pulsing caress of death. For it rolls on at his back, alive and malignant and indefatigable; something beyond life, beneath life. Coming.

He flies like a bolt into lurid purple cloud, out again, his flesh alive with crawling sensation. He tries to call out in his terror, cannot. Down and down he plummets until he sees the surface of the ice sea, dull and flat and comforting. It rushes by beneath him.

It was useless, and worse than that, suicidal. Through the curtains of blinding snow, dense and dark and turbulent, blotting out all else from sight and hearing, Ronin went aft, mindful of the slick layer of ice already forming on the deck.

It had hit with an electric jolt, one moment behind them, the next surrounding them in a frenetic shroud, dancing, swirling, driving. The gale was far too strong; even with both of them gripping the wheel, the ship was being hurled about as if it had abruptly lost all weight. Better by far for them to be belowdecks. He was especially concerned that Borros could be blown overboard.

He skidded once as the ship lurched to port, tilted, trembling in the howling winds, and righted itself. Slowly he unwound his freezing fingers from the rigging and moved now as a mountaineer would, using handholds at every step.

Borros, obsessed now by the thought of the pursuing ship, clung maniacally to the wheel, his blanched face a frozen mask, lips pulled back in a grimace of fear. And Romin, coming alongside him, was reminded of the visage of the newly dead. Clawlike, Borros' fingers were white bones against the wood. Ronin yelled at him, but his voice was drowned in the mounting shriek of the gale. He seized the Magic Man, chopping at his frail wrists to force him to let go of the wheel, and dragged him, lurching and sliding, to the cabin, thrusting him down the companionway. Then he turned and lashed the wheel firmly in place, went forward and slid along the icy deck, fetching up against the starboard sheer-strake. On hands and knees against the fury of the storm, he crawled to the mast and, pulling himself to his feet, reefed the flapping storm sail. He choked in the crush of whipping hail and frozen snow as it beat at his face and shoulders. He secured it to the yard, doubling the knots.

Only then did he go below.

Borros sat on the cabin's deck shivering in a small pool of water. Ronin sank wordlessly to his berth and thought that perhaps it was after all too much. Too many new situations arising each minute and neither of them yet fully acclimated to the surface. For Ronin, it was not so bad; he was young and strong, with a warrior's body and adaptability. But just as importantly his mind was open and flexible. He could accept. He knew that from his journey to the City of Ten Thousand Paths.

But for Borros, huddled pathetically upon the wooden deck, more concerned with an imaginary ship carrying his all too real tormentor than he was with the realities of the storm hurling itself at their craft, it could not be the same.

The howling outside increased and the ship shuddered and swayed dangerously as it sped within the storm. We live or we die and that is the sum of it, Ronin thought. But, Chill take it, I will not die!

Borros had gotten up and was making his way drunkenly up the companionway to the secured hatch. Ronin caught him.

"What are you doing?"

"The sail," said the Magic Man, his voice almost a whine. "I must be sure—that it is up."

"It *is* up."

He squirmed in Ronin's grasp. "I must see for myself. Freidal comes behind us. We must make all speed. If he catches us, he will destroy us."

Ronin whipped him around so that he could look into the tired eyes. They were clouded with panic and shock. It is too much for him, Ronin thought for the second time.

"Borros, forget Freidal, forget the sister ship. Even if it is following us, the storm will protect us. He cannot find us in this." The eyes looked blankly back at

57

him, then they turned toward the hatch. Ronin shook him, finally out of patience.

"Fool! The storm is our enemy! There is death out there. It is the sail which will destroy us in this wind!"

"Then you have taken it down!" It was the irrational wail of a disillusioned child.

"Yes, Chill take you, I had no other choice! If I had not, we would be on our side now breaking up."

Frantically Borros clawed at Ronin. "Let me go! I must put it up! He will overtake us if I do not!"

Ronin hit him then, a swift blow at the side of the neck, breaking the nerve synapses and blood flow for just an instant, and the Magic Man collapsed, eyes rolling up, his body folding onto the companionway. Ronin put him on his berth and turned away disgusted.

The ship groaned under the onslaught and the hanging lamp swung crazily on its short chain, splashing the bulkheads with bursts of sullen light and geometric shadows.

After a time Ronin reached up and extinguished the flame.

He lay listening to the howling darkness, feeling the felucca shudder and lurch under him, smelling the thin trail of smoke from the doused lamp. The gale tore through the rigging, moaning as if alive, spattering hail against the hull in furious bursts.

The darkness deepened and the sounds modulated subtly downward in pitch, becoming muffled as if heard through layers of viscous fluid. Yet other aspects of the sounds, unnoticed until now, were supraclear. Then the volume altered, increasing and decreasing in a slow rhythm that was comforting. The sounds lengthened, as if stretched out of their original shape by the swell.

He was deep, deep, and the towers of the world

rose above him in cyclopean grandeur, steep walls of hard volcanic rock with thick-knuckled ridges of darkly gleaming stone as obdurate as obsidian. Pale fronds and spreading algae partially obscured their faces. The foundations, hewn and sculpted during an age so ancient that Time was but an abstract concept and Law was unknown. An age of great upheaval and movement, when the world was forming and crying out like an infant; when red and yellow molten rock spewed forth in sizzling rivers from the innards of the earth, crawling down new rock edifices, boiling into the violent seas; when land masses arose, glistening and foamy, in the middle of the oceans; when cliffs slid like cataracts into churning waters white with slate and pumice. In an age when all was beginning.

A shadow; he is not alone.

In the awesome canyons of the foundations of the world he feels a presence, diffuse and elemental.

Large it is; unutterably immense so that he does not know whether it moves or is at rest. Perhaps it has features; perhaps it is acephalous or again quite shapeless. There is no way of discerning. Its sides pulse with energy, the source it seems to him of the oceans' very tides. He glides silently over the slippery mountains of its body, a metonymical terrain without end. And he wonders. But in the absolute silence no answers are forthcoming.

He awoke with an enormous thirst and a need to urinate. He ventured on deck. The storm was still raging but the sky appeared somewhat lighter. Dawn, he thought, or just after; impossible to tell in this weather. He relieved himself, then bent and stuffed snow into his mouth, returning to the cabin, shivering.

Borros was still asleep, which was just as well, Ronin thought, since he would wake with a headache.

Ronin crossed to his berth and, leaning across it,

ran his hand experimentally along the outer bulkhead. The craft was obviously built as well as it was designed. He could detect no sign of weakening and, satisfied that it was withstanding the gale's fury, he sat and ate a spare breakfast.

Borros groaned and rolled over but he did not wake up. Ronin saw the blue bruise along his neck. He crossed the cabin and bent over the frail figure. He saw then that the Magic Man was shivering.

Quickly he turned Borros onto his back. He was hot and the skin had a dry, taut look about it. The eyes came open slowly. They were enlarged and abnormally bright.

Ronin reached under the berth and pulled out a woven blanket. He stripped the spare frame of its suit and found that the material was dry but the flesh underneath was damp from the residues of melted snow and fever sweat. The suit was superbly designed to keep out the cold and the damp but conversely, if the body was wet, the material would not allow it to dry.

The body shook with the force of the fever and Ronin, covering Borros with the blanket, cursed himself for a fool. He should have realized sooner that their enormous differences in physical stamina and mental adaptability would result in the Magic Man's eventual collapse. Because he had been the one to continually urge them onward, Ronin had ignored the signs of utter exhaustion on the other's face. How much did Freidal's terrible probings take out of him? Ronin wondered.

Outside the storm smote the ship in monotonous abandon. From time to time Ronin attempted to cool the Magic Man's face with water. The bare skull, gleaming waxily in the diffuse light of the waning day, seemed a constant reminder of his vulnerability. At sunset the fever appeared stronger. Borros had slept fitfully, eating not at all. Now he was delirious and

Ronin felt certain that if it did not break soon Borros would die.

There was nothing he could do and his helplessness vexed him. He had searched the cabin in an attempt to find medicine, but he soon realized that there was no way of knowing what the potions and powders he found were meant for. The wrong choice could kill the Magic Man more effectively than any fever could. So he had left what he had found in the cupboard below the berth, unused, unknown. Borros moaned and the gale shrieked in the rigging.

Abruptly he heard a sharp grinding noise and was sent tumbling as the ship lurched. The motion has changed, he thought as he regained his feet. And then: Chill take it, we have hit something!

It was true. He felt now the slender felucca sliding over the ice at a precarious, oblique angle. If I do not right the ship, our momentum combined with its mass will topple us.

Pulling on his hood, he raced up the companionway, through the hatch, and out into the blinding storm. Needles of ice struck at him and the high winds tore at his torso. Over the screech of the gale he heard a rhythmic heavy flapping and, shading his eyes, peered across the deck. A long strip of rigging had worked loose and was whipping itself against the hull. There was no visibility.

He went aft with the ship trembling as it sped on its oblique and unnatural course. Slowly, he felt the felucca turning broadside into the gale. We shall break up for certain then, he thought. Hand over hand he continued aft, stepping cautiously through the calf-high mixture of ice and snow covering the deck.

A gust of wind tilted the ship and his grip loosened in the slippery iced rigging. He stumbled and skidded along the ice and as his momentum built he knew that he was going over the side. He struggled to regain his balance on the heaving deck, could not, and desperately reached out for the gunwale with his gauntleted hand. He saw with intense clarity the scales of the Makkon hide slide, frictionless, along the slickly iced wood. He tightened his grip, feeling the might of the wind against his body slamming him against the sheer-strake, and he was tossed upward as if weightless over the side, into the howling storm, almost gone, the dark and featureless ice unraveling in a blur below him so close now. His breath caught in his throat and his mouth clogged with flying ice dust. A fire running along his arm and into his chest as the wind pulled at him, moaning and crying, and he twisted in its fierce grip. And through a haze he thought, Now, now or it will surely claim me.

Calm at the core.

Momentum, he thought. And used it. With the gale tearing at him, he used the last of his strength, concentrating it into his gauntleted hand, exerting the pressure, the scales now biting through the ice, gripping finally. And still the wind battered him.

But now he had a pivot and, using it, he no longer resisted the powerful tug of the storm, but rather relaxed into it, letting it swing his body. At the height of the arc, he pushed. Up came his feet, his legs, his torso and he lunged at the gunwale with his boots, feeling them slide along the icy top. Then he had one boot over and he hooked his leg until the second was over the gunwale, and he was aboard, climbing carefully onto the deck.

He slid gasping along the sheer-strake of the stern, recalling what he had seen as he swung aboard. Just to port of the stern was a long gash in the hull. What did we hit? he wondered.

The thought was thrust aside as he scrambled for the wheel, realizing that he had lost precious time because they were still moving broadside. The rope holding the wheel on course had snapped. He gripped the curved wood and leaned against it with all his might. He took deep breaths, seeking to restore his energy, his lungs on fire, and his exhalations made harsh plumes of smoke before him. The wind howled in his face and the felucca juddered as he strove to right its course. He pushed from his feet, hauling at the wheel, using the mass of his body, and heard at last the agonized squeal of metal against ice as the runners fought friction and the storm to turn. Muscles jumped and contracted along his arms and back and thighs.

The craft was frozen in her arc; it no longer swung to starboard. But she was still sliding obliquely and he knew that he could not push the wheel farther, that there was only one chance now before a fierce gust caught the hull across the beam and turned her full broadside to the storm.

Quickly he found another piece of rope and lashed the wheel in place. Then hand over hand he went forward to the mast. His hands moved deftly over the knots, unfurling the storm sail. He pulled at the yard, plucked at the rigging, strung the storm sail.

An ice shower flung itself upon him, heavy clusters, black and jagged as exploded metal, slamming him to his knees, boot soles slithering in the ice. The rigging flew from his hands and the felucca leaped forward, shivering, as the storm sail took the wind.

He tried to get up, sliding in the ice as the gale tore at the ship, and did not attempt it again. Instead he sat, back braced against the port sheer-strake, boot soles buttressed by the base of the mast. He had regained the rigging and was hauling now, hauling to shift the yard into the proper angle.

He became one with the craft. All the creakings and moanings of joints under stress, the trembling of the hull, the incredible singing tension of the mast as it gave in to the wind and thus derived its sleek power, all these were now extensions of his arms and hands and fingers as he fought for the life of the ship.

And slowly the crosstree swayed, moving centimeter by centimeter toward the needed position. It was not a steady process because the storm railed against him, shifted by gusts at odd moments so that he had to be extremely sensitive to the currents.

At first, so minutely that he was not even aware of it, the stern began to swing to port. He thought then that he might fall from exhaustion before he saw any change at all and in that suspended instant of time felt the shift. Like the first long pull of potent wine, a sense of overwhelming exhilaration warmed his chest and new strength flowed into his rigid arms.

At length he lashed the rigging in place and went aft to reset the wheel. Once at the stern, he had time to peer over the side at the gash in the hull. Curious, he thought, the damage is high up. If we had hit a rock outcropping, the mark would have been lower down. What could we have hit? He took another quick look and judged that the damage was not serious. Still, we cannot afford to let that happen again.

Day was done. The purple had deepened, drowning the gray cast of the long afternoon. And now darkness fell with a completeness that was awesome. Still the storm raged and all about him was the dizzying swirl of ice and snow. Just before he went below, he went forward and reefed the storm sail, securing the yard. He was of two minds about it but in the end he felt that it was safer to run the storm without the sail.

"You must tell me."

"Wait, my friend. Wait."

"Borros, too many have already been slain over this. I must have answers."

Dawn, almost. Faint pearled light an incipient glow at the cabin's thick ports. During the night the fever

64

had broken and since then Borros had been breathing easier, the rattle gone from his lungs and throat, the inhalations deeper and more regular. When he awakened after the fever's cresting, he had drunk the warm liquid that Ronin had prepared, gulping greedily and asking for more.

"Later," Ronin said.

Borros lay back for a time, his energy spent, and drifted off into a deep sleep that his body demanded. Just before dawn he had awakened once more, appearing stronger. His eyes were clear and the color of his face was near normal.

"How long?"

"A cycle. A day and a night."

He ran a thin hand across his face. "Can I have something to drink, do you think?"

"Of course." Ronin offered him a bowl. "Not too much."

The whine and whistle of the wind, the muffled patter of ice crystals against the hull.

"You know," said Borros after a time, "I have for so long dreamed of the Surface, imagined what it would be like—in every detail, I mean—wished to be free of the Freehold for so long—and then for my time with Freidal I wished just to die up here—that is why I told him nothing, because I knew that if I did I would die in that hole—and that terrified me more than anything, even"—— He shuddered and his eyes closed. He looked bleakly at Ronin. "Can you understand?"

Ronin nooded. "Yes. I think I can."

They had begun talking and, inevitably, the subject of the scroll arose.

"Answers, Borros."

"Yes, my boy, quite. But I can only tell you what I know." He sighed deeply. "The scroll is a key of some sort. The writings spoke of it as a door to the only pathway that could possibly stop The Dolman. He is destined, it said, to return to the world. First the shift in the laws, then the Makkon and the gathering of his legions and, finally, when the four Makkon are all there, they will summon The Dolman. They are his guardians, his outriders, his messengers, his reavers. Of all the creatures at his command, only the Makkon communicate with him directly. Once the four are here, their power multiplies. That is all the writings told me."

"And where are we bound?"

"Ah, that I can answer with more certainty. We go south; to the continent of man. There I trust we will find those who can translate the scroll of dor-Sefrith."

"And if not?"

"If not, Ronin, then The Dolman shall indeed claim the world and man shall cease to exist."

Ronin thought for a time. At length he said, "Borros, tell me something. If we hit a protrusion of the ice's surface, it would scrape us low on the hull, correct?"

The Magic Man looked puzzled. "Well, yes, I suppose so. It is hardly likely that the weather would allow any high ice formations to develop. Why?"

"No reason," said Ronin, turning away. "No reason at all."

It was dusk when it came. They had been so long with the background static of the storm that at first they thought that they were going deaf and it was not until the white noise filled their ears completely that they realized what it was. The gale had spent itself, leaving only the uncertain silence of the ice sea.

Ronin helped Borros don his foil suit and together they went on deck. To the east, banks of dark cloud gravid with moisture and lightning scudded against the sky and overhead rolled remnants of thunderheads, the last flutterings of torn banners; but to the west the air was clear, the long horizon virtually unbroken, colored by a sliver of sun, lowering like a swollen ember in a banked fire. The sky was the color of cold ash, tinged magenta and pink about the sun's arc. And then it was gone, night stealing over them so swiftly that it seemed as if the sun had never been there at all. Ronin held the image of the sunset in his memory, his heart lightened after so many days of seamless gray and claustrophobic white.

They set about clearing the deck of the debris of the storm. But Borros was still weak and he was forced to stop, moving aft to see to the wheel and their course. While he did this, Ronin stowed the storm sail and set about erecting the larger mainsail to block and tackle along the yard and mast. When he unfurled it, it immediately caught the stiff breeze, billowing out. They shot forward as if fired from a bow. Blue ice flew at the bow.

"Ronin!"

A cry of desperation.

And he knew what it was before he turned his head aft; had known from the moment he had been in the process of swinging back aboard during the gale and had seen it high up on the hull. Too high for any ice, he thought. We did not hit a protrusion. Something hit us. He turned his head and then saw it.

Borros cried out again. Both of them stared sternward. In their wake, in the clearing weather, in the silvered light of the sleeping sun, reflected off the ice, was silhouetted the unmistakable shape of a lateen sail.

"You see!"

Limmed for a moment, before it winked out with the wisps of light, it appeared to have a sinister cast.

"I told you!"

No time for that now. It was indeed a sister ship to

67

their felucca, now perhaps half a kilometer behind them and closing. Could they have lightened the craft somehow? thought Ronin. And how did they find us in all of the vast ice sea? True, they knew our exact starting point; knew that we would head due south. Yet still it disturbed him. He gazed at the spot where last the sail had been. The storm, he mused. The storm should have made this impossible. It blew us about; it blew them about surely. How could they now be so close; what were the chances . . . ? He shrugged resignedly and gave it up. No matter the reason, they are just behind us now.

The Magic Man was clever. Whatever other reading he had done, he had somehow managed to learn a good deal about sailing. That knowledge stood him in good stead now. With the sister ship giving chase, he steered them with the wind so that, with Ronin using his muscle to keep the yard at the proper angle, they caught each gust, using it to its fullest advantage, making top speed. It was all they could do. Here on the limitless expanse of the ice sea, with not even a hint of land on the horizon, evasive maneuvers were useless. But that we do not seem to be doing, thought Ronin as he ran the line through its block so that the yard swung several centimeters to starboard.

"We can outrun them," Borros called from his position aft at the wheel.

Ronin thought not. How is Freidal managing to sail that ship? he asked himself. Even with his daggam; they have no knowledge of ships? But it was merely another question that had no answer. In any case, he thought savagely, I do not believe I wish to outrun them; I have a score to settle with Freidal. I care not for what Borros said.

"It is not death so much," said Borros, "that I fear. It is all that shall come before it." The fear haunted his eyes, making them appear bulged and glassy. "You are but one Bladesman; they will cut you down and make you live through it as I have. And I," he said heavily, "will have to endure it once again." His thin lips quivered. "I cannot, I cannot."

Unwilling, Borros went below. The night was but half gone but he had almost fallen to the deck and he had no choice, his body betraying him despite the overwhelming fear in his mind.

"Go to sleep," Ronin had urged him as he helped him to the cabin's companionway. "You are safe."

The Magic Man looked at him sardonically.

"You are like all your kind," he said sharply. "Every Bladesman thinks himself invincible; until he feels the life streaming out of him."

Now in the silence of the night, Ronin stood against the trembling mast, oblivious to the delicate shhhing of the runners against the ice, the tiny sounds of the fittings. He stared ahead into the darkness, deep as obsidian, black as basalt, his mind a theater.

Freidal, you madman, you defend death. The Freehold is no more. The Saardin scheme for greater power, a power as hollow as this vessel. The lower Levels are in chaos, the workers mad and destitute. And you are pledge to uphold the laws of this place.

Freidal, you slayer, you destroyed Stahlig, slowly, joyously crushing the life from him, the terror mounting until the laboring heart burst. You have destroyed Borros too; he still lives but he is not the same man; he lives in total fear of your retribution. And you wanted to destroy me; I saw it in your face, etched as clearly as a stylus shapes warm wax, when you captured me after my return from the City of Ten Thousand Paths. You had already sent your minions after me: on the Stairwell with K'reen, my beloved, my sister; in the Square of Combat with Marcsh. Now you come for us again. Well. I will not run, for it is time we met, you and I, in Combat.

In the pale wash of first light, the sky a feathered shell of mother-of-pearl, Ronin leaned hard on the wheel.

Sunrise flew to starboard as the bow swung round, describing the beginning of its long arc, and shortly it pointed directly at the sail of their sister ship.

Prepare yourself now, Ronin called silently to Freidal. Time has almost run down.

They closed with terrifying swiftness, Ronin guiding his craft from out of the southeast quarter. The contours of the other ship bloomed abruptly from harmless toy size in the strengthening light. The day was overcast, with layers of stratified cloud, white in the sunrise. A strange light fell across the scene, oblique and somehow harsh as the sun crept over the horizon, so that every edge had a sword-blade shadow and all shapes turned angular.

He could discern now dark figures on the deck of the sister ship, dark robes fluttering thickly, white faces staring intently at him. Then there was the briefest flash of cold light, thin as a bolt, and his gaze swung to the tall slender figure at the bow. He knew even without the coalescence of features that it was Freidal. The Security Saardin's false eye had caught the light of the rising sun as it broke momentarily from the gray cloud cover, reflecting it back at him.

Ronin swung farther into the quarter, turning, feeling the adrenalin rising in him now that he was sure that it was Freidal who pursued them, turning until he ran parallel to the other felucca. They sped now across the ice sea linked together more surely than if they were physically one vessel.

Ronin watched, outwardly impassive, as Freidal went slowly aft until he was near midship. The right eye, the real eye glared at him.

"Of course you were behind this," Freidal called across the frozen expanse as the ships drifted closer. "I have come for you, sir; you and the Magic Man. He willfully escaped my custody." Ronin's eyes roved the other ship. How many? "You were taken from me but I still have many questions to ask you." Certainly two daggam. Were there more below? "The Surface is forbidden to all of the Freehold. I am charged with your return." They will be the best Bladesmen under his command; he will not underestimate me now. "The Saardin wish to question you." Discount the scribe, writing tablet strapped to his wrist, stylus scratching across its face, recording for Freidal. "Unfortunately, neither of you shall survive the journey back. I am no longer concerned with where you were or what you were doing." His good eye blinked and burned. "My daggam are sacrosanct; no one attacks them without being charged with the consequences. You broke Marcsh's back. Now you will pay. Death without honor awaits you, sir!"

Ronin heard a shout aboard ship, saw Borros' head and shoulders emerging from the cabin's hatch.

"Oh, Frost, they have caught us!"

Ronin was fed up. "Get below," he yelled. "And stay there until I come for you!"

The Magic Man stared at the tall figure of the Security Saardin, so close now over the narrowing slice of ice, transfixed with terror at the glowering visage.

"You shall die now, sir!" Freidal called.

"Get below!" Ronin shouted once more and the figure disappeared. The hatch slammed shut.

The twin ships raced on before the wind, and now Freidal motioned to the daggam and they lifted cables with black metal hooks, swung them over their heads, hurled them toward him. They hit the deck and they hauled on the cables, the hooks scraping across the

71

deck until they bit into the wood of the sheer-strake and held.

Now the feluccas were fairly touching and, securing the cables, the daggam leapt to the gunwales. Ronin lashed the wheel in place as they came aboard. Freidal stood silently, his false eye a milky round; the scribe was immobile, stylus poised.

They were tall, with wide shoulders and long arms. They had brutal faces, feral but not unintelligent; one narrow and hatchetlike, the other with a nose wide across the flat planes of his cheeks. Triple brass-hilted daggers were scabbarded in oblique rows across their chests; long swords hung at their hips.

For Ronin it was a moment of delicious hunger, these last still instants before Combat, when the power surged like a flood within him, controlled and channeled. He licked his lips and drew his blade. They advanced upon him. Now the waiting was at an end.

Over the ice they fled, the white spray of their swift passage rainbowed the light, the ships rocking, locked together in an embrace only death could now sunder.

They were a team. They swung at him from different angles, but at the same instant, seeking to confuse him. The blades caught the rising sunlight and, because he was watching their descent, he was blinded momentarily, his eyes watering, and it was instinct that guided his parry, the sword up and twisting broadside on. He got one but missed the other and it sheared into his shoulder, no help for it now. The nerves numbed themselves and the blood began to flow. The daggam grinned and came on.

Everything, said the Salamander, *every thing* that occurs during Combat may be used to your own advantage if you but know how. A strong arm but holds the sword; the mind is the force which guides it. They were more confident now, seeing how easily he was cut, and they swung at him in tandem, with co-ordinated precision, chopping and slashing, moving him backward in an attempt to cut off the number of angles through which he could attack them. They passed the bulk of the cabin as they moved forward along the ship. Let your opponent make the first moves if you are unsure of his skills; in his actions will you find victory.

And so they battered him as he catalogued their offensive strategies, attacking occasionally to gauge their defenses. They were excellent Bladesmen, with unorthodox styles, and he lacked the space to effectively attack them together.

At midship, he split them, using the yard as a barrier. It was done most swiftly, for they were not stupid and they would counter almost immediately. Almost. He had one chance only and he went in fast at hatchetface, slashing a two-handed stroke that slit the daggam's midsection just under the ribs. His innards glistened wetly as they poured upon the deck. The mouth opened in silent protest, so quick had been the blow, and the tongue protruded, quivering. The eyes bulged as the body collapsed, hot blood pumping, congealing on the frigid deck.

But now the second daggam hurled himself under the temporary barrier of the yard, furious at being separated from his partner. Ronin parried his first attack, moving away from the center of the ship, toward the gunwale across which the hooks had been thrown. The second daggam had glanced briefly at his fallen companion and, noting this, Ronin kept his blows low so that the flat-faced daggam would assume that he was attacking the same spot now. Their blades hammered at each other, sparks flying as they scraped together, then snapped apart, only to clash again in mid-air. Ronin parried again and then, instead of the oblique strike he had been attacking with, swung his

73

blade in a horizontal arc. Too late the daggam brought his own sword up and the flat-faced head, severed now at the neck, flew from the jerking body and landed not a meter from where Freidal stood on the other ship. Ronin heaved at the corpse with its curtaining fount of blood, sent it overboard as he sprinted, gaining his ship's gunwale. He leaped, landing with his soles firmly on the deck of Freidal's vessel.

The rigging vibrated, singing dolefully in the breeze as the Security Saardin turned to face him, the tight cap of his blue-black hair gleaming, his long lean face swiveling like that of a predator's. His hand at his chest; a blur, and if Ronin had had to look, he would have been dead. But he was already turning as the blur came at him, whispering past where he had just stood. And he was off across the deck, sword up, knees bent, searching with his peripheral vision for other daggam. He passed the scribe, solitary and unmoving, stylus poised until words rather than weapons filled the air. His cloak flapped sullenly in the wind; otherwise he could have been carved from rock.

"Ah, sir, you have come to me at last." Stylus in motion, then he was off, circling in a shallow arc so that he could see the entire length of the ship. "The corps are unleashed first." The voice emotionless. "A basic rule of warfare." Past the creaking mast, the straining sail. "Soften the enemy with a preliminary attack." Mind the yard, swinging. "Deplete his energy with the soldiers." Past coils of rope, lashed kegs, the spare mast as on his own craft fixed to the port sheerstrake. "Then come the elite." Slick patches of ice near the starboard gunwale. "To finish the task." *Shhhhhh*, the runners peeling the ice below. "An admirable plan, sir, do you not agree?"

The face closer than expected, white, the thin-lipped mouth, long and cruel, pulled back into a

74

sneer. "Not too much trouble to kill a traitor!" The two remaining daggers caught the light as they lay nakedly strapped to his chest. Freidal, Saardin and Chondrin in one man. "The Freehold cannot tolerate your kind. You are a disease that must be cleansed. You see, I cannot allow you to return to the Freehold." At last he drew his great sword. "Now I will crush you; with great care and equal skill, paying attention to the finer points." He twisted sideways until just his right shoulder was presented, leaving Ronin the smallest target to attack. "Of pain." He advanced obliquely. "And fear."

The first was a downward thrust twisting at the last moment; the second a horizontal slash of enormous power coming from the opposite direction. Ronin parried them both and then Freidal had a dagger in his left hand, holding it before him, point tilted upward.

The scribe observed them impassively as they moved slowly along the deck in a strange and deadly dance. They were just forward of midship when Ronin's booted foot hit something on the deck and he stumbled. At that moment, his eyes still on Freidal's face, he saw the barest flicker of the Saardin's good eye and instead of struggling to regain his footing he relaxed his body and fell to the deck. He heard the angry whine as the dagger buried itself in the wood of the sheer-strake above his head.

Now there was but one yet it would be enough and he had to close immediately before Freidal got to it and he sprang at the tall figure looming over him. The ship shuddered in a heavy gust of wind and the Saardin, shifting to compensate, avoided the full brunt of the blow of Ronin's gauntleted fist. It scraped along his cheek, missing the bone which it would have otherwise shattered, dragging shards of skin as it flayed the flesh, split the corner of his mouth at the end of the arc. His head snapped back, recoiling as Ronin flew by, momentum carrying him into the port gunwale, striking him in the ribs, forcing the breath out of him. He gasped and tried not to double over. Freidal swiped at the blood whipping from his torn face in long droplets and swung a two-handed blow. A haze had descended over Ronin and with only his hearing now, not even fully comprehending what was occurring, he threw up his mailed fist, the scaled hide of the monstrous Makkon his only defense now. The blade hit the gauntlet and its hard peculiar surface rippled with movement. It absorbed much of the force of the blow and the sword slid against the scales as if they were oiled, glanced off, the killing blow turned aside, and it sliced into Ronin's already wounded shoulder. The pain woke him and he pivoted off the gunwale, blood whirling like a crimson scarf about him and, renewing his grip upon the hilt of his sword, staggered away from the sheer-strake while Freidal stared in disbelief at the dull hide of the gauntlet.

His bloody face twisted in fury and he came in low and fast and their blades rang like angry thunder as they met. Ronin kept close to him and now the Saardin attempted to retreat as if he was being forced to give way under Ronin's attack. But Ronin knew it for a ruse, knew that he wished only for room to throw the last dagger. Ronin drove into him, crowding him back against the mast. Freidal gripped the gleaming hilt of the dagger and Ronin's gauntlet closed over it. Their blades locked, scraping edge against edge down their long lengths. Freidal shook himself, twisting lithely, and tore free of Ronin's grasp to withdraw the dagger. They moved at once, as if provoked by the same impulse. The dagger's bright blade came at him and it could not be avoided because Freidal was not throwing it as Ronin had assumed he would, but slashing, and Ronin's momentum took him toward it. Freidal had aimed for the neck and missed, the point

76

hitting Ronin's collarbone, abrading the flesh. And then Ronin was past him, a dark blur, his sword held now in a reverse grip so that the blade trailed behind him. Plant the feet, breathe in with a long suck, swing the mass of his frame, pushing from his ankles, the sword like living lightning striking backward at the Saardin, who was just turning to face Ronin, the point ramming into his mouth. A bubbling scream choked off. A twist of the blade and Ronin was pivoting, his sword raised above his head for another blow. It was white in the light, darkened near the tip by red rivulets.

Freidal writhed upon the deck, the lower half of his face covered by his hands and arms. Blood was everywhere. Then he was still and Ronin looked up, awaiting more daggam. The deck was clear save for the scribe. He stood watching Ronin approach.

"You have written your last line."

The stylus dipped to the surface of the tablet, scrabbled there. Ronin left him, went aft, and threw open the cabin's hatch. Down the companionway and into the cabin. No one.

Across the deck and leapt for the gunwale and, crouching there momentarily, turned. Below him, blurred ice like marble. Freidal was where he had fallen. The scribe had not moved. Ronin scanned for the last time his impassive face, then with one long stride he was aboard his own felucca. With a mighty sweeping stroke, he severed the cables holding the ships as one. They parted and, helmless, the sister felucca gradually swept away to port, into the east, growing smaller and smaller, a memory now to some.

Borros did not believe him of course, but that was to be expected; it did not concern him.

"He is dead," said Ronin as he moved about the cabin. "Believe it or no, as you will."

The sun was setting dully behind curtains of blank cloud, colorless, featureless; a deflating end to another day. Just before he went below, Ronin had peered into the west, thought he had seen the outlines of land, but he could not be certain. As it turned out, it did not much matter.

"We still have far to go," Borros said somewhat brusquely when Ronin gave him the news. "And I do not believe that he is dead."

"Perhaps you would have us turn around and make sure," Ronin said acidly.

"If we but had the time, I would insist on it," the Magic Man replied obstinately, "so that I could kick his head in."

"Of course you would. Now."

"I do not regret," he said with a trace of self-righteousness, "that I lack your zeal for Combat."

Ronin sat on his berth and, having found a piece of material, began to clean the blade of his sword.

"My zeal for Combat, as you put it, is all the protection you presently have."

"From the vengeance of the Freehold. Their power is severly limited now that we are on the Surface."

One edge at a time, upward from the thick middle to the tapered tip.

"You would not have said that this morning."

"Ronin, you do not yet comprehend. We have been locked away for generations, progress checked, choking on your own detritus." A nerve in Borros' face began to spasm. "You are as much a product of that as is Freidal. You are proud to be a Bladesman," the voice dry and pedanic, "an artificial life style created by the Freehold." His hand described a sweeping gesture. "It is totally useless here."

"It has not been so far."

"Yes, by all means mock me. What I mean is that we shall soon reach the continent of man. It will be a civilized society. Man has already learned the bitter lessons of the sorcerous wars—"

Ronin stood up.

"What is it you fear, old man?"

"I?" The gray eyes blazed momentarily. "I fear that sword you wield and the arm which wields it. I must speak plainly. I fear that your presence may jeopardize our contact with civilization. I am a man of science and knowledge; I have studied much. They will listen to me but you—you are a barbarian to them. The blood instinct runs strong in you and the chances are quite good that you will misinterpret a movement or a gesture and someone will die."

"You know me not at all, then."

"I know only that you are a Bladesman and that is sufficient. You are all alike; you know how to do only one thing."

"Tell me," said Ronin, mounting the companionway, "how you would have fared on the Surface without me." And went up into the night.

Its tremulous light spilled like wan petals onto the ice sea, over the flying ship's deck, across Ronin's hunched shoulders. He opened his eyes—lashes, brows, stubble of beard rimed with frost—to the pinks and saffron yellows dimly streaking the south. Still sleep-fogged, still feeling the dream-warmth of K'reen's smooth, supple-muscled body sleekly trembling beneath him, still inhaling the perfume of her hair, tumbling, the last parting of a forest dark before him, he turned his head to behold the ripening spray of red-orange-gold in the east as the sun rose behind low lacquered clouds on the horizon. Above him the vault was cloudless, immense, cerulean and translucent, for the first time open to him.

For long moments he sat transfixed. Then he rose and stretched his knotted muscles, warming them with motion. He crossed to the starboard sheer-strake and watched the land unravel itself perhaps four kilometers away. He withdrew a poignard from his belt and thoughtfully scraped at his whiskers while contemplating the view; it was good to see land again after so much time in the center of nothingness. He breathed deeply. The air was fresh and bright, sparkling with a chill brittleness that was not unpleasant, all the more enjoyable after the oppressiveness of the storm.

"Land at last," Borros said from behind him.

Ronin turned.

"Here."

He sheathed the poignard, took the food the Magic Man offered him. The old man appeared to be somehow smaller in the light of the new day, as if his ordeal on the surface had actually shriveled him. Ronin thought he could see new lines scored in the taut, yellow-tinged face, under the slender almond eyes, at the corners of the downturned mouth. He was peering at the oblate sun which, having quit its low cloud cover, was rising with the lassitude of age.

"We are farther south than I could have hoped."

"But we still have ice," said Ronin, pointing to the low humped shore, covered completely with ice and snow.

"Yes, well, that is to be expected for a while. But the storm propelled us far beyond what would have been possible otherwise. Can you feel that the temperature rises? It does so excedingly slowly yet there is already a difference. And the ice too, I believe, has been affected. See there, the difference in color; its thickness diminishes."

The wind had slackened somewhat and they ran gently across the ice sea, an occasional gust billowing the sail. Ronin sat against the port sheer-strake, honing the double edges of his sword, feeling the heady beat of the strengthening sunshine.

Borros was near midship, checking the spare mast and yard and clearing the last residue of ice and frozen snow from the deck.

A calmness had crept over them both during the day, a liquid lassitude, dreamy in its warm stillness, which they both welcomed as respite from the kineticism of their journey since descending the ice plateau. Now they were content to drift through the long afternoon without speaking or even thinking.

They ate a cold supper below and then returned to the deck just before sunset. To starboard the cliffs of ice and snow had given way grudgingly to less forbidding rock faces of scarlet and gray. Snow was still plentiful, but for the first time the land appeared to be able to lift itself from beneath the white carpet. Farther off, seeming flat in the dusky haze of evening, a strong line of mountains marched across the horizon, deep violet, snow-capped, jagged and indomitable, wreathed in mists of mauve and lavender. Abruptly the sun broke onto their summits, light like shards across their peaks, and they lapsed all at once into black paper silhouette with a backdrop of crimson.

Ronin heard it just as the top edge of the swollen sun disappeared behind the mountains. He was near midship and immediately ran to the port gunwale. Borros was at the bow, searching for a spare block to replace one that had cracked during the gale. It was a sound that Ronin did not comprehend, for it had no analogue in his life. It was a dream-sound, as if the world was being split.

It came again. Louder. Longer. Two sounds simultaneously: a deep rumbling roar that vibrated the ship; a high screaming that set the teeth on edge. Borros' head came up.

Then Ronin saw in the lowering light a dark jagged

81

line growing in the ice off the port quarter in front of them. The ice lifted and, in a sledge-hammer blast, flew apart. Chunks of ice were hurled into the air, raining over them. The craft lurched and Ronin reached for the gunwale, hanging on.

He stared awe-struck as, through the widening rent in the sea, a black shape was rising, monstrous and swaying. It rose over them now, blotting out the sapphire twilight, and in a sudden flash of movement Ronin glimpsed a huge eye, baleful and alien, beneath it a narrow ugly jaw. And then it was past him, swooping onto the high stem of the felucca. Shivers ran through the frame and Ronin was hurled into the mast. The runners screeched as the vessel was thrown obliquely across the ice, then shuddered to a halt with an enormous squeal of protest. The deck splintered as the thing lashed itself against the bow for a second time. Fabric tore and Borros screamed. Ronin staggered to his feet and, drawing his sword, scrambled forward, its tip stained crimson in the last of the light.

He heard a violent hissing and inhaled a fetid stench, rotting flesh, slime, and salt and other odors he could not define. It was above him and he felt the chill of the sea depths and the drip of stinking water. Thickets of slimed weed dropped against his face and shoulders. He was in total darkness. Felt rather than saw its presence close to him off the port side and he swung the sword in a vicious two-handed blow. The keen edge cut into scaly hide, into strange flesh. A high keening sound came to his ears as he swung again and again into the thing's side.

It heaved itself away and he caught another glimpse of that terrifying eye, double-lidded, green with black-rimmed iris. He turned and nearly vomited as he confronted the gaping maw of the creature; the stench was overpowering. The jaws were all teeth, enormous and triangular, green with scum and bits of

82

decayed flesh. The head lunged forward and he leaped away, hearing the horrendous snap of the closing mouth.

The head came up and he saw its visage, nightmarish, a great saurian face with a long narrow snout and underslung jaw, blazing filmy eyes on either side of the swaying head and, farther back, rows of crescent slits fluttering along the glistening hide. Then the sight was blotted out as the snout came for him, propelled by a sinuous neck that was the beginning of its great body. Salt spray and seaweed flew at him and he was forced to duck behind the insecure protection of the mast and flapping sail. Too late he realized his mistake. The thing threw itself after him with complete abandon, slicing into the mast and, with a snap and a splintering sound, it collapsed among a forest of shroud and rigging.

The ship rocked under him as he fought his way clear of the clinging tangle to see the dripping jaws hovering over the cowering form of the Magic Man. Ronin raced forward, knowing that he was too far away. His right hand was a blur in the night air as the poignard flew at the thing's head, burying itself just behind the right eye. The terrible head shot forward with incredible acceleration, jaws agape. They snapped shut with a hideous metallic popping. Borros screamed and a geyser of blood and torn viscera showered the air, misting over Ronin as he drove his blade point first into the unblinking eye.

Had he not been as strong, the creature would have jerked the heavy hilt from his hands; but it was his sword and he would not let it go. He was whipped about as the thing writhed in agony. He tried to pull the sword free of the bone into which it had been thrust—an outcropping of skull beneath the destroyed eye. With a grinding sound, he at last pulled it free and dropped to the deck. The saurian head, green viscous blood oozing from the gaping eye socket, quested vainly for its tormentor. Ronin, crawling along the deck, barely missed a blind swipe of the jaws; human blood spattered over him in the thing's wake. Then it reared up and crashed into the ship. The port gunwale near the bow splintered and flew into the air.

It was imperative now that he get to the creature before it tore the ship apart. He had to get it to see him and he moved around so that its good eye stared directly at him. He stood and the head ceased its writhing. It shot at him with alarming speed and he swung at the snout. The blow glanced off the thick scaly hide and he was nearly decapitated by the snapping jaws. He would not attempt that again. But there must be a way.

He turned, searching, and spied the lower half of the mast, the top splintered and sharp. He sheathed his sword and ran aft, the great head following. He ducked another swipe and heaved at the mast. Slowly it pulled up from its mounting. A searing pain scoured his back and he was flung to the deck. Nausea assailed him and his back was on fire. He shook his head and his nostrils dilated at the stench; the head was returning to finish him. Now, he thought through the red haze threatening to engulf him in unconsciousness.

He regained his feet and hauled again on the mast, feeling the thing closing again. Agony shot through him and then he had it and turned to see the glistening jaws. He rammed the broken mast into the gaping maw at an almost vertical angle. The jaws snapped shut and the mast, braced against the lower jaw, slammed its upper end through the roof of the creature's mouth, through the soft palate and into the brain. The head rose into the night, spurting upward, a scaly fountain, crying.

And then it was gone, slithering back beneath the ice, dying or already dead, drifting languorously down and down with only the cracked surface of the ice sea, the blood and slime coating the deck of the felucca to mark its passage.

Ronin, on his knees, fell forward to the deck, forehead against the coldness. He panted, gulping at the air, clearing now after the creature's descent, then crawled painfully forward.

Borros lay in a pool of blood and rent flesh. His legs were gone and the lower half of his torso was a pulpy mass without recognizable form. Ronin stared blankly. Dead.

Onward, he thought. Onward.

But they were motionless on the ice sea. He tried to stand. A wave of dizziness and pain caught him and his knees buckled. He clung to the port gunwale and waited. Moments later, he was able to stand and, putting the pain into the back of his mind, he went carefully over the side and along the ice until he came to the leading edge of the runners. Chunks of ice, thrown up by the ascent of the creature, blocked the ship's way. He moved off cautiously to port, to the gaping rent in the ice, went down on hands and knees. Too dark to see anything but he listened. A gentle lapping came to him, echoing and distant. Water! The ice was thinning. He raised his head, peering southward. Out there. An end to the ice sea? The beginnings at last of civilization? Men.

And then what? he asked himself. He shook his head like a wounded animal. First things first.

He climbed painfully aboard the stalled ship, went forward and lifted the ruined body of the Magic Man. Down to the black ice, to the slippery edge of the obsidian pit. Home at last, thought Ronin. It slid easily from his arms, a pale, smeary flash in the starlight before it disappeared. Just for a moment the splash broke the rhythmic wash of the subcutaneous waves.

He worked for what seemed an interminable time,

clearing the rubble from in front of the runners. His back burned and he was sweating and trembling by the time he had finished.

He went aboard and sat on the deck trying to regain his breath. Moments passed like centuries and he crawled along the length of the ship beneath the cold carpet of stars and in the platinum luminescence broke out the spare mast, fitting it carefully into its mounting, then attached the yard. Ran the rigging through block and tackle while the breeze sighed about him. He attached the sail and went down to his knees, a blackness in his brain, a buzzing in his ears. He pushed himself up and, sitting, raised the sail, lashed the ropes to. It was almost dead calm and the canvas flapped uselessly. He did not care; tried to make it to the warmth of the cabin but fell in a stupor of shock and exhaustion before he could take two staggering steps.

The pain inside him grew and he weakened. Sometime during the long night a strong wind sprang up and the boat lurched uncertainly, then slithered forward, picking up speed. He awoke toward dawn but the movement of the vessel lulled him back to a feverish sleep.

It was night again when he next opened his eyes. He lay unmoving for long moments, his mind attempting to retrace the events of the journey. It was too much. At length his hands went to the pockets of his foil suit but the last of his food was gone. His teeth rattled as a dull bassy booming broke upon him. It took some time for the sound to penetrate, then he flopped over and crawled slowly across the deck.

There was a fitful glow to starboard, flickering smears of reds and oranges lighting the sky. It appeared to him that in the distance a mountain was on fire, belching ruby smoke, casting burning effluvia into

86

the obsidian night. He squinted, fascinated, convinced that he was dreaming. A dense pressure came to his ears. Great chunks of dark soapy stone were hurled high into the air and liquid fire, saffron, pale green, violet, shot from the summit of the mountain, igniting the air as it rose, then cascading downward to the earth. Blue flame, ghostly and luminescent, wrote itself inscrutably upon the tumultuous darkness while the land seemed to shiver and shift in a great upheaval. A roaring vibrated his body, filling him with the incandescence of energy. The entire world was kinetic. He imagined that he heard a mournful wail and the mountain seemed to bleed as rock, white and yellow and crimson, poured steaming and thick down its side, and forests of vapor rolled ponderously into the dulled sky. Then the night and all it held was obscured by a blackness darker even than sleep and Ronin began to choke on the soft dust.

The ship sped southward away, away from the trembling land, the red and onyx sky, over the thinning ice and, when once more the oblate sun cracked the horizon, still steeped in clouds glowing amber from its light, the morning was less chill, promising a day cool, not cold.

Still Ronin lay upon the maimed deck, delirious, the tatters of his foil suit fluttering over his gouged back. Perhaps it was better thus: that he did not see the vast chunks of ice shearing off with great cracks like barks of thunder, floating now out onto the dark green water.

The ship hit the last thin sheet of ice with a noise that was part groan, part splinter. The crust disintegrated under the weight, and at last the ship was afloat. The bow dipped precariously, then righted itself, the stem coming up in a shower. The cascade streamed over the gunwale running aft, eddying around the prone form lying on the deck.

He awoke briefly, snorting salt water from his nostrils, lifting himself weakly, grasping the gunwale, peered over the side. Water! his numbed brain screamed. Water! But he could not think why that was so important. He lifted his head and the sun blinded him. He looked again at the water, blue-green, sun-dazzled golden, and then beneath the surface at—what?

A shadow? Its immense bulk flickered deep beneath the waves without outline or contour. He stared at it for what seemed a long time. Then all that winked back at him were the green waves, tipped with reflected light, chopped into ten thousand minute crescents bobbing and dancing. What? Then he passed out, his body falling limply to the salt-slick deck.

The day turned chill as billowing clouds, dark and gravid, passed before the face of the sun, blotting out its warmth. The sea changed color, becoming slate gray; and now here and there whitecaps appeared. A heavy, gusty wind sprang up from the northeast and tore at the sail. Moments later, in the gathering gloom, the squall hit with full fury. The seas rose and the ship, unmanned, began to founder. She was turned beam on by the wind, into the troughs of the oncoming waves whose high crests now swept incessantly over the felucca. She began to take on water as she lay heavily in the crashing seas. Rain came in sheets and the day turned gray-green, dark and featureless, filled with the hiss and drum of the downpour.

The ship was sinking and nothing could save her. The wind hit her just as a wave crested broadside and she began to break up. The rain slackened but the wind intensified, as if it knew that the vessel was in the throes of going under.

The deck beneath Ronin's body buckled and collapsed and he was washed unceremoniously into the turbulent sea. He awoke in the water, gasping and choking for air as the sea filled his mouth and throat. He rose to the surface, hearing the grinding roar of the splitting ship all around him. Disoriented, heavy with the weight of his sword, he went under, clutched for a floating piece of the mast, missed, regained the surface, lungs bursting, back a glyph of agony as the salt drenched his wounds, reached again for the mast, felt its slippery length for only an instant before it rolled away from him. He tried to go after it but he had no strength and he knew with a peculiar calmness that he was drowning and there was nothing he could do about it. He went down into the cold green depths, watching the light recede from him, taking with him in his lungs a fast-diminishing piece of the sky.

THREE

·Sha'angh'sei·

Even when Rikkagin T'ien looked him full in the face, he was never sure what the stubby man was thinking.

"Tea?"

As now.

"Please."

What rules him? Ronin wondered not for the first time. Rikkagin T'ien was solid, built low to the ground. His wide shoulders, muscular arms, and short legs made him seem almost other-wordly. Then there was the fact that he was hairless.

"So pleasant to relax every now and then, so?" He lifted the small pot, lacquered in a multicolored wheel pattern. "You must excuse the lack of a lady," he continued as he delicately turned the small cups. "It is most unseemly for a rikkagin to perform this function." He poured the honey-colored liquid. It steamed the air. He tilted his head. "However war causes us to make do with so many things that we would normally find abhorrent." He shrugged as if talking to an old friend. His yellowish skin gleamed in the low lamplight, his wide oval head with its small ears, black almond eyes, and smiling mouth seemed almost regal in this atmosphere. The distant sounds of the ship wafted around them like a fragrance, dominated by the rhythmic singing. Rikkagin T'ien ceremoniously presented Ronin with a filled cup. He smiled dazzlingly and sipped at his own cup. He sighed broadly.

"Tea," he said, "is truly the gift of the gods." Then his face fell. This made him appear oddly childlike.

91

"How strange that your people are ignorant of its existence." He sipped once more from his cup. "How tragic."

They sat cross-legged on opposite sides of a low wooden table lacquered in squares of green and gray.

"You are comfortable in your new clothes?"

Ronin put a hand to his loose shirt, looked at his light pants.

"Yes," he said. "Very. But this material is new to me."

"Ah, it is silk. Cool in the heat, warm when it is cold." Rikkagin T'ien sipped again at his tea. "Some things are changeless, so?" He placed his cup precisely in the center of a green square. "Now that you are at your ease, please tell me again where you are from and why you are here."

Something pulled on his feet. His descent was checked. He was cradled, the sea washing over him. Then he rose toward the rippling emerald pool of light, rising from the depths, from the awful liquid silence, from the buoyancy of death, into the clean sweet air, the churning of the waves. Gripped again by gravity, he coughed and retched sea water, his lungs working like bellows, automatically, independent of his brain, which was still fogged, in the coruscating quietude of the ocean, not yet ready to accept the return to life. Then he rose into the air, a gasping, wounded phoenix.

"So," Rikkagin T'ien said, nodding. "A Bladesman you call yourself." He stared hard at Ronin; at his face, at the muscles along his arms, at the deep chest. "A soldier you are, a tactician. Well. You are ill and the injury to your back is quite serious. My physician informs me that you will carry those scars for the rest of your life." He stood up, planted his bare feet wide apart, bending his knees slightly. Three men came into the room, swiftly, silently, all armed, and if he had made a move to summon them, Ronin had not seen it. "Yet a soldier knows one thing. He knows how to fight, so?" He beckoned Ronin to stand. "Come," he said in a light tone that held no overtones, no rancor. "Come against me."

A song in his brain. A song. It dominated his senses, filling the air with a smoky tang, washing over him like the sea. It was a singsong tide of voices, rhythmic, sleepy, and muscular at the same time.

Slowly, numbly he turned over. Dazed. He had been drowning, tumbling gracefully down, twisting on the currents. He stretched out his arms. And now?

He was looking down through the slimy web of a net within which he lay. Below him, the swell and suck of the sea against long wooden planks. Curved. His eyes traveled upward and a word forced itself into his brain. A ship, he thought dizzily.

Drenched and dripping, he swung perhaps thirty meters above the water. Above him, the ship rose another forty meters. Its immense side sloped outward near the botton. The hull was painted a deep green from the gunwale until almost fifteen meters from the sea. From there down it was red. From the side of the vessel myriad square ports had been cut and from these jutted long slender staffs, it seemed to Ronin, cleaving the water at an oblique angle. A forest of staffs; on separate levels. Two? Three? Staring upward, the sun struck his eyes and he vomited the last of the sea water before he passed out.

" 'Rikkagin,' " said Rikkagin T'ien, after Ronin had for the first time told him the story of the Freehold, "is a title not dissimilar to that of Saardin, so?"

That had surprised Ronin because at no time since

he had been brought aboard had he ever been disarmed, even when he was in the presence of Rikkagin T'ien. Slowly he had come to realize that this was because they did not fear him.

Rikkagin T'ien beckoned to him and these thoughts flew through his mind like doves fleeing before a chill wind. What the little man said to him was true; he was not yet fit. Much of his strength had been sapped by his ordeal and it would be many days before he returned to good health. Yet he was a Bladesman and T'ien was again correct: he would have to prove himself.

He stood and Rikkagin T'ien bowed to him, a curious solemn gesture which he had sense enough to return. Two of the men came forward and, stooping, removed the low table from between them.

Slowly Rikkagin T'ien withdrew his sword, the light gleaming along the single slightly curved edge. Ronin withdrew his blade.

"Ah," said Rikkagin T'ien as if he had been holding his breath.

Heat. He sensed it even before he opened his eyes. The polyglot odors hit him then: sweat and briny salt, tacky tar baking in the sun and aromatic pitch, fresh fish flopping in the warmth. The singing was in his ears and the deck rolled gently under him to its thudding tempo. Heat. Against his chest and cheek.

He was stretched out on the deck. The burning along his back had somehow lessened. He sensed movement around him. A shadow crossed his face and the heat lessened. He tried to rise. A hand, gentle, firm, stopped him and he obeyed, understanding now that someone was working on his back. He felt weak and drained, not even sure, if he were pressed, what reserves of energy remained within him. The situation was unclear. He had no idea where he was. On a ship.

Just a ship. With that came the thought of the mast of the felucca. Bend, he told himself. Bend or you will break. Thus he willed himself to relax in the midst of the unknown. Thus did he survive.

He closed his eyes and let the breath flow out of him completely until his lungs sucked in the air of their own accord. He repeated this, cleansing his respiratory system and energizing himself by oxygenating his blood. His eyes opened. He stared at Rikkagin T'ien. He forced all speculation from his mind.

The curving sword was a blur, flashing upward, and simultaneously Rikkagin T'ien screamed. Ronin parried the blow. Just. The intense sound had surprised him. The clang of the blades echoed off the cabin's bulkheads. The rikkagin whirled and his sword hummed in the air again, the force of the blow stinging Ronin's wrists.

Back burning anew, Ronin lifted his blade; it was as heavy as a drowned corpse. Pain flared in his chest, making him gasp, and his guard dropped. Through the veil of agony, he saw Rikkagin T'ien advancing and, sweat rolling down his head and torso, he attempted to defend himself. Slowly, his sword came up, trembling. The end, he thought.

But instead of striking, Rikkagin T'ien stood as still as a statue, lowered his sword, sheathed it. The deck whirled, seeming to rise toward Ronin, and then he was in the powerful arms of the two men who had stepped behind him. They set him gently on a mat of rushes, carefully sheathed his sword.

Rikkagin T'ien's oval face hovered in Ronin's line of vision. He smiled reassuringly. Ronin struggled to rise.

"Stay still now," said T'ien. "I have found out what I needed to know." He shrugged, a totally pragmatic gesture, free of any theatricality. "Do not regret your pain, Bladesman." His face was a great yellow moon planted in the sky. "You see, we saw your boat break up and your story was most convincing, especially with the evidence of your back. But still"—the moon waned before his eyes, blood pounded in his temples—"we are at war and I must tell you that my enemies would do anything to discover my plans. Please do not think me melodramatic; it is quite true. And frankly the distinct possibility arose that you were in their employ." Pain was rippling through his chest, making breathing a labor. The moon smiled benevolently in the cloudless sky. "Rest now; you have proven your story; you are who you claim to be. Only a lifetime of training would have allowed you to come against me with three broken ribs." The moon wavered and broke apart. He strained to see it. "Now my physician is here. He will give you a liquid. Swallow it. He must set the ribs." Then the moon went out and he was falling, falling.

The passage of the days and nights were as puffs of smoke to him, blooming briefly, evaporating on a jasmine wind as if they had never existed; they were replaced by others, an ephemeral progression blending into a canvas of tonal colors, snatches of sounds, watery whispers of almost heard words. Most of the time he slept deeply, dreamlessly.

When at last he sat up he felt the constriction of the bandages fastened tightly across his chest. Immediately, one of the men in the cabin went out. The other leaned forward and poured tea from a clay pot into a small cup set on a lacquered tray. He held it for Ronin, who sipped gratefully until his thirst was slaked. He sat back and regarded the sailor. He had a sharp aquiline nose and a wide thin mouth. His deep-set eyes were blue. He wore an open shirt and wide-legged trousers. A scabbarded sword hung from his right hip. The cabin's door opened and the physician entered.

"Ah," he exclaimed, smiling, "you have had tea already. Good." He knelt and pushed Ronin gently down onto his back, his fingers moving deftly over the contours of the bandages. He was yellow-skinned as was T'ien, with almond eyes and a wide nose. He clucked to himself, then looked at Ronin. "It was a very bad fracture, yes. You were hit with great force." He shook his head as the fingers continued their probing travels. Ronin winced once and the physician said, "Ah," quite softly.

"He is better, so?" said Rikkagin T'ien from close by. Ronin had not seen him enter.

"Oh my, yes," nodded the physician. "Very. The ribs are knitting faster than I had anticipated. A very fine body. As for the back"—he shrugged almost apologetically—"it will heal but the scars are forever." His face brightened. "Still, not so bad, eh?"

"So," said Rikkagin T'ien, addressing Ronin. "When you feel fit enough, you will come on deck. Then we talk." He turned and left.

"Give him as much tea as he wants. And rice cakes," instructed the physician before departing. And Ronin was left with the men. Soon he drifted off to sleep.

A dense and smoky tangle, it climbed into the hills. It spread upward and outward from the wide harbor, the shores of the yellow and muddy sea, in a jungle of one- and two-story buildings of wood, dark paint, brown brick. In many places they seemed set so close together that he could not tell where one ended and another began.

"Sha'angh'sei," said Rikkagin T'ien.

Ronin could discern movement along the vast front of docks and wharves thrusting out into the slowly lapping waves. Dark masses milled like ants over an earthen mound; they were still too distant for him to pick out individuals. A peculiar haze hovered over the immense city, a component of its clutter and sprawl, obscuring its loftier reaches so that he had no clear idea how high the houses extended.

"Welcome to the continent of man." There was a harsh edge to the laugh.

Ronin tore his eyes away from the domination of the city and looked at the man who stood on the deck beside Rikkagin T'ien. He was tall and muscular with cerulean eyes and short-cropped thick blond hair. An ivory bar was run through the lobe of one ear. He wore a light-colored, loose-fitting shirt of silk tucked into tight black leggings. A long curving sword hung in a battered leather scabbard on one hip. A wicked dirk of extraordinary length, its hilt studded with rough-cut emeralds, a rather nonchalant statement of their value, was stuck into his sky-blue waist sash. T'ien had introduced him as his second in command: Tuolin.

"It was I who fished you out of the sea," said the blond man. "It was reflex, really. Most of the men believed you already drowned; you were under a long time."

Ronin shook his head. "I recall sinking, holding my breath, then darkness and a beating silence and then—"

Rikkagin T'ien called out an order and half a dozen men sprang from the deck, racing up the rigging lines. He turned back, observing them both.

"What happened to your back?" asked Tuolin.

"Have you been north?"

Tuolin shook his head, no.

"On the ice sea," said Ronin softly, "far enough south so that the water was already coming up on the ice, thinning it, a—some kind of creature broke through the crust and attacked us." Tuolin's eyes narrowed; he glanced quickly at T'ien, back to Ronin again.

"What kind of creature?"

Ronin shrugged. "I cannot truthfully say. The world, it seems, is filled with strange and monstrous things. In any event, the light was almost gone. It took us totally by surprise. There was no time for anything save death. The men in the rigging had reached the highest yards and they began to furl the topsails, using darting rapid motions. "It tore my friend in two; ate his legs."

They stood like three statues on the high poop deck, near the stern of the ship. A soft breeze brushed their faces, the tentative touch of a reunited lover.

"You must understand," Rikkagin T'ien said, "that death means little to us here in Sha'angh'sei; it is our way of life." He peered up briefly. The men were returning down the rigging. "War, Ronin. That is all we have known; all we shall ever know. Death waits for us behind every doorway, beneath every bed, down every dark alley of Sha'angh'sei." The ship began to slow as the command was given for the rowers to slacken their pace. "We would have it no other way."

"We have lost the ability to mourn for our dead," said Tuolin regretfully. "Still, I would very much like to know more of this creature of the ice sea."

"I am sure there is little more I can tell you," said Ronin. "However, I am most curious about this craft's mode of travel. It I could see—"

"The rowers?" said Tuolin. "I hardly think that you—"

"Tuolin," interrupted Rikkagin T'ien, "I do not think that under the circumstances we have much choice. It is a simple exchange of information." His eyes sparkled. "By all means, lead us down to the rowers."

Tuolin's face had set into hard lines and ridges and Ronin wondered what he was missing in this dialogue. He understood only that he dare not interrupt.

It seemed as if there was no air and one had to take short breaths because of the concentrated stench but over all it was cleaner than he would have expected. The men sat along low wooden benches, three to each oar. They were naked to the waist and the ridges of their working muscles along shoulders and backs glistened in the low light. They moved in perfect unison to the cadence of a drum and the rhythmic singing. Three tiers of men along three quarters of the length of the ship. He stopped counting at one hundred. They were dark-haired and swarthy, thick-boned and short, fair-skinned and fair-haired, yellow-hued and almond-eyed; a jumble of humanity, inhabitants of the continent of man.

"You can plainly see," said T'ien expansively, "that we refuse to rely solely on the inconsistencies of the weather. Canvas is fine when the wind is up, otherwise—" He shrugged.

They walked slowly down a narrow central aisle between the oarsmen.

"They are continually manned," T'ien continued. "The men work in shifts."

"They do not mind this work?" asked Ronin.

"Mind?" said Tuolin incredulously. "They are soldiers, bound to Rikkagin T'ien. It is their duty. Just as it is their duty to fight and die if need be for the rikkagin's safety." He snorted. "Where is this man from that he does not understand this? He cannot be civilized, surely."

Rikkagin T'ien smiled somewhat absently as if he were enjoying some private jest. "He comes from a long way off, Tuolin. Do not judge him so harshly." Tuolin's eyes blazed and for just an instant Ronin believed that he was going to turn on his rikkagin.

100

"Teach him if he does not understand our ways," said T'ien placidly.

"Yes," said Tuolin, the cold light receding from his eyes, "patience is its own reward, is it not so?"

T'ien walked on and they followed, a pace or so behind.

"You see," said Tuolin, "we carry with us many moral obligations which we are taught to honor virtually from birth." A dark blur at the corner of Ronin's vision. "To be bound to a rikkagin has many benefits." Oblique approach, ballooning. "One eats well, one is clothed, one has money, one is trained—" And Tuolin had seen it too because even now he was moving, the long dirk no longer in his waist sash. There was a scream, disturbing the heavy air like a sudden breeze parting a velvet curtain, and the figure was upon them. Tuolin leapt forward, his dirk flashing in a savage thrust. The body, long and thin, sweat-coated, wielded a curving single-edged sword. The face was pinched, the mouth screaming, lips pulled back from rotted stumps of teeth in a rictus, the eyes glassy and bulging fanatically. Then the figure was spitted on the blond man's blurred weapon. The legs kicked violently and then the eyes rolled as the blade ripped through the naked chest, spewing forth blood and bone fragments. The man's sword clattered uselessly to the wooden boards. Rikkagin T'ien watched impassively as Tuolin withdrew the dirk and with a deft economy of motion slit the man's throat. Ronin noted that T'ien had not even drawn his sword.

Now the rikkagin sighed and without looking at either of them said, "It is best if we return abovedecks." And stepped nimbly over the crumpled corpse.

Sha'angh'sei loomed over them as they maneuvered the sea lanes clogged with vessels large and small and eased into the port. The ship plowed slowly through the thick sea, yellow-brown and clinging, past square-rigged fishing craft and high-sterned cargo vessels. Off to starboard, Ronin thought he could just discern the broad mouth of a river spilling into the sea.

He stood on a high poop drinking in the city while all about him was movement as men raced through the catwalk rigging, reefing the last of the unfurled sail, securing yards and lines, the forest of oars high in the air, dripping and shining, as the rowers prepared to ship them. It lay before him in the inky twilight like a vast fat jewel, dusky and dim with age, smoldering with fitful movement, heaving itself from the spume and effluvia of the land.

The low buildings closest to him appeared to be built on a delta and he looked again for the river's mouth for confirmation but it was lost behind the thick clumps of buildings. Beyond the flat of the delta the city rose like the arched spine of a frightened animal and many of the dwellings in this area seemed to need the aid of wooden columns sunk into the hillside, which supported their jutting balconies, fluted and columnated, dark hardwoods gleaming in the smeary glow as lamps and torches were abruptly lit throughout the city as if by some prearranged signal. The deepening haze, sapphire and mauve, softened the flicker of the flames so that the individual sources blended and blurred and the city seemed to glow with an ethereal incandescence.

Ronin's pulse quickened. By chance he had come to Sha'angh'sei, and it was obviously a major port on the continent of man. Here, he felt confident, he would find someone who could unlock the riddle of the scroll of dor-Sefrith. The wash of light reached out for him as the ship maneuvered toward the waiting warf. Perhaps, he mused, Rikkagin T'ien will know of someone.

Men swarmed along the long arm of the wharf in

anticipation of their arrival and Ronin, observing the frenzy of activity, felt the muscles of his stomach contract momentarily as his spirits soared. The continent of man: Borros had been correct all along. So many people here, such a teeming world; even now, though it was before his eyes, it was a shock; so long talked of, it was a dream world that had been an integral ingredient of the fantasy that had kept them alive with a goal as they flew across the featureless platinum ice for endless days and nights with nothing but the cutting wind and cold as their reality. This dream had kept Borros alive until the end, Ronin was sure; his body had been beaten and, save for this land beckoning him on, Borros' mind would have let go in the midst of Freidal's torture within the confines of the Freehold. And now: now I step upon the cluttered foreshore of the continent of man. A dream no more.

There came a brief command and the ship touched the creaking timbers of the long wharf.

There was an electric hum, the live-wire abrasive intensity of rushing bodies, the cacophonous atonality of voices raised in argument, laughter, command, the chunky slap of cargo continually being loaded onto ships ready to sail to other ports, unloaded from just-docked vessels, the brief slam of working doorways, the beckoning cries of vendors, the lilt of hoarse monotonous work songs, the crisp cadence of soldiers' booted feet, the clangor of arms, the tolling of far-off bells, a whiff of mysterious chanting, and beneath it all, the heavy wash of the yellow sea lapping at the belly of the city, caressing it, washing its soil, eating its bedrock.

He stood on the wharf, an alien island in an ocean of moving bodies. The debarking soldiers passed him in formation, elbowing aside the scurrying workers, bare-chested and barefooted, tattered pants rolled up their legs, sweat streaming down their laden backs, some bent double under their immense loads, others in pairs trotting with crates of food-stuffs suspended from bamboo poles supported on their shoulders. Overseers screaming their instructions, orders being barked, sellers frantically hawking their wares, bodies coming against him like breakers, sounds like waves beating upon the shores of his ears, engulfing him. He breathed deeply and his nostrils flared to the steamy air laden with the fragrances of man, the pungency of fresh spices and syrupy oils, the mingling of exotic perfumes and thick sweat, the briny scent of the sea, rich with the myriad animal flavors of life and death.

Tuolin found him eventually.

"The rikkagin will see you tomorrow in the morning." Caftans of silk and cotton, tight blouses over firm breasts, long earrings clashing softly. "He is most anxious to speak with you at length." Gold rings glinting, a wooden leg with a worn shoe stuck on the end, colored skirts swirling, armbands dully shining, flash of yellow feathers. "Now he has many preparations to make and we could both use food and drink." Carts bumping, green eyes flashing, strange two-wheeled carriages pulled by toiling runners, dark hair floating in the soft scented breeze, music skirling. "Especially drink, eh?" Faces hidden by veils, faces covered with long beards, greased and curling, the savory mouth-watering perfume of roasting meat, a black and terribly empty eyeless socket, laughter, mouths gaping wide, black teeth, eyes crinkling, flash of dirk. "And afterward, a very special place, Ronin. Oh yes."

Along the sweep of the wharf the crowd thinned momentarily and Ronin was transfixed by a constellation of bobbing lights along the waterfront. Low, wide boats, some with makeshift shelters, most without, rocked gently on the evening tide. Lanterns were hung, illuminating the occupants. Families crowded the vessels, men, women, scrambling children and screaming infants, old ones still as statues, all assembled now for the meal at day's end; sitting with cracked shallow bowls of rice close to their faces, eating with long sticks, throats working as if they were famished.

"Home for many people," said Tuolin. "Generations have worked on land and have lived on the tasstans." Bodies closed over the view in an unwashed tide, blotting out all but the sea lanterns' mobile glow reflecting off the restless water. They began walking again. "There is no room for them in Sha'angh'sei." Shouts and the sounds of running feet. "There never was."

"Yet they work here, do they not?"

"Oh yes." A scuffle beside them; coarse curses, receding, drowned in the sea of bodies. "There is always work from dawn until dusk: for a copper coin which the merchants take at the end of the day, for the mildewed rice that they must eat. There is always work in Sha'angh'sei for a strong back, day or night. But nowhere to live." Tuolin laughed abruptly and clapped Ronin on the back. "But no more talk now. I have been too long from this city." He guided them skillfully through the jostling throng, moving at an increasing pace.

"Come," he called as he moved ahead. "We go to Iron Street."

Night lights flared along every street they took; black iron lanterns, wrought in openwork grills, the flames within licking smokily at the darkness. The packed streets were cobbled, lined with buildings variously assigned as apartments or shops without any discernible pattern. Men, thin and fat, lolled in open doorways, picking at their teeth or smoking pipes with long curving stems and tiny bowls, squatting against

105

grimy wooden and chipped brick walls, talking or dozing. Off these thoroughfares were ubiquitous narrow twisting alleys, blacker than the night, down which people would sometimes wander, disappearing within instants, leaving behind only a dissipating breath of sweet smoke.

They passed many soldiers, of differing types and obviously bound to various rikkagin. They seemed to be the only people in these noisome streets not in a hurry. Ronin was pleased to be able to walk; it gave him a chance to test his body. His back had ceased to pain him days ago and the wound in his shoulder was almost healed but he knew his ribs needed more time to mend. His chest was stiff and sore but most of the sharp pain had left him and this exercise was invigorating, not tiring.

On Iron Street, two men threw a set of five dice against the side of a wall, talking softly to each other, intent on the faces of the cubes. A woman in filthy clothes sat in the dust of the street, a bawling baby in the crook of one arm. She held a grimy hand, nails torn and black with dirt, palm upward.

"Please," she called in a pitifully weak voice. "Please."

Her sad eyes caught Ronin's and they were filled with pain.

"Ignore her," Tuolin said, noting the direction of Ronin's gaze.

"But surely you can spare something for her."

Tuolin shook his head.

"Please," the woman called.

"The baby is crying," said Ronin. "It is hungry."

Swiftly Tuolin crossed the crowded street and, thrusting aside the folds of the woman's robe, grasped the hidden wrist and Ronin saw that she held a dirk which she had been digging into the baby to make it cry. Her almond eyes flashed angrily and she

106

wrenched her wrist from his grip, lunging at him with the blade's point. Tuolin stepped back out of harm's way and they resumed their walk along Iron Street.

"A lesson of Sha'angh'sei," he said.

Ronin glanced back through the crowds of people. The woman sat, palm outstretched, the other hand hidden. Her lips moved; her eyes searched the passing faces. The baby cried.

"War is the reason Sha'angh'sei was built and it was built in a day."

"Surely you are not serious."

"Perhaps I exaggerate just a bit."

"How long?"

"To build the city?"

"No. How long has the war been on?"

"It is endless. I do not remember. No one can."

"Who is fighting whom?"

"Everyone against everybody."

"That is not an answer."

"Yet it is the truth."

They were sitting in a low-ceilinged tavern, at a plank table located along the back wall which ran almost the entire width of the establishment. A wide wooden stairway to the second story took up the remainder of the wall.

The air was thick with smoke and grease and burning tallow. Before them lay platters of broiled meat and steamed fish, raw vegetables and the inevitable rice. Cups of a clear rice wine, hot and potent, were constantly refilled as they ate using the long sticks. The men aboard ship had taught Ronin how to use these peculiar eating utensils.

"All the races of man are here, I think," said Tuolin between mouthfuls, "in differing strengths. And they have never gotten along."

"Borros, the man I traveled with over the ice sea,

107

believed that the sorcerous wars had ended all conflict."

Tuolin smiled as he swallowed but his eyes showed that he was not amused; they were as coldly blue as ice. "Man will never learn, Ronin. He is eternally at war with himself." He shrugged. "There is no help for it, I am afraid."

Six soldiers in dusty uniforms came into the tavern, pulling up chairs around a table near the door. They ordered wine and began to drink, laughing loudly and pounding on the table. Their long swords scraped against the floor boards.

"This city is composed of factions," said Tuolin, "all of them mistrusting the others because the war allows you to make much money if you are shrewd."

In the far corner two cloaked men, tall and light-haired, sat with arms around a pair of sloe-eyed women, slight, with high-cheekboned, flat-nosed faces, long black hair falling sleekly to the middle of their backs.

"The city is filled with many, many hongs—merchants—who are rich and fat from the war."

"They live here?"

One of the couples was kissing now, a long and passionate embrace.

"Hardly," Tuolin snorted. He gulped at his wine. "They live on the upper reaches." He refilled his cup. "In the walled city."

"Another city?"

"Yes and no." He took more meat with his sticks. "It is still Sha'angh'sei."

Along the opposite wall a woman with long eyes and a curiously simian face whispered to three men in dark cloaks. She wore her shiny hair piled upon her narrow head and long earrings of a green stone spun as she moved her head.

"What about the war?"

"It is everywhere. It is why we returned to Sha'-angh'sei. An army of bandits have massed to the north and west." Three children ran in from the street, thin and filthy and hollow-eyed. The tavernmaster called to them as they clattered up the stairs. He shouted and the tallest one returned and laid a number of dull coins in the man's hand. The tavernmaster slapped the boy so hard that his frame shook. The boy dug a dirty hand into a pocket and extracted several more coins, then he ran up the stairs after the others. "The hongs are paying us to protect their interests before the bandits become a nuisance by descending on the city itself."

Even to Ronin, so short a time with these people, it seemed an implausible story; however, he could not guess why Tuolin should lie to him.

"Then you will be leaving Sha'angh'sei?" he asked.

The simian-faced woman was gesturing now with narrow bony hands. Her long nails were lacquered green and, Ronin saw with some surprise, her teeth were black.

"Yes. The day after tomorrow. It is a three-day march to Kamado, the fortress in the north."

One of the men got up and walked out. The remaining two resumed talking to the simian-faced woman with increased animation. Her teeth gleamed darkly.

Ronin was about to say something but Tuolin's hand on his arm stopped him. He followed the blond man's gaze.

Two men stood in the doorway. They wore dark baggy pants and black cloaks over silk shirts. They were almond-eyed with flat wide faces. Their long hair was waxed and bound in queues. An errant gust of wind plucked at their cloaks and Ronin caught a glimpse of short-hafted axes thrust into their sashes.

"Keep still," whispered Tuolin, his eyes drifting

slowly away from the tall figures. His voice carried a peculiar note, of fear perhaps? He looked at Ronin and said in a more normal tone, "The rikkagin will require you at a specific hour tomorrow. Until that time, he requested me to be your guide around the city." Ronin stared at him. "Sha'angh'sei is a most complex and at times bewildering city. The rikkagin does not wish for you to get lost."

The men were still in the doorway, their black eyes sweeping the room. The tavernmaster glanced up from serving a table and, wiping his hands on his apron, hurried across the room. He drew from some inner pocket a small leather sack which he handed to one of the men. The other said something to him and laughed. The tavernmaster bowed. Then the two were gone without a sound.

"Who were they?" asked Ronin.

"The Greens," said Tuolin as if that were all the answer needed. He drained the last of his wine. "I have had my fill of this place. What say you, Ronin, shall we move on?"

Tuolin paid for their meal. The green stone earrings of the simian-faced woman danced as she spoke.

Outside in the fragrant air, there seemed less people about than earlier in the evening. Tuolin looked both ways along the street, then he seemed to relax, stretching.

"Now," he said, "the evening begins."

The gold plaque said "Tenchō." It was fixed with golden spikes to the brown brickwork to the left of the high yellow double doors at the head of a curving iron stairway on Okan Street.

Twice he had caught Tuolin glancing behind them as if he thought they were being followed. However, it seemed quite impossible to tell among all the bodies darting in every direction.

Tuolin knocked on the yellow doors and after a moment they opened inward.

"Matsu," he breathed, smiling.

She stood between the two armed men, her slender frame appearing smaller for their presence. She had an oval face with long almond eyes and thick black hair which she wore straight and loose so that one eye was continually blanketed by its cascade. She word a silver robe with a high neck and flaring sleeves, embroidered with gray doves. Her skin was very white; her lips were unpainted. The oval lapis pin at her throat was the only relief from the black, gray, and white.

She smiled at Tuolin, then gazed for a long moment at Ronin. Then she murmured to the guards, who relaxed somewhat.

She led them wordlessly through a narrow foyer. Strips of thin carpeting covered the wooden floors; a tall gold-framed mirror briefly disclosed the small procession. They went through open doors on the left from which yellow light wavered and danced.

They were in a wide, deep room with blond wood paneling along the walls to a height of an average man's waist. Above this, the walls were painted a muted yellow. The high ceiling was bone white. From its center hung an immense oval lamp constructed of faceted topaz; perhaps five hundred crystals had been cunningly mounted so that the lamp's myriad small flames, set in its center, shone through the facets. It was this singular light which gave the room its tawny aspect.

Scattered about the lacquered wooden floor were small intimate couches and groups of plush chairs upon which sat the most diverse assortment of women that Ronin had ever seen. Some were with men, drinking and smoking, others were in small groups talking languidly among themselves, turning their exquisite faces to the prowling men like petals of a flower following the path of the sun. Young girls in quilted jackets and wide silk pants of pastel colors moved between these groups, ships in the indeterminate voids separating these trembling constellations.

Matsu left them, crossing the room to a group of two men and a woman. After several moments the woman detached herself and approached them. She wore a floor-length saffron silk dress, slit up one side so that with every step she took Ronin could see the length of one naked leg. The dress was embroidered in patterns of fantastic flowers in the palest green. Like Matsu's, the dress was wide-sleeved and high-necked and this style managed somehow to highlight her figure.

But it was her face that was most extraordinary. She had long dark eyes, the upper lids dusky and sensual without seeming to be painted. Her face was narrow at the chin, accentuating her high cheekbones. Her lips were painted deep scarlet; glossy, half opened. Her hair was so violently dark that it appeared blue-black; she wore it very long and brushed to fall delicately across her left shoulder and breast.

She smiled with small white teeth and lifted her hands, pressing them together.

"Ah, Tuolin," she said. "How good it is to see you again." Her voice had the tonality of a bell, far away, lilting. She dropped her hands. They were small and white with delicate fingers and long nails lacquered yellow. She wore topaz earrings in the shape of a flower.

Her head turned slowly and she gazed at Ronin and at that precise moment he had the peculiar sensation of seeing double.

"Kiri, this is Ronin," said Tuolin. "He is a warrior from a land far to the north. This is his first night in Sha'angh'sei."

112

"And you brought him here," she said with a musical laugh. "How very flattering."

A young girl in a light blue quilted jacket and pants came up to them.

"Liy will take you to bathe. And when you return, you shall decide." The dark eyes regarded him.

The girl led them across the room of topaz light, through a wide teakwood door into a short passageway of rough-hewn stone. The contrast was absolute.

They went down a narrow stairway lit by smoky braziers set high up along the walls. The stone steps were damp and somewhere, not far off, Ronin could discern the soft slap of water. The stairs gave out into a wide room with rock walls and a low wooden ceiling, lamplit, warm. Into one wall had been hewn an immense fireplace within which hung an equally enormous cauldron steaming as the fire boiled its contents.

The room itself was dominated by two large square wooden tubs set upon raised wooden slats; one of the tubs was half filled with water. Four women, dark-haired, almond-eyed, naked to the waist, stood as if waiting for their arrival. Water steamed and gurgled.

"Come on," Tuolin called happily, stripping off his dirty sea clothes and hanging his weapons on one of a line of wooden pegs set into one wall. Ronin followed suit and the women directed them to the empty tub. As they climbed in, the women drew up buckets of hot water, filling the tub. Then they climbed in and, taking soft brushes and fragrant soap, began to wash each man thoroughly.

Tuolin snorted and blew water from his mouth.

"Well, Ronin, what do you think of this? Was home ever so pleasant?"

The hands were soft and gentle and the hot soapy water against his skin felt delicious. The women murmured to each other when they saw his back, the scars long and livid and newly healed, and they took great care in cleansing this part of him so that he felt no discomfort, only pleasure. They stroked his chest, gently massaging his muscles almost as if they knew of his recently broken ribs. They murmured to him and he and Tuolin moved, creators now of their own waves, commanders of tides and currents, to the second tub to which clean hot water was added. Two of the women began to clean the first tub while the other two gathered up the pair's dirty clothes and went out.

Ronin lay back, stretching out his legs, letting the heat slowly soak into his body. Gradually, his muscles loosened and much of the tension drained out of him. He closed his eyes.

How unexpected this all was. How utterly different were the circumstances than what Borros had pictured. How— Abruptly the realization came that he had had no idea of where he might be headed or even if he could survive when he had ascended onto the surface from the Freehold's forbidden access hatch. He had followed Borros blindly, not caring, wanting to escape from the Freehold as much as he had wanted to solve the mystery of the scroll of dor-Sefrith. The heat climbed into him like the presence of a naked woman close beside him.

And with that the barriers which he had so painstakingly erected folded in upon themselves and he thought of her. Oh, K'reen, how you must have been tortured. He destroyed you day by day with the poison he fed you. The lies!

The water rippled and Ronin looked up, into the present. One of the women had climbed in beside Toulin.

"Do you want the other one? It is perfectly all right but you must ask."

Ronin smiled wanly. "Not just now. The water is enough."

The blond man shrugged and splashed the woman, using his cupped hand. She giggled.

Strange. The Freehold seems like so long ago; as distant as another lifetime. But she does not. She is still with me and there is nothing, Chill take him, that the Salamander can do about that.

He glanced at his great sword, swinging a small arc, brushed by one of the women as she slipped out of the room. Within it was the scroll and perhaps, if Borros was right about this, the key to man's survival. And he could no longer doubt the Magic Man. He had already grappled with the Makkon; felt its awesome power. And instinctively he had known that such a creature was not of this world; it held its own kind of monsters.

Of this he was certain: at least one Makkon was already here. If the scroll has not been deciphered by the time the four converge, they will summon The Dolman and mankind will surely be doomed.

"Ready?" asked Tuolin.

They both stood up, dripping.

"Let me look at you."

The scarlet lips opened. The tiny pink tongue brushed the even white teeth.

She laughed. "She is always so clever about these things."

He wore a silk robe of a color that could have been light green or brown or blue or any one of a dozen colors. Yet it was none of these but perhaps a subtle blend to cause the finished cloth to appear colorless. Along the body and arms were fierce dragons, rampant, eyes seething, taloned limbs seeking, embroidered in gilt thread so that their hides seemed molten. Tuolin was clothed in a robe of deep blue with white herons on front and back.

"Ah, Tuolin, you must have brought me a remarkable man." Kiri directed her eyes to Ronin's. "You know, I will not say this to all who come to Tenchō, but Matsu chooses the robes to fit each person who enters here. She is rarely wrong in her matching."

"And what does this mean, then?" asked Ronin, glancing down at the glittering dragons.

"Why, I am sure I do not know yet," she said with a small smile. "I have never seen that particular pattern before."

She turned to Tuolin then and took his arm. Her perfume came to Ronin, rich and subtle, musky and light. The three of them strolled across the room of topaz light, stopping momentarily as one of the girls offered them tea and rice wine, and Kiri introduced them one by one to the women who were not already engaged with men. All were beautiful; all were different. They smiled and stroked the air with their ornamental paper fans. At length, Tuolin made his choice, a tall slender woman with light eyes and hair and a generous mouth.

Kiri nodded and turned to Ronin.

"And you," she said softly. "Whom do you wish?"

Ronin looked again at all the women, the jutting landscape of femaleness, and he came back to her black dusky eyes.

"It is you," he said slowly, "that I wish."

When the organism does not comprehend, sight and sound become meaningless. The light-haired woman therefore looked strange to him as she opened her mouth wide and emited a sound.

She gasped, then half giggled, stifling it with a swallow as the three others stood quite still watching her. Around them the movements continued, the languid flutters of a fan, the flashes of naked legs, the sweet smell of smoke curling, the steaming of hot tea and

116

spiced rice wine, like the slow immense wheel of the stars.

There came then the chink of a cup being set down on a lacquered tray, as separate and distinct a sound as a crack of thunder of a rainwashed night.

Tuolin said: "But that is im—"

Kiri's delicately upraised hand halted him in mid-sentence.

"He is," she said, "from another land. That is what you told me, Tuolin, yes?" The yellow nails were like slender torches in the light. "I asked and he replied as he wished." Now she was gazing into Ronin's eyes but she spoke to the blond man. "You have selected Sa, as *you* wished. Take her then."

"But—"

"Think no more upon it, lest your harmony be broken and this house become worthless. I take no offense." The yellow nails moved fractionally, spilling light. "I shall take care of Ronin. And he shall take care of me."

"What happened?" asked Ronin after Tuolin and Sa had departed.

She took his arm and laughed softly. They began to walk in the room of topaz light. "Death," she said lightly and without any trace of coyness. "It is death to ask for me, foreigner."

A tiny girl in a pink quilted jacket came up to them to offer rice wine.

"Please," Kiri said and he handed her a cup, took one for himself. He sipped at the wine; it was quite different from the rice wine of the tavern. The spices added a tang and sweetness that he appreciated.

"I will choose another then."

There was muted laughter and the sinuous rustle of fabric against scented skin. The sweet smoke was heavier now.

"Is that what you wish?"

117

"No."

"You told me what you desired."

He stopped and looked at her. "Yes, but—"

"Hmmm?" The scarlet lips opened and curled in a smile.

"I wish also to abide by the rules of your people."

She urged him to begin walking again.

"The one thing you must remember about Sha'angh'sei, the only thing worth remembering is that there are no laws here."

"But you just told me—"

"That it is death to ask for me, yes."

The yellow nails traced the gilt dragons of his robe, over flaring nostrils, open mouth, and snake tongue, down the serpentine body, across the rampant claws, following the sinuous tail.

"But everything is yours for the taking. The factions of this city bind themselves in codes and unwritten rules." Her eyes were huge and mysterious; he felt the pressure of her nails through the cloth. Her voice was a whisper now: "Who dwells in Sha'angh'sei but the dominators and the dominated?" He drew toward her. "Yet law is unknown here."

It was less dense in the room of topaz light as the couples began to disperse. The girls were cleaning up in perfect silence and soon its tawny splendor was left to them alone.

"No," she said, and when she shook her head her hair was like a forest in the night, "you are not from Sha'angh'sei or anywhere close. You are totally untouched by the city."

"Is that so important?"

"Yes," she whispered. "Oh yes."

"Tell me again why you have come to Sha'angh'sei."

"You have heard it before."

"Yes, but this time I wish Tuolin to hear it."

"I had never heard of the city until you told me of it."

"Of course," he said, not unkindly.

Rikkagin T'ien sat cross-legged behind a green lacquered table on which stood a fired clay teapot, a cup showing the dregs of many fillings in its bottom, an inkwell, and a quill pen. He put aside the sheaf of rice papers upon which he had been writing a vertical list of figures.

"Begin, please."

Ronin told the story of the scroll of dor-Sefrith, the gathering of the Makkon, the coming of The Dolman.

There was silence in the room when he had finished. Yellow light streamed obliquely through the leaded glass panes beyond which, one story below, lay Double Bass Street where the rikkagin and his men were quartered and from which they would depart at dawn tomorrow for the long march to Kamado.

He saw T'ien glancing at Tuolin, who stood, hands clasped behind him, facing away from the windows. With the light at his back, his face was in deep shadow. It occurred to him then that they did not believe him; that, despite Rikkatin T'ien's words to the contrary, they perhaps thought him still an enemy. Nevertheless, I must ask.

"Perhaps you could help."

"What?" T'ien had been pulled from some deep thought. "Help in what way?"

"By deciphering the scroll."

The rikkagin smiled somewhat sadly. "I am afraid that is quite impossible."

"Perhaps the Council could aid him," said Tuolin.

Rikkagin T'ien looked bewildered for a moment and he stared at the blond man as if he were a statue which had just spoken. Then he said, "Yes, now that you have brought it up, that might be the answer." He seemed lost in thought again.

"You see," said Tuolin, "the city is governed by a Municipal Council: nine members with the major factions represented and the minor ones currying favors through taels of silver and other commodities. If any in this city possess the knowledge you seek, they would."

"Where does the Council meet?"

"In the walled city, on the mountain above us. But you will have to wait until tomorrow; I do not believe there is a Council session today. Is that not correct, Rikkagin?" Tuolin smiled.

"Hmm? Oh yes, quite so," T'ien said, but his mind still seemed preoccupied with other matters.

In the small silence, the soft clatter of the rikkagin's men attending to their preparations drifted lazily through the open windows.

There came a knock on the door and Tuolin crossed the room before T'ien had a chance to say anything. A soldier bowed his way in, handing Tuolin a slip of folded rice paper. The blond man opened it and read its contents, his brows furrowing in concentration or anxiety. He shook his head at the soldier, who immediately departed. Then Tuolin crossed the room and laid the paper open in front of the rikkagin. While T'ien read it, he said, "I am afraid that a number of last-minute administrative problems have arisen and they will require the attention of the rikkagin and myself for the remainder of the day. Please feel free to see the city but we should like it if you would return here and take the evening meal with us." The smile came again.

T'ien looked up. "Ask one of the men downstairs for directions. They have been instructed to give you a bag of coins. You cannot get anything in Sha'angh'sei without paying for it."

Outside, he turned left and then right, walking down a street of some incline. The day was overcast and a yellow mist was still rising. He caught himself thinking of T'ien and Tuolin. Again he had the feeling that he had missed something vital in their exchange, yet the answer remained elusive. He shrugged and put the problem out of his mind.

He came to a broad avenue after several minutes and the noise of the city welled up at him. Rows of stalls lined the crowded street. One sold fowl. They were hung by their necks, cooked and varnished with a shiny vermilion sauce so that they looked wooden and unreal. As he watched, people stopped, putting down a few coins. The stall's owner brought out bowls of rice and sticks and commenced to cut up pieces of the cooked bird into the rice. The people ate standing up. For another coin they received a small cup of green tea to wash down the meal.

Elsewhere, a tailor of leather worked, making boots and cloaks. And at a busy intersection a fat man with a thin drooping mustache sat within a square metal cage, lending money at the day's going rate, which, Ronin surmised, was somewhat higher than yesterday's.

He heard the cadence of boots and a group of soldiers tramped by, moving disdainfully through the clouds of people.

He walked the city's twisting fluid streets, caught up in the rapid pulse, repeating and changing, flashes of color, a riot of sound, aromatic spices drifting across his meandering path.

He observed transactions of all kinds, handled in quick sharp movements; he watched people who seemed to do nothing but watch other people, standing by shopwindows or sitting along the sides of buildings.

He was staring at a line of six barrel-chested birds

on a thick wooden perch, preening their long saffron feathers, when it came to him, strained through the myriad sounds of the city, yet perfectly clear as it gyred in the wind. Following his ears, the sound pulling him in like a net, through the turnings of broken streets and dank alleyways until at length he stood before a stone wall and listened to the tolling of the bells, coloring the air. An ancient wooden door was set into the stone wall. Without thinking, he opened it and went through.

The tonal wash of the city faded as he crossed the threshold and he heard the bells more clearly now although their source seemed still far away.

Across a sudden background of misty silence he heard a horn sound once.

The bells tolled sweetly once again, in the garden neat, precise, beautiful. Glistening flowers of white and yellow and pink were arranged amid rocks and furry moss and feathery ferns in exquisite patterns.

Water burbled and farther on he found a tiny waterfall and a pool filled with small fat fish with long silver fins fanning the green water like veils. He walked on a path paved with brilliant white gravel.

The bells ceased and the horn sounded again. A quiet chanting began, lilting, pleasing to the ear, drifting somnolently on the still air. Ronin strained his ears but could discern no sound from the city without the stone wall.

In the center of the garden was a large metal urn, of brass perhaps. Beside it sat an ancient man in brown robes. His wrinkled face was serene, his eyes were closed. His sparse hair was white, his beard long and wispy. He sat still as stone.

Ronin reached out and touched the bulging metal sides and felt—nothing. So pure a nothingness that it was tangible. An immutable space yawned, years falling like dry leaves, centuries passing like silent drops of rain, eons emerging, merging, sundered. And an immense quietude entered him: the thunder of eternity.

He was shaken.

He found that he had closed his eyes. When he opened them, the bells were tolling again, high in the air. He went on stiff legs through a wooden doorway and it was as if a gust of melody had transported him to another world. The air was humid with incense, the light was dim and brown as if it were ancient. Stone walls and marble pillars, a ceiling indistinguishable in the gloom.

In the distance, masses of squat yellow candles were lit, the tiny flames swaying like a chorus of dancers preparing for a performance. The incense and the tallow caused the air to take on a third dimension. Thus he moved now, feeling like the fish in the pond outside, as slowly as through water. The centuries hung upon him as taels of silver, dense and beautiful.

Then from somewhere he thought he heard a coughing, low and questioning. An animal presence. Perhaps a voice, so distant that he heard but the echo, said, *Find him*. Soft pad of paws, a scratching as gentle as the rustling of autumn foliage. *You must find him*. Echoes echoing. Away.

He looked dreamily about him. The chanting came again, pellucid, peaceful, scenting the air. Shafts of tawny light fell obliquely through the high narrow windows, lacquering the store floor and the reed mats. He was alone.

He thought of the bronze urn and the man who sat so still beside it.

He was there when Ronin returned to the exquisite garden. Eyes closed. A statue. The fish swam lazily. The water gurgled throatily. The bells were silent.

He approached the stone wall, went through the wooden door, and as he closed it behind him the discordant noises of the city, frantic and desperate, descended upon him like a horde of locusts in the heat of summer.

He walked randomly, still half dazed, until he realized by the waning light that the day was almost done. He asked a corpulent merchant lolling indolently in the doorway to his store, waiting impatiently for customers, gap-toothed and sweaty, for directions back to the rikkagin's quarters. The man looked at him, his clothes, the sword at his hip, the bag of coins in his belt.

"You go to dinner, gentleman?" His breath was foul.

"Yes, but—"

"A goose perhaps. Or a fine fresh-slaughtered pig for your host." His voice took on a wheedling tone. "A magnificent gift, very generous and at a most modest price. Twenty coppers only."

"Please tell me where—"

The merchant's brow wrinkled. "If you are thinking of Farrah's, his meat is not one tenth as fine as mine." He clasped his fat hands as if in anguish. "And the prices he charges! I should inform the Greens."

"Double Bass Street, is it near here?"

"I would, you know, but I am not a vengeful person, ask anyone on Brown Bear Road. An honest businessman only. I mind my own affairs. Do not ask me, as many do, what goes on around the corner or"—he rolled his eyes—"upstairs. If I told you—"

"Please," said Ronin. "Double Bass Street. How far?"

"If they want to do those vile things, well, who am I to say—"

Ronin left him, walking blindly down the street.

"Go to Farrah's then, as you planned all along," the fat merchant called after him in his high whine. "You deserve each other!"

124

He passed up a carpet shop along Three Peaks Street. It was crowded with customers and an army of clerks who all looked as if they were related. Next door was an apothecary, its huge stone jar hanging above the doorway on ancient creaking chains, a dusty window filled with small colored packets, phials of gritty-looking powders, liquids in tall tubular jars. In the center of this display was a lidded clear glass bowl filled with a slightly yellowish liquid suspended in which was a root in the singular shape of a man. It was dusky orange-brown and had many threadlike tendrils. The thing stirred his curiosity and he went inside the shop.

It was long and narrow, dusty and tired-looking. A high wood and glass case ran the length of the shop's right wall. Within it lay neat piles of containered liquids and stacks of cartoned powders, a hundred and one items, he supposed, for headaches and stomach pains, muscle pulls and swollen feet. The proprietor stood behind a counter along the back wall.

He was small and old and stooped as if he carried his years about with him as a tangible burden. He was a sad man, with almond eyes and yellow skin as thin as rice paper, almost translucent. Long strands of hair hung down from the point of his chin, otherwise he was hairless. He was measuring out portions of a sapphire powder upon clean white squares of rice paper.

He looked up as Ronin approached.

"Yes?"

"Am I near Double Bass Street?"

"Well now, that depends." The gnarled yellow hands continued their work.

"On what?"

"On which way you go, naturally." He stoppered the container of powder, put it carefully away on one of a series of shelves behind him that ran all the way to the ceiling. He turned back. "If you cut through the

125

alley there to Blue Mountain Road, well then, you are but five minutes away." He began to pour each mound of powder into blue glass phials. "However, if you were to walk farther down Three Peaks Street until you reached the Nanking it would be infinitely safer." He had two of them filled now. "Longer but safer." His head nodded. "Yet"—he looked up at Ronin—"you did not come in here merely to ask me the way to Double Bass Street." He pointed with one crooked finger. "Anyone out there could have told you just as well. No, I believe you came in to inquire after the root."

Ronin did not hide his surprise. "How could you have known?"

All the phials were filled now. One by one, he stoppered them.

"You are not the first, by any means. It is not there for decoration, though many passers-by think so."

Ronin was fed up.

"Will you tell me?"

"The root," he said, lining the phials up on a shelf, "is ancient. And as with all things ancient, it has a history. Oh yes! Not a very pleasant one I am afraid." His nostrils dilated and he shifted several times. "Come closer." He nodded. "Yes. It was you, then, who was at the temple." He closed his eyes for just a moment. "There is a lingering trace of incense."

"But what—?"

"I heard the horn sounding, after all."

"The horn?"

" 'A visitor,' it said. 'A visitor.' "

"What foolishness. It was merely a Sha'angh'sei temple."

The old man smiled oddly and Ronin saw that his teeth were lacquered black, shiny and square-cut. He thought of the simian-faced woman in the tavern:

what mysteries had she been selling, and for what price?

"Ah no." The old man shook his head. "The temple was here long before Sha'angh'sei came into being. The city grew up around it. It is the temple of another folk, being gone from this continent before the beginnings of man." He shrugged deferentially. "Some say so, at least."

"But there was a man in the garden of the temple."

The smile was released again, oblique and inferential.

"Then perhaps what they say is not the truth. You know people often tell you only what they wish you to know." The old man put a hand to his head as if it pained him. "Such as the house on Double Bass Street."

Ronin stared at him. "What?"

"Take the Nanking."

"But that is the longer way, so you said."

"It does not matter. There is no use in your going there."

A crawling along the back of his neck.

"Why not?"

"Because," said the old man flatly, "there is no one inside."

Ronin went out the door fast without bothering to close it, weaving through the throngs of bodies, his eyes searching ahead for the alley leading to Blue Mountain Road. He almost overran it, so narrow and dark it was. The braziers and lanterns of the city were just being lit, luminescing the deep purple haze that seemed to cover Sha'angh'sei each evening.

Three Peaks Street was still dusky with the lingering dregs of afternoon so that he did not have to pause in the gloom of the alley for his night vision to become effective.

The darkness deepened and he knew at once there was trouble. There should have been at least a glow from the lanterns of Blue Mountain Road, even from around this turning just before him. He slipped his sword free. Silent and deadly now, he advanced along one dank wall, went around the bend.

The smell of raw fish, putrefying; human excrement. There were hard, scraping noises. Panting. A grunt. He froze and listened intently. More that one person; more than two. That was as exact a determination as he could make. But that was all right because the adrenalin was pumping through him; his sword had been sheathed far too long. Now he ached for battle. He did not care how many men awaited him. He advanced.

Whites of eyes peered up at him as he approached at a run and he counted quickly and precisely because he knew there was little time and he had to prepare his entire body. The battle lust would not impede him because his training automatically took care of the organism. Six.

A man lay on the ground, the six over him. Brief glint of a curved blade, heavy, twisting, then the image was gone from his sight, lost in the night. But something lingered and he reviewed it because it might be important. The glint was not silvered, but black on white, wet-looking. Red is black in dim light. Blood.

He heard the faint whirring and let that guide him because he knew now what it was and they would not expect that.

Speed.

He thrust in a blur and there was a piercing scream. A chink on the stone as the ax hit the paving. He had deliberately aimed low, to open the soft viscera of the stomach and intestines to make a mess. He lifted the blade as he withdrew, flicking it, so that a fountain of black blood and wet organs spewed forth as the man collapsed.

He was already moving forward with a two-handed thrust as the second man leapt for him and the blade whistled in the air as it clove the man from shoulder to belly. The corpse danced drunkenly, dead before it hit the ground, twitching still.

The fever mounted and it seemed as if everything around him slowed as his own speed increased. He saw the ax peripherally and knew that he could not get the sword up in time because of the angle, so he let it fall and allowed the crescent blade to come at him, gleaming, whispering scythelike. At the last instant his gauntleted hand came up, closed over the blade. The hide of the Makkon absorbed the force of the blow. There was a gasp and he saw the whites of his opponent's eyes all the way around as they opened in fear and surprise.

He laughed then, and it boomed through the close corridor of the alley, echoing menacingly off the wood and brick walls, dank and covered with slime.

The sound of running feet, the breathless air fanned, muttered voices, cursing, and the lights of Blue Mountain Road at last glowed at the far end of the alley. Ronin rubbed the scales of the gauntlet as he retrieved his sword, sheathing it.

He turned then to the man who lay twisted on the ground. He bent on one knee, searching for the pulse at his throat.

The man coughed. He was dark-haired with almond eyes but there was a strange cast to his face that, even in this dim and uncertain light, looked vaguely familiar to Ronin. He was clad in a tight-fitting suit of dull black cloth.

"Uk—uk—uk."

Blood came out of his mouth, black and wet in the night. His hand reached up convulsively and clutched at his neck. He coughed once more, blood and something more. Then he died.

Ronin stood up, then impulsively he bent again and opened the man's clenched hand. A slender silver necklace with something on it. He took it from the dead man for no reason at all and slipped it into his boot. Then he went down the alley and out into the confusion and flaring light of Blue Mountain Road.

Silence.

The night still and calm.

The old man had been right. There was no one at Rikkagin T'ien's quarters, not T'ien, not Tuolin, not a soldier, not a porter.

Ronin turned on the step and surveyed the street. He was absolutely alone. They had all gone. To Kamado, he assumed. Early. Not a good sign. Perhaps the situation to the north had deteriorated. If they had told him the truth; and he was not at all sure now that they had.

Abruptly, he remembered the strange root. In his haste to get here, he had not had the time to hear its history. He shrugged. Well, it was too late now, the shop would be closed. He could stop by tomorrow before he went up the mountain to the walled city to see the Council. And in any event he was hungry. He had not eaten since the morning and then only rice and tea. He went down the steps of Rikkagin T'ien's house and along the street in search of a tavern.

"Someone will come for you."

"But—"

"No instructions."

"All right. And the payment?"

"Now. In taels of silver."

"Just a moment—"

"You wish to be there? You wish to see it?"

"Yes, but—"

"Then you will do as I say."

The simian-faced woman was wrapped in a green cloak. A hairless man sat by her side tonight, narrow-skulled, flat-faced, a bright ring through his nose. He smoked a pipe with a long stem, curved downward slightly, and a small bowl. The simian-faced woman was speaking to a man with russet hair and light eyes. His skin was milk white and he sat in a peculiar position as if he could not bend one leg.

"It is too much," said the man with the russet hair. The other man was impassive, pulling on his pipe.

The woman leaned forward and Ronin could see the sheen of her black lacquered teeth. "Think of what the silver will buy you. The Seercus is not an everyday occurrence." She laughed tautly. "And I need not remind you of the restrictions. Consider yourself fortunate." The odd head nodded, up, down. "Most fortunate."

They were sitting at a corner table, near enough to Ronin so that he had no difficulty in hearing their conversation over the steamy noise of the tavern.

It was a large, smoky room off the Nanking, one of Sha'angh'sei's main roads. Low wooden beams crossed the ceiling; the air was thick with wax and grease. It was, in short, like every tavern in the city.

Ronin pushed away his rice bowl, lifted his sticks, and put a last morsel of broiled meat into his mouth. He reached for the rice wine.

"Perhaps I can get a better price elsewhere," said the man with russet hair, but there was little conviction in his voice.

The simian-faced woman laughed, a soft silvery tinkle, surprising in its delicacy. "Oh yes, by all means. And the Greens will—"

"No, no," said the man quickly. "You misunderstand. Here." He reached out a leather pouch from beneath his cloak, counted out forty silver pieces.

The woman stared at him solemnly, did not look down at the taels. The hairless man swept them off the table, his yellow hand a blur in the light for only a moment.

"And ten more," said the woman evenly.

The man with the russet hair started.

"Ten—but you gave me a price—"

"For this ten, I will not inform the Greens."

She laughed as the man reopened the pouch.

"The Seercus," she whispered.

The hairless man took the coins. He pulled again on his pipe. There was a cloud of smoke. They got up and left.

The man with the russet hair ran a shaking hand over his face, reached for the small flagon of wine on his table. Drops beaded the wood as he poured.

Two men came in and sat down at Ronin's table. The proprietor wandered over and they ordered steamed fish and wine; Ronin asked for another flagon of wine.

"And how were the fields, now that you've seen them firsthand?" asked one.

"The poppies are not good." This one had a large nose, red-veined and wide-nostriled.

"Ah, the Reds again. This time we must enlist the Greens to—"

"Not the Reds." He was still brushing the silt of travel from his gray cloak.

"Eh?" He looked suspiciously at the other. "This is not another of your tricks, is it? You know I agree that what the Greens ask is enormous, but we stand to lose much more if the harvest is ruined. I should well think that you would understand that by now."

"No, I tell the truth."

"Well, what then?"

The proprietor came over with a tray laden with

132

food and wine and they remained silent until he had served them and drifted away.

The man with the large nose sighed and poured himself wine. "I wish I knew. Truly." The fish looked at them from the center of the table. He picked one up with his sticks, bit into the head. "The Reds in the north have, I believe, split apart."

The other laughed uneasily, pouring wine. "I hardly think that is possible."

"Still, that is what I have heard." He began to shovel rice into his mouth with his lips close to the rim of the bowl. "Every day, more kubaru disappear and the crops themselves are not producing as they should."

"Well, if they are not being properly attended—"

"I am afraid that is only part of it." He took a gulp of wine, perhaps to steady his nerves. "It is as if the land itself has changed, become less fertile—" He began to cough thickly.

"Are you ill?"

"No, a chill only. The weather is much colder than it should be at this time of year."

At first Ronin had been listening peripherally. He wanted to understand this complex city. To do so he had to understand its inhabitants better. Listening in on conversations seemed as good a way as any to start. It was another reason why he had chosen to go to a tavern instead of visiting one of the many street stalls selling an infinite variety of foods. But his rather casual eavesdropping became more intent the further on this conversation went. Perhaps this was the beginning; perhaps he had less time than he had thought. If so, it was more imperative than ever for him to gain admittance to the Council of Sha'angh'sei; to find someone who could decipher the scroll of dor-Sefrith.

Now the merchants talked of other matters, prices and the fluctuating market. Ronin paid for his meal and left. In the Nanking, he asked a boy for the way to Okan Road and had to pay for the information.

She was not there and so he waited.

It was already late. He asked for rice wine and it was brought to him by the tiny girl in the pink quilted jacket. He remembered her.

"How old are you?" he asked as he savored the spices.

She lowered her painted eyelids.

"Eleven, sir." So low he had to strain to hear her.

He opened his mouth again and she ran off.

"He tried to relax, opening his ears to the soft sounds of silk brushing satin thighs, liquid pouring, low talking that was almost like the murmuring swell of the sea. The tawny light. He closed his eyes to slits, hearing in his mind a horn sounding, far off and alone. A gentle laugh intruded. A giggle, stifled. Perfumes drifting upon the languid air. A hint of sweet smoke from somewhere and he thought of the poppy fields. "There is much fear in the north," the merchant with the large nose had said. Why?

"Ronin."

He opened his eyes.

It was Matsu. Skin white as bone; eyes like olives. Her body small and supple.

"She will be very late." Black hair drifting over one eye. "Please let me take you upstairs."

She offered him her hand. Firm and warm. He stood up, rubbed her palm with his fingers. He towered over her as they went up the broad polished wood staircase to the second story. Yet he felt her support, strong and comforting. One arm was around her slender shoulders. He stroked her cheek as they rose. The yellow light grew brighter as they ascended toward the great crystal lamp. The tiny flames shivered, sparking pinpoints of light across their faces.

He peered down, drunk with wine and fatigue, at the grand, deserted room with its golden couches and low lacquered tables. Even the serving girls had gone to bed by now. The room was spotlessly clean, not a stained teacup lay about, not a spill of wine, not an ash-laden pipe remained.

The tawny light streamed down endlessly, it seemed, until Matsu shut the door of the room. She did not light the small lamp on the black lacquered table next to the wide bed. The room had a high domed ceiling and across the patterned walls flowers were tossed and dripping in a summer rainfall. The curtains had not yet been drawn and through the window he could see that the moon was up, pale and ghostly but perfectly clear in the night sky.

He sat on the bed and stared out the window at the pulsing carpet of pinpoints, blue-white like rare gems and startlingly close. Matsu knelt and pulled off his boots. A part of the sky was lighter, as if a translucent scarf had been laid over the blackness of the night; a bridge of light formed by the closeness of the stars within its width. She removed his clothes and he donned the dragon robe which she held out for him.

She put him under the covers and then came into the bed. her naked body trembling from the cool of the night sweeping in from the open window, her soft skin raised in gooseflesh, and he put her head in the hollow of his shoulder, stroking her hair, his thoughts over the hills and far away.

She smoked a little, the sweet smell engulfing them as she inhaled deeply with a quiet hiss. Sounds drifted up to them from the city that never slept. A dog barked, far off, and rhythmic singing wafted up from along the waterfront. Something metallic clattered on the cobbles close by and feet pounded briefly. A hoarse shout. The rattle of a cart and someone whistling tunelessly. Matsu's eyes glazed and the cold pipe

135

fell from her open fingers spread like the petals of a small white flower on the dark covers.

She was asleep against him, close and warm now, her shallow rhythmic breathing a soporific. At last he relaxed. Carefully, he put the pipe away. The moon was huge in the black glittering square of the window, flat and thin as rice paper. Then a cloud rode across its face and his eyes closed. He dreamed of a field of poppies shivering in a chill wind.

It was still dark when she woke him.

"She will not come tonight."

The moon was down but the sky had not yet begun to lighten.

"It is all right."

"Do you want me to stay?" Her voice was tiny, like a child's.

He watched her at the side of the bed, the light silk robe clinging to her firm slender body.

"Yes," he said. "Stay with me."

A sinuous rustle as the robe slithered off her and she climbed into bed. Black and white.

There was silence for a time and he listened to the leaves trembling in the trees on Okan Road. Footsteps and muffled voices briefly heard. Matsu pulled the covers closer around them.

"Cold."

Ronin felt her lithe body against him and held her close.

After a time, she spoke again. "Do you know Tu-olin well?"

Ronin turned his head to look at her.

"Not well, no."

She shrugged. "It does not matter. He will die at Kamado."

He lifted himself on one elbow and stared at her.

"What are you saying?"

136

"He told Sa many things in the shallows of night. I have heard many others. Tales of evil."

"What," he asked, "have you heard?"

"The rikkagin's armies no longer fight the Reds in the north. I have heard that they fight side by side now: the lawless and the law."

"Against whom?" But he already knew.

"Others," she said, giving the word a strange overtone, as if that were not the word she wished to use. "Creatures. Men who are not men."

"Who told you this?"

"Does it matter?"

"Perhaps very much."

"My friend's husband is a soldier with Rikkagin Hsien-Do. So is his son. They spent much time in the north, near Kamado. They returned three days ago." She clutched at him and he felt the shivers in her frame, thought of the green leaves on the trees outside. "My friend's husband is blind now. They had to carry the son back to Sha'angh'sei. His back is broken." Her voice came in little gusts now. "They did not fight the Reds; they did not fight bandits. They fought—something else." Another shudder went through her frame. "Even the Greens are talking among themselves about the situation in the north."

There was a thin line of the faintest gray now, visible only if he looked away because at night vision is better around the periphery. He held onto the shaking body and, from the corner of his eye, watched the line of gray widen with agonizing slowness, bringing the burden of another day.

She was still sobbing so he said, "Who are the Greens?" Because he wanted to stop her; and because he wanted to know.

"The Greens." She sniffed. "You must have seen some of them."

137

Two men in black in the tavern's doorway, axes at their sides, demanding payment.

"I am not sure."

"They are," she said, "the law."

He was surprised. "I had assumed that the rikkagin were the law."

She shook her head, her hair fanning his cheek, and the last of the tears fell from her cheeks onto the darkness of his arm as it lay along the covers.

"No," she said quietly, calmer now. "You must understand that the rikkagin are not native to Sha'angh'sei, or this land. Oh, they are the reason that it has grown and become——the way it is. But many are from far away. They brought their legions here to fight for the wealth of the land, the poppy fields, the silk farms, the silver, and more. They twisted the land and its people to their own ends." She sighed a little as if she were not used to speaking so much. She moved her head against his chest; he inhaled her fragrance, clean and sweet. Her feet twined with his, their soles rubbing together. Friction warmth.

"But this is a most ancient land," she said. "Here there are still many who have not forgotten the ways of their ancestors, handed down carefully from father to son and daughter. A legacy more precious to us than land or silver, even after the coming of the rikkagin, the turning of the hongs."

Her hand sought his, lightly, a feathery touch, yet it conveyed to him an intimacy most singular. "The Greens and the Reds have been at war for all time, or so it is told; from the moment of their births there was enmity. Now each seeks to gain each other's territory."

"What is the nature of the enmity?" he asked.

"I cannot tell you."

"You mean you will not?"

Her eyes flicked at his face, surprised. "No. I do not know. I doubt if they do themselves now."

On the Okan Road, the sky was pearling the roof-tops of Sha'angh'sei. A fine rain began to fall, sighing among the trees, misting through the window, blown on a gentle morning breeze. A sea horn sounded in the distance, muffled and melancholy.

She kissed his broad chest as she opened his robe, the dragons writhing. "They are," she whispered, "the terrorists of tradition." And she offered up her mouth, moist and panting.

It was the angle that made it so dreadful.

Matsu choked and turned her head away and he held her as her body convulsed.

There was nothing there and that was why the head was at such an inhuman angle; he could imagine her shock. She seemed steadier now and she turned, needing to look once more, to help dispel the shock. The head remained attached to the shoulders only by a sheet of skin glinting readly in the dismal light.

The scream had burst in on them like a thief in the night and he had unsheathed his sword and was out the door before it had entirely died away, the gilt dragons fluttering in his wake. There was noise on the wide landing from behind myraid closed doors; movement as the sleepers awoke. The scream tried to force itself out again, like a caged animal, but it was choked off and he heard instead a liquid gurgling.

He raced down the hall, toward the head of the staircase. A dull thud, leaden with finality, and he knew he had just passed the door. Matsu was coming after him, tying the sash of her robe, closing the gap now because he had stopped. Raising his sword, he opened the door, slamming it wide with his shoulder, and leaped into the room.

He saw the window first because it was directly in

139

his line of sight and because he knew it was the room's only other egress. It was open to its fullest extent. On one side, the curtains were completely gone, on the other, the tatters fluttered uselessly. There was an increasing clatter from the hall but he ignored it. He inhaled the stench.

She was on the bed, her head at an impossible angle because everything had been torn out: throat, larynx, neck musculature. Just the frayed skin and a great pool of blood. He looked at last at her face. Sa.

He took Matsu outside into the hall, though he had to force her, because there was nothing either of them could do. He closed the door behind them.

"I have never," said Matsu, "seen such a death."

The hall was crowded now, mainly with women; the men preferred their anonymity.

"Has anyone seen Kiri?" Ronin asked them. No one had.

He took Matsu back to the room of dancing, crying flowers and once there began to dress. She pulled her robe tighter about her; peach marsh with pale green ferns.

"The Greens?" he asked because he wanted to be absolutely certain.

She shook her head, hair like a thick mist, fanning out. "No, the Greens use axes and"—she shuddered—"not that."

He buckled on his belt and went to her, drawing her up to him. Her pale hands were like ice.

"It is most important that I go out; and I must go now. Do you understand?" Because her eyes were clouded like the sky on the dawn of a stormy day. "Will you be all right?" His fingers gripped her shoulders. "You will stay with the guards?" He wanted to make certain.

She looked up into his colorless eyes now. "Yes," she said and he believed her. "Kiri will soon return."

"Tell her I was here."

The ghost of a smile.

"Yes," she nodded. "I will."

The door closed softly behind him.

It was a disquieting day: overcast, rain falling more heavily now, pattering against the roofs of the street stall, and he pulled his cloak about him. It was somewhat lighter directly overhead but dark clouds scudded across the sky in the distance.

The weather had not diminished the crowds, however. Oiled rice-paper umbrellas and thick cloaks to keep out the dampness were much in evidence.

He paused at a stand on Blessant Street, for rice and tea and to inquire after the surest route to the walled city. But there was a crawling in the pit of his stomach and he found that he had little appetite. He drank his green tea and listened to the forlorn drip of the rain on the stand's meager canopy.

He took Blessant Street as far as King Knife Street, which wound around in such circuitous fashion that several times he believed that he was headed away from the incline of the mountain.

Once he saw a beggar, sprawled in the street, filthy, unmoving. It was only after he had passed the body that he realized there was no life in him. Death was ignored in Sha'angh'sei, as T'ien had told him; at least most forms. Which brought him back to Sa's death.

He had known before he asked Matsu that it had not been the doing of the Greens. The stench was still in his nostrils. But that was a time factor; even if he had been later, the smell dissipated, he would have known by the way she was killed. It was the same manner in which G'fand had died in the City of Ten Thousand Paths. The Makkon.

But why had it killed Sa? He felt that it was important for him to know, but the answer eluded him.

141

As King Knife Street began to wind upward, the old dustworn shops thinned and gaps between buildings became more frequent. At first these were mere dirt alleyways into which filth and refuse had been dumped. But gradually, as he continued to ascend, they were filled with wild grass and thickets of fir trees, tall and willowy, their slender dark green tips swaying in the swirling rain.

As the incline increased so the aspect of the houses he passed was transformed. There was more brickwork in evidence here, in good repair and ornately crafted. Different styles of architecture made their presence felt.

The road was well paved now but fairly free of people and it occurred to him that here, on the way to the walled city, was the only area of Sha'angh'sei he had been to so far that was not jammed with people.

It was eerily silent. At once he missed the hubbub and jostle of the throngs, the thick swirl of commingling scents, the filth, the life and the death, the vast mysterious panoply of humanity.

In the absence of the teeming crowds, he was struck by the artificiality of the houses and he recalled Matsu's words, *They twisted the land*. For this seemed an entirely different Sha'angh'sei, at once cleaner and crasser. It seemed to him that here, among the columnated houses, with their plaster and wrought-iron scalloping, the natural tones and inclinations of the land had been pushed back, held at bay along the foothills, and that here the brand of the legions of rikkagin from faraway lands, squatting, growing fat from the wealth of Sha'angh'sei's land, was very apparent.

He topped the last rise of King Knife Street and went into the chill shadow of the walled city. The wall itself was some six and a half meters high, constructed of enormous yellow stone blocks joined so cunningly that he could barely distinguish the joints. Heavy metal doors stood open to the inward side but a latticed metal grillwork gate barred the entrance.

Men in purple quilted jackets and wide black leggings stood just inside the gate. They all were armed with curved single-edged swords and short-hafted throwing axes. They were almond-eyed and their long greased hair was bound in queues.

A thickset man with a flat face and wide nose came and opened the gate.

"Why do you come to the walled city?" asked the man. "You are a new compredore, perhaps?"

Another man drifted over in a cloud of sweet smoke. He took the pipe out of his mouth and regarded Ronin with heavy-lidded eyes.

"No, I seek an audience with the Municipal Council."

The flat-faced man guffawed and walked away.

"They will not see you," said the second man, pulling at his pipe.

"Why not? It is most urgent that I see them."

Smoke swirled in the air and the man turned languidly, pointing at the trees of the walled city running in thick rows away from them, lining the quiet avenues; the large, stately buildings, flat-roofed, terraced, with carefully sculptured gardened fronts.

"Here the fat hongs and sleek functionaires of Sha'angh'sei live and build their fortunes, unseen and, for a price, safe."

"From what?"

The black eyes studied Ronin with unwavering intensity.

"From Sha'angh'sei," he said.

He sucked at his pipe but it had gone out. He knocked the bowl against the wall, began to refill it from a leather packet within his quilted jacket.

"No one sees the Municipal Council, my friend." His eyes were unnaturally bright. "At all."

143

The rain beat down. The avenues were slick with wet, gleaming dully. The trees rustled in the wind, flinging moisture, and somewhere a bird sang sweetly, enfolded within brown branches and green leaves.

"Where is the Council building?"

The man with the dark eyes sighed. "Take the avenue to the left. Second turning." He moved into the shelter of an overhang.

The echoes of marble. The soft sighing. The prolonged susurration of whispering. The quiet click of boot soles.

The hall was cold and columnless and empty of ornamentation. Its only furniture was low, wide, backless benches of the same pink and black marble.

The hall echoed to his footsteps as he crossed the polished floor. Ahead of him, the desk.

He passed people sitting humped on the benches. There was a peculiar air about them, as if most of them had been here for so long that they had forgotten their purpose in coming. Expectancy had perished a long time ago.

The desk too was of marble, curved and thick, a heavy shield for the woman who sat behind its imposing façade. Although she had the black hair and almond eyes of the people of the Sha'angh'sei area, her face was nevertheless less delicate, with a more pronounced bone structure so that he knew that she had other blood in her. She had light eyes and a square chin which she knew gave her the appearance of strength. She spoke accordingly.

"Yes, sir. State your business, please." She had before her a long list of names and was in the process of drawing a line through the third name from the top with her quill.

"I seek an audience with the Municipal Council of Sha'angh'sei."

144

The quill dipped into the inkwell. "Yes?" Scratch.

"I come on a matter of the utmost urgency."

She looked up then.

"Is that so?" She smiled charmingly with small white teeth. "I am afraid it will do you no good."

"I am sure that when the Council hears—"

"Pardon me, but you do not seem to understand." She wore a tightly cut green and gold quilted jacket that showed off her jutting breasts and narrow waist in a way that was severe and, because of it, sensual. Her startling sapphire nails plucked at the jacket. "One must make an appointment to see the Council." She brandished the list in front of her. "It will be many days."

"I do not think you appreciate the gravity of the situation," said Ronin, but already he was feeling rather foolish.

The woman sighed and pursed her lips.

"Sir, everyone who seeks audience with the Council is on an urgent mission."

"But—"

"Sir, you are in the Municipal Building of Sha'angh'sei, the seat of government for not only this vast city but the enormous area of land in the surrounding vicinity. Maintainence is a most complex and problem-filled task. Can you understand that?" She leaned forward, her face intent. A strand of hair came loose from its binding, stroking the side of her face as she spoke. "In the event that you do not, let me tell you that this city must feed and house not only its numerous inhabitants but also many of the outlying communities. We also must take care of the constant flood of refugees from the north." She threw her shoulders back as if it were an act of defiance; it had a double effect. She knows her job, he thought. "Sir, through the port of Sha'angh'sei comes the bulk of the raw materials to sustain much of the continent of

145

man. It is more than a full-time task in these evil times to keep this city running." She finally swept a hand up, flash of deep blue, tugging the wayward strand over her ear. "Now you can appreciate why we cannot allow the Council to be errantly disturbed. Why, if everyone who came to this building were allowed an immediate audience, I cannot imagine how this city would function." She took a deep breath, leaning back in her chair. Her breasts arched at him, an unsubtle offering of consolation.

Ronin leaned over and stared into her eyes.

"I must see the Council today. Now."

He did not expect her to be intimidated and she was not. She clicked her sapphire nails and two men appeared armed with axes and curving dirks.

"Would you care to have me add your name to the list?" she asked sweetly, her eyes never leaving his. They laughed.

"All right," Ronin said, and gave it to her.

"Yes," she said, the quill moving. Then she sat back and her pink tongue strayed for a moment between her lips. "That is most sensible."

The rain was heavier and they were all within the roof's brown overhang, squatting around a brick pit. Flames crackled and sparked. They were drinking rice wine when he came up. The man with the dark eyes peered at him through the smoke of his pipe; the others ignored him.

Ronin came unbidden out of the rain, shook the water off his cloak.

"The Council would not see me."

"Yes," said the man, "a predictable course." He shrugged his shoulders. "Lamentable but what can one do?"

Ronin squatted beside the man. No one offered him wine. "What I want," he said, "is a way in."

The man with the flat face looked over at him. "Throw him outside, T'ung," he said to the man with the dark eyes. "Why waste your time?"

"Because he is not from Sha'angh'sei?" said T'ung. "Because he is not civilized?" He turned to Ronin. "What would you give me as payment?" The flat-faced man grunted knowingly.

Ronin lifted the bag of coins at his waist, letting the fat chink of the coppers speak for him.

T'ung eyed the pouch and screwed up his mouth. "Mmm, much too small, I am afraid." His face assumed a sad expression. "Not nearly enough."

"What, then, would you want?"

"What else have you?"

Ronin looked at him.

"Nothing."

"That is most unfortunate." He sucked on his pipe, blew smoke lazily. It held on the humid air, a translucent pattern, a mysterious glyph.

"Wait: Perhaps there is something." He dug in his boot. "A chain of silver."

Ronin drew out the dead man's chain. The silver blossom gleamed in the diffuse light. He handed it to T'ung.

The rain dripped dolefully, pattering against the overhang, making the leaves on the trees dance to its rhythm. T'ung sat very still, staring at the silver blossom. It flamed orange as he twisted it and it caught the firelight. Slowly he put down his pipe.

"Where," he said softly, "did you get this?"

"What?"

A brief flash in darkness.

"Tell me."

Black blood. The scythe blade blooming silver as it swung at him in the alley.

"I want an answer." The voice turned harsh and grating. Heads turned. The flat-faced man rose.

147

Too late, Ronin thought savagely. He stood up, staring at the scythe-bladed ax hung at T'ung's side. Greens.

The flat-faced man saw the silver blossom and his hand went to the haft of his ax. T'ung stood and the others, alerted now, dropped their cups and pipes and came toward him.

Ronin backed away, thinking furiously, Chill take me for a fool! Those were Greens in the alley.

T'ung was between him and the open gateway beyond which teeming Sha'angh'sei beckoned like a sweet reward.

T'ung clutched at the chain and withdrew his ax. And the others came on.

"Kill him now," said the flat-faced man.

He crouched in the tangle, panting, taking deep breaths, swallowing to get the saliva back into his mouth. He listened for the sounds he knew would come, magnified by the rain. But all he heard was the rustle-drip of the soaking foliage. The sky was all but gone. The rain beat against him, running down his face. He blinked, lifted one hand across his forehead to clear his vision. He heard the sounds then.

The right arm had decided him. It was out and up, about to begin the ax's deadly descent. They had been expecting him to use his sword and to retreat defensively. He did neither. He launched himself head-long at T'ung, lifting his forearm and knocking the ax blade aside as he smashed into the body. Taken by surprise, T'ung crashed into the wall and the way was clear.

Then he was through the gate and running in an erratic zigzag through the rain, acutely aware of the axes at his back, knowing that they could be thrown as well as swung.

Boots pounded behind him and he heard the flat-

148

faced man screaming and, farther behind, T'ung's voice, curiously calm and remote.

He heard the panting coming closer; the flat-faced man was gaining on him because he ran in a straight line, did not have to dodge.

He turned then, planting his feet and withdrawing his sword in one motion. The flat-faced man was quick and agile but he was angry and that would help. Ronin swung first and his foot slipped on the wet paving. Idiot!

Grinning now, the flat-faced man dodged the blow, came on, and the blade of his ax was a blur in the rain. Ronin was moving away when it bit into his arm with a searing white heat. Ignore. He swung his own blade in a reverse arc and the Green, not used to double-bladed weapons, was slow to react. Ronin's blade caught him beneath the arm, sinking deep into the socket. He cried out, his body jerked, and the bloody ax fell from his trembling fingers. His gaping mouth filled with water. Ronin wrenched at the hilt to free it and the arm came off. The flat-faced man shrieked and folded like a paper doll. Rain washed at the running blood. The others were coming now and Ronin took off down King Knife Street.

Through the beat of the rain he heard the boots and the echoing shouts; he kept his body low and the sounds were amplified. Then voices came to him on the wind: queries, shouts of anger. He risked some movement in order to get a visual fix. Led by T'ung, the Greens fanned out, searching for him. One was coming directly toward him.

In the end, the cart had saved him. It swerved out of a walkway blind to King Knife Street and he almost ran the owner down but there was just enough time and he missed it. It was now, however, directly in the path of his pursuers. The delay was brief but sufficient. Around the next turning, rows of houses and an

149

explosive tangle of wild greenery, within which he promptly lost himself.

Still and calm, he remained behind his house of trees and tall ferns. Drip, drip. The rain beading and streaking the leaves. They quivered before his face. A bird fluttered in the branches above him. Crunch. The sound very close indeed and he felt the presence, separated only by the tenuous curtain of greenery. He held his breath. Perhaps—no, the branches low down swayed and began to part and he had no choice. Silently he put down his sword, then turned away from its mirrored surface, his reflection distorted by the moisture.

After a time, with Ronin's forearm jammed against his windpipe, the Green's eyes rolled up and he collapsed without a sound, his face white and pasty. Ronin crouched, listening. Still. The pinging of the rain. He dragged the Green behind a dense section of foliage, went back to where he had left his sword. He wiped it down and sheathed it, then crouched again behind the sheltering leaves until he was certain that they had gone back to the gate.

The rain had ceased by the time the shops of Sha'angh'sei built themselves around him once again on the cluttered level ground of the lower reaches of the city. Through the filth of the milling throng he pushed himself, his left arm soaked in blood and the pain a constant thing now that he attempted to clamp down on.

He passed a large group of people, wide straw hats, torn and uneven, feet bare and black with the muck of the streets, all carrying sacks and hurriedly tied bundles. Soldiers were directing them to a building farther along the street.

"Refugees," said a soldier in response to Ronin's question. "Refugees from the fighting in the north."

"Is it worse?"

"I do not see how it could be," the soldier sighed. "This way," he called sharply to a straggling few, staggering in exhaustion. One of them, a frail figure, fell into a puddle of brackish water. No one paid the slightest attention.

Ronin moved toward the still form.

"He is beyond help," said the soldier.

Ronin knelt and turned the body over, wiping the black mud from the gaunt face. The mouth was slack, the eyes closed. It was a woman, young and still beautiful despite the ravages of near starvation. Ronin pushed back her stiff wide-brimmed hat, felt along the side of her neck. He opened her mouth wide and breathed into it, slowly, deeply.

The soldier sauntered over. Most of the refugees had been herded inside now.

"Save it," he said, taking a large bite out of a tightly rolled brown stick. "She is gone."

"No," said Ronin. "There is life within her still."

The soldier laughed, a dark and evil sound. "She is less than worthless." He hawked and spit. "Unless you lack the coppers for a woman. Still she seems a poor—"

But Ronin had risen, turned, hand on sword hilt. Jaw set, muscles rigid, staring into the soldier's eyes. He said something, his voice like the whistle of a steel blade as it strikes.

There was a long moment when he saw the soldier weighing it in his mind. He looked for his comrades, found none.

"All right," said the soldier. "Do whatever you wish. It is no concern of mine. Let the Greens handle it." He turned away, heading toward the building into which the refugees had gone.

She was taking shallow breaths now but her eyes were still closed and clearly she was seriously hurt or

151

ill, perhaps both. He could not leave her here and, since he had been on his way to the apothecary's, he hoisted the frail form carefully onto his massive shoulder and disappeared into the hurrying masses of humanity.

The enormous jar hung suspended, creaking on its chains in the lowering light, the metal burnished. The dust seemed thicker in the shop, as if he were returning here after a century instead of merely a day.

"Ah," exclaimed the old man without much surprise. "So you went through the alley after all." His long chin whiskers trembled with the movement of his mouth.

Ronin went down the narrow aisle, put the woman onto a stool. The apothecary came around from behind his counter. He wore a wide-sleeved yellow silk robe and strange shoes which seemed but wooden platforms for his feet. He glanced at Ronin, then looked at the huddled figure.

"She is not from Sha'angh'sei—"

"Yes, I can see that." The hands moved deftly.

"She is from the north, the soldier told me. Fleeing the fighting."

The old head shook from side to side. He touched her face, then went behind the counter, reached out packets of powders, red, gray, gold, mixed them with a milky liquid. He pushed the contents across to Ronin.

"Get her to drink that." He turned. "You will take her with you?"

"Yes, I cannot leave her. I am sure that they will take care of her at Tenchō."

Something inexplicable came into the apothecary's eyes and he nodded.

Ronin pressed the hinge of her jaw and the mouth gaped open. She was still unconscious. He cradled the

152

back of her head, mindful of the angle, and let the thick liquid dribble into her lips. Half of it went down her neck and he had to depress her tongue to prevent her choking, but he got a fair amount in her.

The apothecary returned from the musty interior of the shop and began to work on Ronin's arm, laying a square greasy pad along the wound, then wrapping it in white cloth. Over this he poured a clear liquid which seeped into the cloth and thence into the wound. For a moment the pain was exquisitely sharp. Then, almost immediately, it was gone.

There was time now, he thought.

"Tell me about the root."

The apothecary poured more liquid, wiped at the seepage.

"It is said that it was found by a warrior." The voice was dry and dusty like the wind of the ages. "The greatest warrior of a people now long dead. The warrior was out riding, for he was bored. His skill was so great that none could stand against him, so that that thing which he desired most—the conquest of a powerful foe—was denied him." He wrapped the shoulder in dry bandages.

"As evening drew nigh," the apothecary continued, "he came upon a glade in the high forest of his land. No other thing grew near it and a pale new moon, already lambent in the sky, illuminated the root. The glade was quite large and as he dismounted he found that cracked and weathered stone slabs were set in the earth, as if this place were an ancient burial place, but of what people he could not imagine, for time had long ago beaten the writing on the stones."

Dust swirled in the shop, as if a wind from an unmentionable quarter had sprung up.

"The warrior went to the root and pulled it from the soil. He found that he was suddenly ravenous and he cut a piece of the root and ate it." The apothecary was putting the last of the packets away.

Ronin stared at him.

"The warrior, so the tale goes, became more than man."

"A god?"

"Perhaps." The apothecary shrugged. "If you wish. It is but a myth."

"Not a pleasant one, you told me."

"Yes, that is true." The old man's eyes blinked, looked huge. "The warrior indeed became more than man but in so doing he became a danger to the old laws because now surely there was none to stand against him. So was unleashed upon him a terrible foe. The Dolman."

The vertigo was so severe that he thought for an instant that the tiled floor of the shop had become a river. He worked to control his breathing. Somewhere the echo of laughter.

"What was The Dolman?" It sounded like someone else's voice, faraway and indistinct.

"The ancient of ancients," said the apothecary softly. "The primeval fears of man. The terrors of a child alone and afraid at night. Nightmare given free reign, embodied now, substantive."

A dry wind at the core of his being, plucking.

"It does not seem possible." Merely a whisper in the aged dust.

"It is a most monstrous creation."

"Where did it come from?"

"Perhaps the root?"

"Then where is the root from?"

"The gods themselves cannot know—"

"She wishes to see you."

"Good, she has returned then."

"She asks for you to wait for her."

154

He regarded Matsu in the tawny light. The slender face, with the planes and angles of a man-made structure. Small, wide-lipped mouth, large black eyes as soft as velvet dusk at the waterside. She wore a robe of pastel blue with brown cicadas embroidered across the body and wide sleeves. It was edged in deep gilt with a sash of the same color. He thought—

"Wait for her here, please." She studied the floor at his feet.

"Will you stay with me tonight?"

"I cannot." The voice barely a whisper. He tried to find her eyes. "Yung will see that you have wine."

She bowed to him, a curiously formal gesture.

"Matsu?"

She went away from him, across the room of tawny light, through the buzzing conversations, the opulent silks, the exquisite bodies, the perfect faces.

These people are still a mystery to me, after all, he thought.

He found an empty chair and sat wearily. Almost immediately, tiny Yung in her pink quilted jacket appeared with a lacquered tray with a wine pot and cups. She knelt at his side and poured the wine, handed him the cup.

He sipped and she left. He savored its warmth down the length of his throat, tasting all the spices, and he was reminded that he had not had a full meal that day.

Afterward, the apothecary had returned to the woman while Ronin withdrew his sword. He removed the hilt and produced the scroll of dor-Sefrith. Once again he studied its glyph-covered face. So many times. It stared at him blankly.

He turned. Evidently the old man had found a wound on the woman. He had tied a poultice in place on the inside of her thigh.

"Do not change the bandages even if they should

become dirty. There is medicine underneath." Then he saw the scroll and began to shake his head.

"Do you know what this is?"

He looked away. "I cannot aid you in this."

"You have not even looked at it." Ronin thrust the scroll toward him.

"It does not matter."

Ronin's eyes blazed. "Chill take you, it does! You know of The Dolman, you alone of all the people I have met in Sha'angh'sei. You know that he exists so you must know that he is coming once again to the world of man."

The old tired eyes stared at him without expression. Desperately Ronin said, "His minions are even now prowling the streets of the city. The Makkon killed this morning."

A faint tremor began at the corner of the old man's mouth and he appeared about to crumble from misery and pain.

"Why do you speak to me of such things?" he asked in a cracked voice made thin by fear and something else. "There is not a day in my life that I have not suffered and I have seen many days; I wish now but an end to the suffering."

"Do you wish the death of mankind?" Ronin cried, suddenly furious. "By not speaking of what you may know, you become an ally of The Dolman."

"A new age is dawning. Man must look after himself."

"Are you not a man?"

"I am unable to help you by reading that scroll."

"Tell me then who can."

"Perhaps no one, any more. But I can tell you this. The Dolman does in fact come and this time the world may be ground into the utter oblivion that is The Dolman's victory. It is the destroyer of all life, war-

156

rior, wielding a power beyond imagining. Already its strengthening forces are marshaling themselves in the north. Ah, I see that you have suspected this. Good. Now go. Take the woman and care for her well. Remember what I have told you. I have done all that I may for now."

Yet what was he to do now? The Council of Sha'angh'sei would not see him for many days and he could not now return to the walled city because the Greens would never allow him through the gate. Kiri was his only hope. She knew many people, a large number of them extremely influential, for through the saffron doors of Tenchō flowed nightly the cream of Sha'angh'sei society and business; Tenchō was for the wealthy and the powerful. Among these were, no doubt, several officials of the Council itself. There leverage could be applied, if she would consent to aid him. He had to ask her now. Time was fast growing short. With each passing day the chill shadow of The Dolman reached farther into the continent of man as his legions consolidated their strength.

Thus he waited for her, as she had bidden, sprawled in the plush chair, his scabbarded sword scraping the polished floor, drinking the clear wine— Yung had already come and gone twice more—his mind drifting, his eyes watching. The women passing were colored reeds, pastel and slender, bending, robes sweeping in perfect folds and rustling in the gentle wind, fans and long lashes fluttering like nervous insects in the oblique rays of the sun at day's humid end as it dazzles the still water. Placid oval faces, helmets, of flowing hair, the fabulous blossoms of impossible flowers, mysterious and erotic.

Two willowy girls in matching quilted jackets came for him then and led him off to be bathed and dressed and he knew that tonight would be special.

"Am I not worth the wait?" she said without coyness.

She was dressed in a formal robe of rich purple silk, like a plum sunset with threads of the palest dove gray woven into a pattern of opening flowers.

Her lips and long nails were purple and she wore an amethyst pin in the shape of a fantastic winged animal in her hair. Her extraordinary black eyes danced with diamond-point lights.

Still, she looked subtly different.

They had bathed him and dressed him in black silk pants and wide-sleeved shirt laced with platinum thread which glittered in the light. When he was ready, they had led him to a small room and she had come in.

"Are you hungry?" she asked now.

"Yes, very."

She laughed and it was like hot sun glancing off a naked blade. "Well, come then, my strong man, and remember well what you have said."

Out into the Sha'angh'sei night they went, of moist wispy fog, lavender and blue, of a thousand eyes and ten thousand knives and one million running feet.

Down the wide sweeping stairs and into a square covered carriage Kiri called a ricksha. They climbed in and the barefooted kubaru lifted his poles and set off without a word, the ride much smoother than Ronin would have imagined because it contained a peculiar rocking motion tied to the runner's gait that he found soothing.

The blazing streets of the city, aflame with the swinging lanterns and the crush of people, the smells of broiling food and boiling rice, fresh shellfish and spiced wine flowed past them in a rippling without end, a vast variegated canvas upon which it seemed all the events of the ages of man must be painted in subtle colors too potent to be real.

He breathed the musk of her perfume and stared into her eyes when he could tear his vision away from the flashing city. They were so huge that he imagined that an entire universe resided within their depths. Platinum flecks shivering and he saw with a start that her eyes were not black but the deepest shade of violet that he had ever seen.

Upward they climbed, away from the crawling delta of the port, onto higher reaches of the city where silver taels made room for spired houses, ornate balconies, sculpted stone walls, and landscaped greenery.

Trees whispered their mysterious messages and the night deepened as the intense light from the multitude of lamps drifted silently away from them, down the mountainside, the fast receding shore of an incandescent isle, remote now and unreal, just choppy splashes on the dense ocean of the night.

Just the panting of the jogging kubaru's breath, the slap-slap of his feet, soles burnished like leather, the intermittent tiny sounds of the nocturnal insects, an owl hooting high up in a tree.

Once he thought about telling her but the pale oval of her face caused his words to catch in his throat and he said nothing, but watched the platinum motes.

The ricksha stopped before a two-storied house of dark brick and carved hardwood, columnated, flamboyant. Slender lamps like torches stood on either side of the wide yellow-metal-bound doors.

Ronin stepped out of the ricksha and turned. Kiri came into his arms. Together, they walked up the stone steps. The doors opened inward as they approached. A rather overly dramatic welcome, Ronin thought.

Two tall men stood before them. They were clad in black cotton shirts and leggings, armed with short single-edged swords which hung unscabbarded on thick brass chains at their sides. They had eyes like slits, mouths thin-lipped and wide, their faces peculiarly canine. They bowed to Kiri and stepped impassively away from the doors, allowing them entrance. They stared curiously at Ronin as he passed them.

They were in a towering hallway the height of the entire structure. The whole of its far end was taken up by a forked staircase curving upward to the second story. To the left were two closed doors. To the right opened sliding doors of oiled fragrant wood through which they entered a large room, warmly furnished with satin-cushioned chairs and plush settees without legs. The floor was covered with an enormous rug of dark swirling patterns. The pale green walls were edged in gilt. The room was windowless.

There were perhaps ten people arranged about the room; less than half were women. A tall slender man turned as they entered and a curiously white smile split his long face. He came toward them. He had round eyes of a pale blue and thick graying hair which he contrived to wear very long. Unbound and brushed, it framed his face in such a way as to give him a startlingly leonine appearance. He was dressed in a formal Sha'angh'sei suit, leggings and loose shirt, in a shadow pattern of gilt on gilt.

"Ah, Kiri."

The voice was deep, well modulated. He smiled again and Ronin saw the semicircular arc of raised white flesh beginning at the left corner of the mouth and terminating at the side of his nose, which at some earlier time had had its left nostril sheared off.

"Llowan," said Kiri, "this is Ronin, a warrior from the north."

The man turned his ice eyes on Ronin and bowed formally.

"I am most pleased that Kiri brought you."

"Llowan is the city's bundsman. He oversees the transactions of all the harbor hongs, collecting for

160

Sha'angh'sei, duties on each shipment coming in and departing the port."

Again that strange smile, unnaturally extended by the livid scar.

"You honor me, lady." Then to both of them: "You must have some wine. Hara," he called to a servant, who served them a sparkling white wine in stemmed crystal glasses.

"Are you really from another civilization?" asked Llowan, leading them into the vortex of figures, beginning the introductions over Ronin's reply, then, coaxed into a peripheral conversation, leaving Kiri to continue, names tumbling like leaves in an autumn wind, and he concentrated then on the faces.

"Rikkagin," said the large man with no chin and tiny eyes like broiled insects, "one is becoming quite alarmed by the tales being told of the fighting in the north."

They were sitting on silk pillows on the bare floor around a low table made of a wood with grain like a stormy sea, polished to a high gloss upon which were laid out glazed pots of hot wine and bowls of various small foods such as pieces of fish, battered and dipped in hot oil, steamed vegetables, small sticky sweetmeats.

"What of it?" said the rikkagin in a tone of voice clearly indicating that he had no wish to discuss the matter. He was a wide-shouldered man with a ruddy complexion vanguarded by a wide red-veined nose. He had a thick gray beard stained yellow around his red lips. "This is a city of tales, Chi'en. Most of them, as I am sure you are well aware, are utterly false."

"Yet these persist," said Chi'en, his yellow jowls quivering. He reclined on the pillows, an ornate fan waving at the side of his sad face.

"Tales to frighten hongs such as yourself are easy

161

to create," the rikkagin said with some disdain. "Do not be an old lady."

The large man bristled. "But the fighting is not——"

"My dear sir." The rikkagin was frowning now, his thick brows beetling like thunderheads. "Without the war Sha'angh'sei would still be a muddy swamp with primitive paper houses collapsing in the first high wind and you would be in the rice paddies with your wife earning just enough to survive. It will come as no great news to any of us here that the war is what has made us rich. Without it——"

"You speak of war," said a thin, dour man with dark eyes and close-cropped hair, "as if it were an object to hold in one's hand and use as one pleases." Ronin thought for a moment, recalled his name: Mantu, a priest of the House of Canton. "Yet war is death for thousands and mutilation, starvation, and suffering for countless others."

"How would you know?" interjected a high-cheekboned woman, another hong. "You who have never ventured forth from the sanctity of your region of Sha'angh'sei."

"I am not required to do so," the priest said acidly. "I have quite enough on my hands with the refugees that daily stream into the city from the north seeking sanctuary and solace at the House."

"Your piousness sickens me, Mantu," said the rikkagin. "Where would the Canton House be without the war? Without the great suffering who would come to fill your cathedral?"

"Tradition would——"

"Do not talk of your tradition."

The voice was harsh and heads turned. The man was slender and muscular, with a bony face dominated by eyes like slatted windows, black as night. He had dark curling hair and a long drooping mustache that gave him a sinister appearance. He alone at the table

162

wore plain clothes and a traveling cloak. "Your people came to this land before the rikkagin but as surely as they preached the faith of Canton you took from my people as much as the soldiers. The House of Canton. My tongue grows thick with rage whenever I am forced to utter that hideous name. Yours is not the religion of Sha'angh'sei."

"Po," said Llowan kindly, "your people are traders, nomads from the west."

The slatted eyes flashed like dark lightning. "You delude yourself if you believe that there is a difference. Are not my eyes the same as Chi'en's? Is not my skin the same color as Li Su's? They were wealthy hongs of Sha'angh'sei just as their parents were before them. They are from the south, their origins far from my people, is that what you would have me believe? Yes?" His fist hammered the table and the sound was like the crash of hammer onto anvil in the green and gilt room. "I tell you no! Ours is a land of unlimited wealth yet my people eat half bowls of rice and, if they are fortunate, week-old fish heads which they find discarded on garbage heaps. And all the while they toil to distill the fruit of the poppy for the lords of Sha'angh'sei."

"The tradition of the Canton House is without reproach," said Mantu somewhat didactically. "It has stood for many years—"

"Growing fat like the rikkagin and hongs from the sweat of our labor," sneered Po.

"You obviously do not understand the Canton teachings and, like most men, you are misdirected," Mantu said. "All men crave permanence." He lifted his arms. "Hence they acquire many things as if in these possessions they may truly find the belief that they will not die." The arms folded in on themselves, somehow communicating pity without condescension. "Yet all life is transient, and man, in desiring per-

163

manence, is inevitably defeated and thus suffers; and in his suffering, makes those around him suffer."

"Philosophy is all well and good for those with time on their hands," said Chi'en irritably, "but I am more concerned with what I have been hearing, Rikkagin, that the war has changed."

"Oh, out with it," said the rikkagin in exasperation, wiping at his beard. "If we must listen to your prattle, best get it over with."

Chi'en ignored this outburst. "The tales," he said quite carefully, "filtering into Sha'angh'sei are that the soldiers in the north no longer fight men."

There was a small uncomfortable silence in the room then, as if an uninvited and unwelcome guest had arrived unexpectedly with news they all dreaded yet wished to hear.

"A tale to be believed by fools," said the rikkagin disgustedly. "Come then, tell us, Chi'en, what these beings 'other than men' are like. No doubt you have detailed descriptions for us."

The large man's jowls quivered and his eyes blinked several times in surprise. "No, I have told you all that I have heard."

The rikkagin grunted and leaned forward to snag a piece of fried fish with his sticks. He sighed rather contentedly. "Yes, it is always most enlightening to hear how the truth is twisted to serve the needs of the individual—"

Po laughed at this, a short discomforting sound like the abrupt cracking of a dry twig in a forest when one had been certain that no one else was around.

The rikkagin looked down his nose at Po and continued. "The Reds have enlisted the aid of a savage tribe, a northern people who, it seems, are much addicted to the fruit of the poppy. From what I understand, they extract the syrup, freeze it, and then chew it."

164

"What?" exclaimed Li Su. "Uncured and uncut? It cannot be! The effect would be—"

"Most extraordinary," said Llowan with his white lopsided smile. "I believe we are all agreed on that point, Godaigo."

"Quite a frightening habit, I agree," said the rikkagin.

"I did not say that," replied Llowan, and they all laughed.

Godaigo wiped his red lips on a silk cloth provided by the host. "Be that as it may, it is this unusual lever that the Reds are using to induce the tribe to join with them against us." He put his hands up. "And I admit that until reinforcements are in place we will be rather inconvenienced. But that is all."

"Still the tales exist," interjected Mantu. "It would be most appropriate if they were true."

"What are you saying?" said the rikkagin.

"I am telling you quite plainly that I would welcome the veracity of these tales because it would likely mean an end to the war. That is, after all, what the House of Canton seeks."

"The House seeks dominion over the continent of man," said Po harshly. "And in that it shall surely fail."

"We seek dominion over no one; you speak out of ignorance."

"Just their souls."

The priest smiled benignly. "Life, my dear Po, is soulless. The essence of each man survives death to be placed in, one hopes, a more worthy body, until the final Nothingness is achieved."

"Their minds, then."

Mantu smiled and shrugged. "Shall we debate semantics, trader?"

"Well," said Llowan, clapping his hands for the servants and seeking to head off another dispute, "I believe that it is time that we get down to the serious business of the evening. I trust everyone has brought that which they need." The white grin.

The servants first filled everyone's glass with a cold clear wine, "to clear one's palate," as Llowan told them. Then they ladled out a rich steaming soup of fish stock into large enameled bowls.

Following this, new glasses were brought into which was poured a sparkling wine while several dishes of spiced raw shellfish were put before the guests.

Ronin was still thinking of what the priest had said when the servants staggered in with huge platters of meat of a bewildering assortment. Each platter had half the meat shorn in thick slabs from the white carcasses. With this was served more of the clear sparkling wine.

"Mantu," Ronin said. "This Nothingness you spoke of. What is it precisely?"

The priest turned to Ronin, seeming glad for the interest. "It is the state to which all men must aspire—"

"Women also?"

Mantu was not sure whether he was being mocked.

"Certainly. Theologians use the word 'man' as a shortening for 'mankind.'" His small mouth glistened with grease. "Nothingness is, in essence, the total extinguishing of the ego."

Ronin was somewhat surprised. "Do you mean that the individuality of each person must be surrendered?"

"Is that so valuable a possession?" asked Mantu. "It is, in the end, no different than land, a house, taels of silver, a work of art or"—he looked at Ronin—"a sword."

"But those are all physical."

"Yes, but all possessions are indistinguishable and

166

must be surrendered before the Nothingness so that wholeness may be attained."

"And what then?"

"Why, then perfection," said the priest, somewhat nonplussed.

"But I do not believe that man was meant for perfection."

Llowan laughed and pounded the table.

"He has you, Mantu."

The priest did not join in the general good humor.

The animated conversations continued as the servants silently removed the dishes only to replace them with fresh ones onto which they heaped portions of steamed and fried rice diced with meats and vegetables. No sooner had this course been devoured by the guests than gleaming tureens piled with whole boiled langoustes were served with cups of rice wine.

Ronin thought then of Kiri's earlier remark and he saw that she was smiling slyly at him. Yes, I was famished, but this—

He cracked into the thin carapace. She had spent most of her time in conversation with Llowan and Li Su and he began to wonder why she had brought him here. He felt now that he was jealous of her soft whisperings and gentle touches because they were directed toward their host. He gulped at his rice wine.

Perhaps she did not own poppy fields or trade in the silver market yet she was a powerful woman, the city's leading merchant of a commodity at times more precious than either smoke or metal or silk for that matter. Was she really privy to the secrets of Sha'angh'sei? If so, she was his only way now into the Council. Yet, even as he thought again on these matters, he felt the ebbing of the urgency. As he stared at her awesome beauty, imperfect and therefore terribly thrilling, as he felt the radiance of her aura, the only imperative was his desire to master her.

The langoustes, empty red and green exoskeletons languishing now in their own congealing liquids, bits of white and pink flesh still clinging to their edges, were slowly carted away.

Hot scented cloths were brought for face and hands and then bowls of pudding, dark and creamy, custard, yellow and fluffy, trays of pastries stuffed with candied fruits were put before each guest.

"A warrior Llowan called you," said Po, leaning over so that Ronin could hear him more clearly. "My folk were such once upon a time."

Ronin bit into a pastry, washed it down with more wine. He was not really interested in what this trader had to say; he could think of but one thing.

"What happened?"

"Very unprofitable." The black eyes regarded him like those of a dangerous reptile squatting beneath a rock, suddenly magnified, unknowable in the brief moments before—

Ronin realized belatedly that he was being baited. He dipped two fingers into a pudding, cool and spicy. It did not seem to matter.

"Perhaps they were not then sufficiently adept."

The dark eyes widened, staring madly for an instant, and Ronin's fingers closed around the hilt of his sword. Then the face relaxed and, like a thunderstorm after a long drought, Po began to laugh.

"Oh yes," he gasped, gulping at his wine. "I might even get to like you." He bit into a pastry. "But tell me, how did my people fail as warriors?"

"They do not rule this land," said Ronin softly.

The smile was gone and the face before him now seemed incapable of expressing any happiness. The mouth opened.

"Yes, warrior. I cannot argue with that." He sighed. "Yet they had no choice, a small tribe from the west." He shook his head. "We lacked the numbers."

"There are many tribes in this land?"

"Many, yes, scattered on the land."

"The unification of many into one might have been a beginning."

The ebon eyes peered at him with keen interest now. "Do you imagine such a task to be a simple one? Words! But it takes—" He was choked with emotion, boiling inside, an unleashed storm, and his hand clutched whitely at his glass. His voice but a sibilant whisper now, controlled and venomous. "But there was no one. We cried out to our gods for help, sacrificed our children, rent ourselves in desperation, and how were we answered?" The unpleasant smile returned. "*They* came. The foreign priests and then the rikkagin and by then it was too late; enslavement seemed almost pleasant by comparison."

The salad arrived in great bowls, accompanied by wedges of yellow cheese and thick slices of a heavy bread made from grain.

"Yes, it is too late now," Mantu observed, "because you failed to keep what could have been yours. It is ours now and it serves you ill to blame others for your own shortcomings."

"Silence, you!" cried Po.

"You see," said the priest blandly, turning to Ronin. "An illustration of the Canton teachings. Man's craving causes suffering to all about him."

"Words!" Po spat.

"My dear fellow." Llowan raised a hand warningly. "You really must learn to control—"

But the trader was already on his feet, swaying. A tall dark creature of the night.

"For too long have the outlanders plundered our land, twisted the ideologies of our people with taels of silver. Too late, is it?" He laughed. "Now! Now the time of retribution draws nigh! Now come the days of darkness and all foreigners shall taste defeat before

169

they are ground into the mud of the Sha'angh'sei delta!" His cloak swirled like the wings of an avian predator as he pivoted and strode from the room. In a moment they heard the door slam.

"A bitter man," said Mantu out of the silence.

"I trust we can all forget that unfortunate outburst," said Llowan.

But Ronin was watching the rikkagin and he did not like the look in the other's eyes.

Llowan clapped his hands and, with that, the last course was brought. Oranges, peeled and soaked in wine, figs, white raisins, and an assortment of nuts.

When, at length, the last of the dishes had been cleared away, pipes were distributed, bone-white with long stems and small bowls. Tiny open lamps were set beside each guest and Llowan commenced to carve chunks from a block of a brownish substance.

They began to smoke and it seemed to Ronin that after a time the light in the room grew dim and diffuse and there were more women around the table than before. He took little of the smoke himself but watched the others relax as they inhaled deeply. The air became thick and sweet. Kiri shared a pipe with Llowan as they continued to whisper together. He leaned over, inhaling her perfume, anger welling within him. He gripped her cool wrist and she turned as he pulled, falling into his arms because he was expecting resistance and there was none.

Her purple lips were at his throat and he felt the press of her breasts as she murmured, "Let us not overstay."

He felt only surprise as he watched her kiss Llowan gently on the lips.

He was rising dreamily, holding her lithe form as they moved off the soft cushions and through the sweet smoke, across the room, speaking to no one, their departure unnoticed, past the guards and out the

170

doors into the chill startling night. He breathed deeply, freeing his lungs of the cloying scent, clearing his head. And the sweating back and jogging feet took them down the mountainside, away from the tall firs and thickets of gardened foliage filled with the chirruping of cicadas, away from the round shining faces, lips slick with gravy and bubbling wine and lust, away from the gilt and the guards bought with precious metals.

He was silent.

She watched him for a short time as if wanting to imprint the outline of his profile on her mind.

"You are angry with me. Why should that be so? I have done nothing to you." The call of a whippoorwill.

"Why did you bring me?"

Light on her brows and cheek like a new moon.

"Must I have a reason?"

"Yes."

"I wished to be with you."

He laughed shortly and she shivered a little. "You spoke with Llowan all evening."

"What does that matter? I am with you."

He closed his eyes for a moment, sensing a tension springing up between them which was both unpleasant and vaguely comforting in its familiarity. *K'reen, why are you crying? You know I hate that*. Oh, you bloody fool!

Not again.

He opened his eyes, found her staring at him, the gathering lights slithering by them reflecting in her impossibly violet eyes. He smiled.

"Yes, it was foolish of me. My mind was filled with thoughts of other times. Let us forget it, yes?"

Her lips opened and she leaned toward him, the heat reaching out to him, her "Yes" a vibration in their mouths.

Into the clearing night with a fresh sea breeze blowing, into the blazing Sha'angh'sei delta, chittering with countless people, past stalls selling rice and frying fish, silks and cottons, knives and swords, past brutal brawling men, drunk and stinking, past women in pink and green parasols, white-faced, red-lipped, long-legged and beautiful, past wine vendors and money-changers hiding behind the protective barrier of their street-corner cages, past marching soldiers and screaming hongs, past thieves and pickpockets lurking in the blackness of the alleyways and drunken cripples living along the edges of the streets, past battling children and slinking dogs, past piles of refuse upon which dark figures slept and crawled, past rotting corpses kicked and stepped upon by the teeming crowd, onto the Nanking and halted now by the festival's milling throngs, the wide avenue a riot of color and frenzied motion.

They were confronted by a giant dragon, thrice colored, undulating to the movement of the crouched figures beneath its paper hide. It eyed them mock malevolently before turning aside and following the turning of the Nanking. Children in tattered clothes danced along its writhing flanks, urging it on. There was discordant music, percussive and staccato, and much shouting as the people accompanied its slow rippling passage.

Kiri, enfolded within his arms, put her lips to his ear so that she could be heard over the tumult.

"The festival of the Lamiae is this night reaching its zenith. This creature before us is the effigy of the Lamiae, the female serpent which lives in the sea at the edge of Sha'angh'sei. It is she who turns the waters yellow by the thrashing of her immense coils, thus lifting the silt from the sea's floor. The festival annually honors her who guards our dragon gates."

"This land is filled with legends."

172

"Yes," she said. "So it has been for all time."

They moved on, their kubaru seemingly tireless as they rocked gently through the endless tumbling streets filled with the sleeping and the dead, huddled families and vacant-eyed ancient men and women alone in the sputtering cracked darkness.

He smelled at last the sea as the blackness of the port quarter engulfed them, the streets slick with salt water and fish blood, the great warehouses windowless, gleaming in the silver light from the moon which had finally managed to slip its cloud cover, looming over them like vast mysterious stone monuments. The sea smell was very strong now and, when they stopped, Ronin thought that he could hear the lapping of the sea against the wooden wharves.

They slipped from the ricksha into a silent black building. He closed the door behind them and in pitch-darkness Kiri went away from him. He heard small sounds and, after a moment, a yellow flame flickered as she lit a lamp.

She led him through the rooms, four on this level.

"This is one of Llowan's harrtin," she said. "Where his produce is stored and where, normally, his compredore lives."

"Llowan is a hong also?"

She laughed lightly. "Oh yes. He is master of many poppy fields in the north." They stepped into another room. "Here," she said quietly, "are stored dreams enough for ten thousand lifetimes. Dreams of passion. Dreams of desperation."

"What?"

She started. "Nothing."

They moved on.

"Look here," she said. "The compredore's office. He is the go-between for Llowan and the stevedores and kubaru. He runs the day-to-day shipping and oversees the storing. A most lucrative position."

173

"And where is he this night?"

She turned to him and smiled. "At Tenchō, my warrior. At Tenchō."

The room on the second story stretched almost the entire length of the building. The far wall was constructed of a series of window doors, wooden and slatted, beyond which the spangled night beckoned.

To the left lay the expanse of an enormous bed, low, with many pillows, which took up most of the width of the room. To the right, rugs were strewn across the wooden floor boards. A massive writing desk took up a far corner. Above it was a large mirror set in a carved wooden frame. There were several low chairs made of a tough resilient reed.

Ronin went across the room and pulled at a window door. It opened, folding back on itself, and he was surprised to find that he could step out onto a wide veranda.

Below him the sea: dappled in platinum moonlight chopped to a shower of rippling shards by the undulating surface, so clear in the night that it might have been a molten pathway building itself, beckoning him to climb to the far reaches of the sky, to illimitable whirling shores. Dazzled now, he listened to the quietude composed of the gentle sea lapping at the wharves' stanchions, the creaking of the dark brooding ships at anchor, the stirrings of sleeping families on the galaxy of tasstans rocking on the waves, the splash of a fish. All these now familiar sounds made more searing to him the absolute alienness of the cosmography arched like bits of a shattered world above him.

He felt her presence behind him just before he felt the touch of her body as it pressed itself against his. Through his silk suit, seeped the warmth of her skin;

the contours of her breasts and thighs, at once soft and firm, defined themselves. The heat.

He turned and pressed his mouth against hers and her small tongue licked at him and the night beat on around them, the eternal lapping, the soft singing of the kubaru as they made ready for the sailings at first light, the distant cries of the festival of the Lamiae. His finger tips traced the indentation of her spine, descending slowly.

She drew him inside and the sea breeze followed them to the edges of the bed, soft and downy, upon which they tumbled as one.

Her hair whipped his face as he opened her robe and kissed the opalescent flesh. His thirst was enormous.

"Ah," she moaned. "Ahh."

And the tide took him.

Floating in the loss of tension.

The window doors all folded back now so that sea and sky were before them.

"You went to see the Council today." Her voice held a note of puzzlement.

"Yes, this afternoon."

"And fought the Greens. That was most foolish."

He sighed. "It could not be helped."

"Did you have to kill one?"

"I have killed more than one."

She made a sharp sound.

The moon had disappeared and they had had to re-light the lamp. He listened to the quiet splash of the sea for a while.

"They will come after you now."

"I am not afraid."

Her hand stoked his chest. "I do not want you to die."

He laughed. "Then I shall stay alive."

175

"The Greens are not to be taken lightly—"

"That was not my intention. I mean only that what has been done cannot be altered. I am a warrior. If Greens come for me, then I shall destroy them."

She stared at him, her eyes unreadable. He thought he could hear the plaintive cry of a sea bird far out on the water.

"Yes," she said at last, "I believe you would." Then, "I cannot imagine saying that to anyone else."

"Is that a compliment?"

She laughed then, a clear sparkling sound, and he reached for her hand in the night, feeling its warmth, the fingers twining in his.

She scraped a nail along his flesh. "Why did you seek out the Council?"

He told her.

"But you cannot mean that the tales are true?"

"That is just what I do mean, Kiri."

"But Godaigo—"

"The rikkagin was not at Tenchō this morning."

Her head twisted so that she could see him more fully. "What has Sa's death to do with tales of beings that are not men fighting our soldiers in the north? My men have already dispatched the murderers."

"Murderers?" Ronin said thickly. "Who?"

"Why, the last men with her, of course, but—"

"Kiri, she was not killed by men."

He felt her quiver and the skin along her arms was raised in gooseflesh. It might have been the strengthening wind.

"How could you know that?"

"Because," he said, "I have fought the creature that killed her. It destroyed a friend of mine in precisely the same manner."

He felt her pull away from him. "I cannot believe that; just as I cannot believe that the war is anything

176

but what it has always been from a time long before you or I were born."

"Still, I ask you to aid me with the Council. I cannot see them without your assistance."

"Why do you believe that the Council can aid you?"

"Tuolin told me of the Council."

A cloud passed across her face, fleeting. She shrugged. "I cannot think why he did. The Council will be of little—"

Ronin gripped her shoulders.

"Kiri, I must see them!"

"There is no other way?"

"None."

She tousled his hair. "All right, my warrior. Tomorrow you will be within the Council chambers."

He drew her to him and kissed her hard, feeling her melt as her sinuous body began to writhe slowly against him. The unbound forest of her hair lifted in the wind, a tremulous bridge between their coiling muscles. The lamp sputtered and went out.

She reached under a pillow and her hand lifted, a signpost, long and white and slender, the nails as black as dried blood in the almost-light. Between thumb and forefinger a small black shape, between forefinger and middle finger, its mate. She put thumb and forefinger to her lips, inhaled, then reached out, the arm extending to him, her lips calling, calling in the werevoice of the sea bird flying lonely above the tossing waves. Fingers against his lips. A cold sensation.

"Eat this."

And after he had opened his mouth, "Do your trust me?"

But it was rhetorical and he felt no desire to reply.

The warmth suffused him, friction like a satin glove stroking yellow ivory.

Again and again her open lips, wet and shiny, spoke a kind of litany of sound and motion and form. Words were a distant concept, dim and unremembered, discarded within a far-off cave of bright light and animal smells.

The wind died and the air grew calm, ceasing its dancing. The darkness of night hung like a black velvet curtain, containing them. The atmosphere paused between breaths and he hung suspended, listening to the lapping of the waves, as clear and powerful as thunderclaps, rushing against his eardrums in time with the throbbing of his body.

And his body changed, filled now with a delicious warmth, a sexual ecstasy suffusing his feet, climbing upward through his legs and groin and torso and into his brain, and in that moment the strength of Kiri's body moving against his became an exquisite physical sensation. Sight, sound, touch, taste, and the visions in the theater of his mind became one while he was made aware of them as totally discrete inputs, savoring them independently and simultaneously, time stretching out before him like a new-found joyous friend, endless and concurrent. A conduit.

He plowed the heaving seas at the prow of a mighty ship filled with warriors bent on revenge, the feeling a taste at the back of the mouth, sweet and hot. He climbed the curving neck of the high prow, carved into the sinuous head of a dragon, brandished a long sword, screamed at the wind. He was the ship, feeling the heavy water washing over his flanks, his bow cleaving the seas, sending shivering spume into the bright air, leaving white spray in his wake. Man and vessel, he was both and more.

He plunged into the sea, yellow and turgid, and felt his legs grasp the slick scaly coils. He reached down and triumphantly brought the head up, ineffably exquisite, Kiri's deep violet eyes, dark as the depths of he sea, platinum flecks like schools of flying fish, with oft seaweed hair and a face as white as snow. The oils writhed beneath him and he rode the Lamiae rom out of the shallows of the Sha'angh'sei sea, past he creaming reefs, teeming with life, and out, away, way, on the great westerly currents, into the deep.

It was then that the cold terror came, a dread resence, and he was swept up like an animal in the ortex of a whirlwind. And for the first time he knew ts name. From his core, which beat like an incandescent stone and which remained unmoving in the lux caused by that which he had eaten, came the ound: The Dolman. His entire being opened now and ttuned, he felt it drawing near. And it was devastation; it was annihilation. A suprahuman observer, he aw the cinder of the world, blasted and lifeless, blown through the fabric of space by a firestorm of incalculable power. The terror gripped him in its fierce claw and he felt his chest contract until all the air was orced from his burning lungs. He struggled against he coming, feeling helpless. Hearing what he could not comprehend. *Thee,* howled The Dolman, the universe trembling. *Thee. Thee!*

He screamed and came off the bed, stumbling, crashing into the wall. The shutters shivered. He was drenched with sweat. Or sea water.

Kiri came after him, lovely and naked, ivory and charcoal, crouching beside him.

"It's all right," she said softly, mistaking his reaction. "I had forgotten that you are not used to the smoke; this was much more. I had thought to give you only pleasure."

He put his arms around her, felt the whip of the chill night wind racing in from the water. He looked out at the black sky and willed himself to breathe deeply, oxygenating his body.

"No, no, Kiri," he said his voice thin and strained.

"I felt it, more than seeing. Whatever you gave me created a—connection of some kind. I felt—The Dolman is close, very close." His voice was now a metallic whisper in the rising notes of the wind.

"And it comes for me."

She would not let them rest and he felt the rising terror within her, as deep as an undug wellspring, although he was calm now, the intensity still with him but a shell forming, replacing the aftershock that allowed normal thought.

They dressed and went out into the narrow shiny streets. It was the time of night when the moon was down and dawn had not yet begun to pull upon the last thread of darkness. It had begun to rain and the air was heavy with an acrid active smell.

They raced the downpour to the patiently waiting carriage and the kubaru took off at his steady rocking pace, across the marshy delta of the port and into the black back recesses of Sha'angh'sei.

Lightning wreathed the sky like the twisting branches of a great ancient tree and peals of thunder echoing off the buildings' walls caused the runner to break his stride now and then.

By the storm's pale flickering light he watched the lovely profile, the eyes pools of shadow, the cheekbones whitely limned, emphasizing the face's strength and sweep.

They were in what looked to be the most ancient section of the city now, traveling down narrow unpaved streets, earth churned to mud by the rain and the fleet passage of the kubaru's soles, slap-slap, slap-slap, black water splashing in a bow wave, presaging their progress.

Small houses of board and reed grew here as if from the soil itself, dilapidated yet with a peculiar sorrowful dignity that was impossible to define. Perhaps

180

it was merely the congruence of meager dwelling to its surroundings that was sufficient to impart this feeling to him. Nevertheless, he understood without being told that he was seeing Sha'angh'sei as it must have been before the Canton priests and the round-eyed rikkagin had come to the land.

The ricksha halted unbidden before the towering columns of a stone temple, squat and thick, its face slick now with rain, cracked and half covered with climbing plants.

They went into the narrow street, following the kubaru through double doors of bamboo bound in black iron. He took them through a crowd of kubaru who milled about the entranceway and who, Ronin suspected, would turn away those who they did not wish to enter.

The gray stone floor, the arching stone walls, caught murmurings and mutterings, echoing them along their length and height like the desultory flame of a guttering candle. This temple had a completely different feel than the one Ronin had come upon in the midst of his wanderings.

"What is this place?" Ronin whispered.

Kiri turned her face toward his and he saw that she had produced a plum-colored silk scarf from somewhere and had wrapped this around her head as if she did not wish to be recognized, though who here would possibly know her he had no idea.

"Kay-Iro De," she said, using a word that was of the ancient tongue of the Sha'angh'sei people and which had no ready translation into modern speech. It meant variously sea-song, jade-serpent, and she-who-is-without-members, and it perhaps had more meanings of which no one spoke.

"I have told you that tonight is the culmination of the Festival of the Lamiae," she said softly, her violet eyes shining. "Yet tonight is more. Every seventh year on the last night of the festival comes the Seercus of Sha'angh'sei." A simian-faced woman wrapped in a green cloak, a hairless man by her side gathering in the taels, her clandestine whisperings.

It appeared now that the temple was immense as they followed their kubaru down a narrow, windowless hall that seemed endless. The dank stone walls, beaded with cold moisture, echoed their footsteps. At regular intervals, stone arches were built into the passageway and from their apexes were hung iron braziers casting a dim, fitful light. At length they reached a wide stairway down which they descended. He noted with some curiosity that the hall seemed to have no other egress at this end.

They went carefully downward, their way lit now by flaring torches set into scorched metal sconces, encrusted with the detritus of the ages. Fifty steps and then a landing, peopled by kubaru who scrutinized all who passed. Down and down they went with the air becoming increasingly humid and chill, the stairs slick with moisture and slime, until he gave up counting the number of landings.

The atmosphere was thick with salt and phosphorus and sulphur by the time they reached the last landing and passed through the guard of the kubaru there. The runner motioned silently to them and they stooped, half crawling through a cramped passageway, utterly dark, rough-cut from the living rock. Small creatures skittered past their feet in the wetness.

The tunnel gave onto a vast grotto lit by immense guttering torches, crackling and smoky in the damp air. Great natural columns of stone, flecked and streaked with minerals winking metallically in the light, rose up from the craggy floor into the dark reaches of the unseen ceiling.

There were so many people crowding the cavern that at first Ronin did not see that which actually dominated the place. Then, in some unfathomable shifting, the throng parted momentarily and he saw the pool.

He stepped closer, mesmerized. It was an immense oval stripped out of the floor of the cavern by some cataclysmic upheaval eons ago and the water that filled it was of the most remarkable color he had ever seen. Not a trace of blue or brown could be seen in its shifting depths, yet surely no water could exist without at least a hint of these shades. Yet the water into which he now gazed was the most extraordinary green, halfway between a forest of firs in deep summer and the translucence of the most exquisite jade. Its depth seemed limitless. Surely it led to the vast ocean beyond Sha'angh'sei's shores.

He thought again of the simian-faced woman and her hissed words, *the Seercus,* her inflection imparting to them a mysteriousness that Ronin had supposed was merely a part of her pitch. Now he found himself at the Seercus and he wondered.

Kabaru continually poured into the grotto from several low apertures in the walls similar to the one they had used. Almond-eyed, black shining hair pulled back into long queues, wearing loose suits of dark cotton and coarse silk. He felt that he was, at last, viewing the true Sha'angh'sei, naked in the arena of Kay-Iro De on this most sacred of nights. They were free now of the immense burden of the fields and of the war, of intruder and of time. The betrayals were held for this moment suspended. Ten thousand years had fallen away like so much dead skin to reveal—what? Soon the answer.

He heard chanting, far off and aloft, and the dimness gave grudging way to warm yellow light as the priests entered the grotto from some hidden doorway, carrying before them immense lanterns constructed from the whole skins of giant fish, dried, blown, and lacquered to stiffness. Various pigments had been used to cleverly reproduce and enhance the original aspect, heighten the character of each creature.

The priests wore swirling cloaks of sea-green which left their strong arms bare. They were long-skulled and yellow-skinned, hairless and quite young.

They set the fish lamps down in prescribed places and now he could see that towering over the pool, on the far shore, was a statue. It was of solid gold, carved most cunningly in the shape of an enormous dragon, its thick coils entwined about a regal throne of gold. But where he had expected a female head to be was carved a skull of semi-canine structure, with long grinning muzzle, sharp-toothed and flaring-nostriled above which large round eyes of sea-green jade sparked in the brighter light.

Kiri gripped his hand in hers and her breathing was heavy as she stared at the priests.

All were assembled now and kubaru were stationed at each entrance, he supposed to discourage intruders though in all the crowd he had not seen any glint of weaponry save his own.

One of the priests now gave a signal and incense was thrown into a wide brass brazier. Clouds of yellow steam rose into the black mists of the grotto and spices came to him on the moist air. A young boy appeared leading an animal that Ronin could not readily identify; perhaps it was a young boar. Squealing, the animal was laid out upon a stained stone slab and the chanting began again from the priests and this time it was echoed by the assembled: "Kay-Iro De. Kay-Iro De."

One of the priests reached inside his cloak and produced a knife with a hilt of yellow crystal. Lifting it high over his head, he spoke in the ancient tongue, words that neither Ronin nor, he suspected, Kiri could understand. Yet the meaning seemed clear and Ronin

184

was not surprised when the gleaming blade flashed downward in a shallow arc and pierced the flesh of the animal. Hot blood spurted from the severed artery, spattering the robes of the priests. Dropping the knife, the priest reached his hand into the still trembling interior of the animal and pulled out the warm heart. This he tied with coarse thongs to the knife and cast it into the center of the sea pool while his fellow priests set about collecting the blood of the animal in a glazed yellow bowl. With the splash a kind of sighing went up from the multitude and the chanting began again.

The priests marched silently around the perimeter of the pool toward the golden dragon on the far side and, laying the bowl of blood at the foot of the throne, each in turn bent to dip his hands into the crimson liquid. One by one, then, they climbed the huge throne and daubed the blood onto the eyes of the dragon until it dripped down the muzzle, into the mouth, staining the teeth darkly and thence from the points into the deep green waters.

Now they returned and with them was a young girl in a white robe with silver fish embroidered on it. He felt Kiri against him now, warm and trembling, as they brought the girl before the multitude. She was white-faced and beautiful, tall and shapely with black almond eyes and dark hair that came down to her buttocks. She seemed very young.

Ceremoniously, the priests washed their hands and, at another signal, more incense was thrown into the braziers so that now a green cloud rose into the thick air. Ronin felt then the heat of the throng and the denseness of the atmosphere and he was obliged to take deeper breaths to get sufficient oxygen.

Their hands still wet, the priests donned masks of papier-mâché that caused them to take on the appearance of articulated fish, scales gleaming, gills starkly

185

delineated, round eyes staring unblinkingly. Slowly, they moved in a semicircle around the young girl and the chanting from the throng took on volume and urgency. With infinite slowness their hands lifted and unwound the robe from the girl.

Naked she was breath-taking, with wide hips and heavy breasts and firm thighs. In that electric instant, the priests' robes fell away and she collapsed to the floor of the grotto.

The chanting was all but a roar now and Ronin strained along with the others to see clearly as the priests followed the descent of the girl to the cavern's floor. For many moments the rhythmic movements of the muscular bodies moved to the cadence of the chanting. "Kay-Iro De, Kay-Iro De," and when the priests had finished they rose as one and servants of the temple clothed them once again and removed their fish masks. The girl lay whitely, her breasts heaving like waves upon an agitated sea, fists clenched between her legs. Kiri moaned softly next to him.

Up from a small side pool was drawn a flapping sea creature of some kind, black and sleek and gleaming. It was surely not a fish, for when the priests slew it, this time with a knife of purest green jade, the thing bled red blood as an air-breathing animal would. Again the priests caught the blood in a bowl and with it drew near the prone girl once more.

They grasped her arms and lifted her until she was standing, cradling her as they forced her head back and made her drink the warm blood. Choking and gagging, she drank and when it was all gone they took her to the far side of the sea pool and thrust her roughly upward onto the golden throne, so that her legs entwined with the metallic coils. She clung weakly to the dragon's slippery hide, her head hanging so that the face was concealed by the black forest of her tossed hair. And in no time her body convulsed and she vomited the red liquid so that it drenched the fierce head of the statue.

She shuddered and her grip upon the thing loosened and the priests' arms were retreating and, like the sticky spume that now dripped from the fanged mouth of the golden dragon, she slid inexorably from its slippery embrace into the cool green waters of the sea pool, into the bloodstained salt sea.

There was a collective gasp from the crowd and the chanting began once more from the mouths of the priests, "Kay-Iro De, Kay-Iro De."

The girl thrashed in the water, choking, seemingly not able to swim. Her head disappeared, then she surfaced again, mouth open in a silent scream and with a thrash, descended into the depths.

At that moment the waters of the pool appeared to swirl as if subject to a swiftly passing current, fierce and unnatural, and the air above the water seemed to shimmer as if from some terrible heat.

Tension stung the crowd like an incipient thunderstorm and they seemed caught between an urge to press forward and an instinctive fear to pull back. As a result, they milled about chaotically as the chanting of the priests rose to the howl of a tornado, the rock walls of the grotto hurling the sounds back upon their ears.

"Kay-Iro De. Kay-Iro De."

And now, though he could scarcely believe his eyes, a whirlpool was forming in the center of the sea pool and abruptly the green waters darkened. Emerald mists rose from the pool's sides and salt foam fountained from its core.

"Kay-Iro De. Kay-Iro De."

And the fountaining presaged the presence of something from deep within the sea. He saw the ill-defined shape, black and monstrous, through the imperfect lens of the water, staining the pool with its bulk.

"Kay-Iro De. Kay-Iro De."

And now it broke the water's surface, a reluctant, elastic barrier, into the molten atmosphere of the cavern, heavy with incense and freshly spilled blood, hot with the body warmth of the frenzied people. Foam flying from the tangled seaweed of its hair, black almond eyes huge and baleful.

"Kay-Iro De. Kay-Iro De."

Oh, surely not, thought Ronin. The black eyes within the human head surveyed the throng, the body arching upward so that within the green foam and white spray of its thrust could be seen thick, sinuous coils, scaly, encrusted with algae and yellow barnacles. And within those twisting coils, a glimpse of a white broken torso, slim legs.

With a crash like the collapse of a building, the thing shot straight down, merely a ripple, dark and remote now beneath the waves clapping at the sea pool's edges. And then nothing, only the trembling of the water, limpid and deep green once again.

For an instant, all sound ceased, and had it not been for the tiny slap-slap of the diminishing wavelets, Ronin might have believed that time itself had stopped.

Kiri, shuddering, gripped his arm.

"Look," she whispered hoarsely. "Look."

And his eyes lifted to the far side of the pool, at the immobile dragon. There, instead of the canine head darkly dripping blood, was the golden head of an exquisite woman with almond eyes carved of sea-green jade.

When he awoke, the sun was already past its zenith. He lay quite still for a moment, watching the bright whips of sunlight rippling like molten lead across the floor, listening to the close sounds of singing, hoarse shouts, the frenetic slap of jogging feet, the creaking

188

of ships being outfitted, the metallic grate and the splash as a ship weighed anchor.

For a moment he floated above the receding abyss of his unconscious where rose . . .

And sat up. Slatted wooden doors through which the salt breeze blew and light streamed and he knew then that he was in Llowan's harrtin, though why Kiri had brought him back here instead of to Tenchō he could not remember. He was alone in the room. He stood up and, naked to the waist, went out into the day.

The veranda too was empty yet still he felt the complex shreds of last night clinging to the edges as if they were real and fluttering in the wind.

He looked out at the sluggish sea, clogged with vessels large and small. It was a bright, clear day with thin high clouds near the lid of the sky and he squinted in the sunshine. Below him, the activity along the long wharves of Sha'angh'sei was fierce with loadings and unloadings, the compredores calling to the stevedores, who in turn shouted at the singing kubaru, jogging under the weight of bales and barrels filled with the wealth of the city, the foods and textiles of the continent of man.

His eyes moved from the white billowing sails studding the near waters to the yellow sea farther out and, like a wave pungent with salt and phosphorus washing over him, the events of last night flooded in on him.

Kay-Iro De. Kay-Iro De.

He shook his head. Perhaps it was only the aftermath of the substance which he had taken. What had Kiri called it? The tears of the Lamiae. Merely an illusion, rising and falling like the tide. Sun dancing on the restless water, shards of liquid gold. A memory elusive and vague, as if it were part of another lifetime, lapped at the edges of his consciousness. What? A shape, dark and vast and inconstant and . . .

He heard a sound behind him and turned, passed through the open shutters into the cool room to find Matsu, serene, lithe Matsu, standing in the center in a pale green silk robe edged in rust, leaves of the same color falling across its surface. She held a deep blue lacquered tray on which sat a clay pot glazed gray and red and several small cups painted in the same pattern.

"I have come to take you to the Council," she said, kneeling and setting the tray down before her. She lifted a slim arm. "Please. Sit. I have brought your breakfast." Her dark eyes stared up at him unblinkingly and for a moment his stomach contracted.

He ran a hand across his face and went to her, knelt, the tray a low barrier between them. He washed his face and hands from a large bowl of water which she handed him. She patted his face dry with a clean white cloth. He sat back.

"Matsu, where is—?"

"She has much to accomplish today and it is already afternoon."

"How is the woman I brought to Tenchō?"

She did not answer but concentrated on the ceremony of the tea, the turnings of the cup, the stirring, the pouring, all the precise movements that made it so special. He sat quietly and watched her deft hands.

At last the tea was steaming in the cup and she lifted it, an oblique offering, saying, after he had accepted it, "She has awakened. Her name is Moeru, she wrote it for me."

He sipped the tea and it tasted better because of the way she had served it to him.

"Has she still a fever?"

"I think not. The sweat no longer rolls off her and she is eating now."

"That is good." Her eyes hiding behind sooty lashes.

190

"She wished to remove the bandage."

"What bandage?"

"The one high up on her thigh. The dressing is dirty."

He put the cup down on the tray.

"Ah, no. The apothecary told me to leave it on. There is a healing poultice beneath the cloth."

"But she says that she has no pain there."

"Then the poultice is working."

There was silence for a time. He continued to sip his tea. Matsu watched him, her small white hands folded on her lap. Leaves rustled as she breathed. Smells of sweat and spices and fresh fish from the wharves. Shouts and hoarse laughter. Oval face like still water, strands of hair floating in the breeze, the perfect column of the neck, slender and ivoried.

"Your friend's husband," he asked. "How is he?"

"Ah," sighed Matsu, her head minutely in motion so that a wave of black hair fell over one eye, across her cheek. "It is most sad. He was knifed last night, fighting in a tavern."

"I am sorry."

She smiled wanly. "It is as well he died. The war had changed him. My friend no longer knew him. He brought only sorrow to those who loved him, even his son who lies paralyzed on a bed in my friend's house."

"I do not understand."

"His back is broken but he still has eyes with which to see. His father resented that." She shrugged. "As I said, it is perhaps better this way."

"Will you have some tea?"

Matsu shook her head. "It is for you."

Outside, the sun beat down out of a deep cerulean sky. They smelled the gutted fish drying in the heat, a hint of cinnamon, of cloves, of coriander, and Ronin's

191

nostrils dilated for a moment as if recalling on their own a distant and odious scent.

Then they were in the ricksha, moving off down the narrow, baking streets, past the blind faces of the harrtin which Ronin now knew opened opulently their splendid verandas onto the bund—the wharves of Sha'angh'sei and the swelling yellow sea.

Deep within the jungle of the city, the kubaru runner stumbled and fell and the ricksha jerked to a halt. Although he had been talking to Matsu and his head had been turned away, the bright line of crimson along the runner's side caught the periphery of his vision and as the two men leaped onto the still rocking ricksha his sword was already withdrawn.

It was the wrong action in the confined space and the man who went for him had the advantage, the hilt of his filthy dirk slamming against the inside of Ronin's wrist with a quick flick, the sword clattering to the muddy street. A professional, Ronin thought, and he did the only thing he could do, grappling, tearing the momentum so that they both fell to the ground.

He inhaled the stench of the body and the foulness of the breath as the man slashed the dirk at his throat. Saw the yellowed stumps of teeth, holes in the gray gums, images flashing across his vision path as the head whipped and the shoulders twisted and the blade blurred into the soft earth just past his neck.

Elbows in and up, using the heavy bone structure, and the man's jaws clashed together with a crack as Ronin hit him. He had the good sense to scramble away then so that he could regain his advantage.

He let Ronin get up before he came toward him, confident because Ronin was unarmed. He was small but very powerful with broad shoulders and lean hips and thick muscular arms. He had a wide flat intelligent face, dark cunning eyes. He was bald save for a long queue of dirty blue-black hair. He was missing an ear.

He was clever and ignorant at the same time. He feinted, the blade of his dirk appearing to whip toward Ronin's neck, canting downward at the last instant, reaching to slit his stomach. Using the man's momentum, Ronin stepped into the thrust, grasping the extended arm, and leaned back, his hip and groin beneath the man's buttocks, a solid base as he planted his feet and stiffened the muscles of his legs. He lifted his right foot, slamming the sole of his boot down onto the stretched knee joint. Resistance was minimal. The kneecap shattered in a shower of white and pink and the vulnerable thighbone cracked as if it were a dry twig. The man screamed and collapsed and Ronin reached for his fallen dirk.

"Stop right there," said a voice.

Ronin turned and in that instant remembered the second man. He stood now several paces from Ronin with Matsu drawn to his side, his dirk at her throbbing white throat, so perfect, like ivory. The blade grazed her windpipe for emphasis. He stared into her eyes, saw in their darkness no fear. What then?

The second man shook his head sadly.

"You should not have done that." He was large, very tall, with a grizzled beard and long greasy hair. He had a high forehead and the eyes of an animal. Ronin froze. "What shall I tell his woman and her children? How will they eat? Now I will take your money and the woman." His feral eyes flicked at the man, broken and unconscious in the muddy earth, came back to Ronin. "She will fetch a high price at the Sha-rida." Matsu gasped in pain as the blade bit into her throat.

"Sha-rida?" said Ronin, edging closer, wanting to keep the man talking.

"Outlander. Fool to travel these streets in a ricksha.

The scent of your money precedes you." He smiled mockingly. "Yet I salute your foolishness because you are my living. Long may it last. Do not come closer," he snapped suddenly. His voice was now cold and hard. "The woman will be breathing through the hole in her throat. You are not that foolish, I trust." The man pulled Matsu in front of him and his blade caught the sunlight in a dazzle. "Now come, let us not drag out this encounter. Toss your money to the ground."

"All right," said Ronin. "Do not harm her." Because he was close enough now and Matsu was in the correct position. He had deliberately moved because he wanted her in front of the man, where he could look at her, read her expression. He needed that advantage. His sword was out of the question. She would die before he got halfway to where it lay.

His shoulders moved minutely, slumping in an attitude of defeat. Back within the depths of the Freehold and his Senseii, the Salamander was before him, saying, "Provide your foe with clues. He will be trained to look for the key to victory through the tiny betrayals of your body. So you must give him that which he wishes to find." These men were sufficiently adept.

His hands were at his belt, slowly unknotting the cord to his bag of coins. He stared at Matsu and she read what he wished her to know, written in his colorless eyes.

The bag hit the soft ground with a heavy chink and the gauntleted hand sped across the short space without warning. The hesitation, the merest split instant caused by Ronin's attitude of defeat and the visual and aural distraction of the bag of coins dropping, was sufficient. Ronin grasped the blade just as it commenced its inward stroke. He wrenched at it and the metal snapped. At the same time, Matsu twisted her body, swung her arm, and her fist hit his stomach.

194

Then she was away and Ronin was closing with the man.

He went for the throat and the man blocked him, turning as he did so, taking Ronin down. There was pressure against Ronin's windpipe and he had to force his breathing. The man's fist smashed into the side of his head and the grip tightened on his throat. He felt the urge to retch as his body rapidly used up the last of the oxygen in his stilled lungs. He fought to breathe, could not, and so turned his attention to bringing up his right hand. It was caught between their bodies and he worked at freeing it while he began to strangle on carbon dioxide. The man's attention narrowed as he increased the pressure and now the hand was free; bring it up, through the maze. Groping, he found the open spot on the side of the neck, jabbed with his thumb.

The man could not even scream and Ronin was up, his lungs heaving in great bursts of air. They were on their knees in the mud and slime and the man was recovering and there was no time to reconsider, the organism out to survive. Ronin's fist, sealed within the hide of the Makkon gauntlet, smashed into the lower end of the man's sternum. The bone cracked, splintered, the force of the fist plunging it upward into the heart. Blood and viscera fountained outward, drenching him as the face before him, drained and white, bobbed like a berserk marionette. The jaws snapped shut spasmodically, biting off the end of the lolling tongue.

Ronin stood and kicked at the body, looking around, but there was only Matsu staring at the ruined corpse.

She started then, looking at him. She went and got his sword and he sheathed it as she bent to pick up the bag of coins. Then she went to the slain kubaru and ripped off his damp shirt, returning to Ronin and wiping the pink foam from his face and chest and arms. She reached out and touched the strange scaled gauntlet, horny and unreflective, glistening now, beaded with dark fluids.

"What is that?" she whispered, stroking the hide.

"A present," Ronin said, watching the thin line of red across her throat where the dirk had crossed the delicate flesh. It stood out like a tear on a shadowed cheek. He licked his finger, wiped it along her neck. Her eyes closed and she shuddered. "It was given to me by a little man who walks with a limp, whose companion is a singular creature. It is made from the claw of the thing that killed Sa."

She seemed not to hear him. "I could not believe that any man could do what you have just done. Was it the gauntlet?" Her fingers dark now with the viscous liquids.

Ronin wiped her hand and the gauntlet on the sodden shirt, then threw it from him. He shrugged. "Perhaps, in part." He reached for her. "Now we must finish our journey. The Council awaits me."

The dark eyes lifted, looked at him strangely. Then she nodded and they set off through the labyrinthine streets, finding at length the Nanking and then, a short time later, a narrow winding road with no name that Ronin could see.

"I came a different way the last time."

"I have no doubt. But it is not prudent to take King Knife Street, is this not so?"

He laughed then. "Yes, Matsu, it would indeed not be wise. But what about the Greens at the gate?"

She smiled. "There are many entrances to the walled city."

The climb was steep this way. No houses lay along the road, only giant firs and lush green-leafed trees. The earth was thick with small plants and wild flowering bushes.

196

Soon the shadow of the great wall blotted out the warmth of the sun and they stood in the cool dimness while Matsu spoke in low tones to the Greens who guarded this gate. The metal door swung open and they went through. The Greens ignored them, returning to the absorption of their dice game.

Within the perfectly linear corridor of the carefully tended trees he asked her, "The Sha-rida, Matsu. What is it?"

She laughed nervously, the sound like shattering crystal in the quietude, and he heard the sighing of the trees before she said, "The Sha-rida is a tale told to frighten outlanders." But he saw the look on her face and did not quite believe her.

"Tell me then," he said lightly. "I am not easily frightened."

Her eyes swept his face and she tried a smile but did not quite make it.

"It is a market, a special kind of market, which, it is said, moves from night to night, through the black alleyways of Sha'angh'sei, opening only after the moon has left the sky."

"A flesh market," said Ronin. "Slave trade."

She shook her head. "No. There are many of those in the city. They conduct their business during the day."

"Well then?"

"It is true that the Sha-rida deals in human flesh, but only the most beautiful women and men, young and healthy."

"Toward what end?"

They walked in silence for a time. The cicadas were singing among the trees and birds called in staccato rhythm above their heads. The avenue stretched before them, white and empty, as if it were some giant's plaything abandoned now for some newer and more elaborate toy.

"Toward, it is said, a hideous death." Her voice was like the first touch of autumn's winds. "The buyers wish only to observe death and the act of dying, and the more they indulge themselves, the more bored they become and the more monstrous the forms of dying they conjure up." She looked at him. "Even in a city such as this, such a thing does not seem possible."

"It is only a tale."

"Yes," she said. "That is all."

Their footsteps shattered the silence of the hall and the still air eddied softly in their wake. The woman with the light eyes and jutting breasts was at her post behind the heavy marble desk. Two Greens, armed with axes and curving dirks, stood watch outside heavy wooden doors with iron rings in their centers.

"Yes?" she inquired, lifting her head. She did not seem to recognize Ronin. He was about to say something when Matsu squeezed his arm.

She spoke to the woman who said, "Ah," softly as she listened, her eyes on Ronin.

"Ah." Her lacquered nails scraping across the cool desk top like articulated insects. "No, I am afraid—" But Matsu cut into her prepared speech and they stared at each other now, a test of power that encompassed more than mere wills. The woman licked her lips with her bright tongue. "Well, I—" Matsu spoke at length and the woman's face came apart, a subtle thing which he observed with some wonderment. "Yes. Yes, of course." She signaled to the Greens who turned and, pulling on the iron rings, opened the doors.

At last, Ronin thought, as they went forward. An audience with the Municipal Council of Sha'angh'sei. They went into the Council chambers. He was already unscrewing the hilt of the sword. An answer to the long riddle. An end to the uncertainty. The way now open to defeat The Dolman and his hordes. The doors closed behind them. His hand stopped as it was about to pull forth the scroll of dor-Sefrith.

He whirled on Matsu.

"What insane jest is this?"

"There is no jest." Calm. The black eyes steady.

"Then surely this is the wrong chamber."

"You can see for yourself that this is the Council's chambers."

It was a high-ceilinged, windowless room dominated by an immense ornate table around which were placed at regular intervals high-backed wooden chairs, richly carved, regal. Save for the two of these, the chamber was empty.

"Why did you bring me on a day when the Council is not in session," he demanded.

"If it were not in session, the building would have been closed."

Ronin's temper broke and he shook her by the shoulders.

"Are they ghosts then that I cannot see them?"

"No," The voice as distinct in the room as a bird call in high summer. "It is quite simple."

His hands moved. "Matsu, I will break your neck—"

"The Municipal Council of Sha'angh'sei does not exist."

The dragon stared at him quizzically. From the chair, its golden eyes sparked in the last oblique rays of sunlight. Its head was erect but its body was distorted, foreshortened by the folds. Ronin crossed the room and, removing his shirt and weapons belt, donned the robe as Matsu had bidden him. The silk moved in the breeze from the open window and the dragons writhed.

Day was almost done. They had not spoken on the

journey back to Tenchō. Although he had been hungry and although they had passed many street stalls filled with a variety of fragrant foods, he had denied himself that pleasure, preferring not to delay the explanation. He had spent too long seeking an answer only to find other riddles.

He had raged at Matsu, threatening to tear the chambers apart, to destroy the Greens outside the door. She had merely stared at him and asked that he return to Tenchō with her. "The answer is there," was all that she had said and had waited him out.

Eventually he had given in. He had no choice.

Clouds were piling up to the west, darkening the lowering sun, turning it from orange to deep crimson, a half-seen oblate, bloated and veiled by the oncoming weather. Another storm approaches, Ronin thought, sliding the dragons over his torso. The silk felt cool on his flesh.

Matsu came to him beside the window and tied his sash in the formal manner. She had changed into a crimson formal robe, the color more vivid than was usual for her. Deep brown reeds on the body, the wide sleeves plain, bordered in deep red.

She studied him for a moment in the twilight, the fast-disappearing sun now a dusky ruby glowing between the buildings on Okan Road. And the strange light, burnished and intense, drew all the color from her face, causing her to appear pale, shadows building in layers around her eyes, across the hollows below her cheeks. The skin was perfectly drawn, not a line, not a blemish marred its satin surface. She stood quite still, all light and dark, and he felt compelled to reach out and touch the face to assure himself that it was indeed flesh and blood, warm and pliant, that he was not staring at some fantastically conceived and crafted mask. Her lashes dipped for an instant and her lips parted as if she were about to say something. Then

200

her lids rose and her slim hand moved startlingly, passing through the light, then black shadow, as she reached down for his hand. And she managed somehow to turn that simple gesture into a tender caress as she led him wordlessly from the room, into the dim corridor, the great lamp not yet spilling its tawny light.

Down the curving stairs in a wide arc and into the rear of the house where he had never before ventured. They went out the back, swiftly silently, through a small wooden door with a large iron lock and, instead of the expected crowded street, Ronin found himself in a spacious garden, lush and green with the plumage of ripe foliage.

Amid the artful jungle of greenery stood a pair of four-legged creatures, saddled and harnessed. They snorted and pawed the earth as Ronin and Matsu neared them so that their attendants were obliged to pull on their bits and talk to them soothingly in meaningless words.

"These are not horses," said Ronin and Matsu smiled.

"No. They are luma. Steeds from the far north, very powerful and quite intelligent." She shrugged. "Horses are quite stupid. They are fine for warfare and that is where they are primarily used. In any event, the luma are quite rare." She lifted one arm. "This one is a present from Kiri."

The animal was a deep red-brown stallion with a thick red mane. It had a long tapering head with flaring nostrils and erect triangular ears. Its eyes, round and large, were a deep blue and, between them, thrusting from the thick skull, were three stubby yellow horns in a vertical row like a miniature trident. The luma had no tail but the lower reaches of its legs were streamered with silky red hair.

Slowly, Ronin approached it. One large blue eye

followed his progress with curiosity and, as Matsu had told him, intelligence and when he reached out to stroke its head it snorted and pushed its muzzle against his hand.

He mounted the luma and Matsu leapt onto her own, a gray mare with a pure white mane. He saw that a double slit in her robe allowed her to sit astride the luma without difficulty.

They rode out from the dense garden, the attendants opening thick iron gates, the luma's hoofs resounding against the cobbles and the close walls of the city's streets like pounding hammers, and blue-white sparks flew in their wake.

The dragons along his arms rippled in the wind, seeming to come alive dancing across his body to the music of their movement. Matsu, riding just ahead of him, cried out frequently, guiding her mount and warning the crowds clogging the streets. Dark figures scrambled hastily from their path, pointing and murmuring, their words jumbled and lost in the swift passage.

Into the dark labyrinth of the delta, the port area less jammed with people but with narrower, twisting streets. Then, all at once, they broke from the confinement of the alleys of the bund, purple and black and deep red in the last of the sun, a minute crescent now against the unmarred horizon as it heaved its bulk into the welcoming embrace of the singing sea.

Along the wooden boards of the bund they raced, the kubaru's songs a spice on the salt air. He inhaled the scents of the sea, pungent drying fish, the cloying sweetness of the poppy's syrup, and the violet faces of the harrtin with their wide verandas, impassively observing the end of another day, swept by them in majestic array.

Until, abruptly, they were alone on the sand, the curving, darkling beach stretching before them in exultant desolation, and Ronin's luma lifted its head in an unmistakable sound of pleasure and triumph, calling, galloping, galloping, the sea to the left now cinnabar solid in the last of the red light, and he felt a tremendous jolt of adrenalin, as if he were joining battle, and his heart thudded and, as his steed leapt over a dark dune, its crest as sinuous as a snake, he unsheathed his sword and lifted it toward the cold pinpoints of light just becoming visible and he thought, Let The Dolman come. I welcome now the Makkon's freezing embrace, for surely I am its nemesis. I am its slayer.

And he rode on into the deepening dusk with Matsu at his side, her shadowed face impassive, thinking her unfathomable thoughts.

When the hazy golden lights of Sha'angh'sei were but a smear behind them, Matsu broke off and called to him, into the singing wind rolling in off the turbulent sea, alive with green and blue phosphorescence.

"I must leave you here, Ronin. Ride on. The luma will take you unerringly."

"But what—"

She was gone, had already wheeled her mount, its hoofs but a whisper against the sand in the night, and he shrugged, dug his heels into the luma's flanks as she had instructed him, and it leapt forward. He concentrated on its power, the concordant rippling of its muscles, the thin film of sweat slickening its rich coat, and then it was slowing, snorting and bobbing its head as if telling him of something ahead.

He peered into the darkness and heard the luma's prancing steps before he saw its silhouette looming up before him. All at once he was close enough to see that it was of a deep saffron with a black mane.

Astride it sat Kiri. The lustrous violet eyes stared back at him. She flicked her head and he saw the unmistakable lines of her proud face. Her long dark hair was unbound, streaming in the wind. It was held back from her face by a narrow band of yellow topaz. She wore a pale yellow robe with golden flowers embroidered upon it in the most intricate pattern. It was different from all the others he had ever seen but he could not tell why.

"Kiri," he said almost breathlessly, the wind moaning between them, "I thank you for this present. It gives me great pleasure to ride."

She smiled. "It suits you well, the luma, and I am told that it welcomed you immediately; they are not easily tamed, the luma."

"Yes, but how in—"

"Come!" she called over the shifting sand, pulling on her reins. "Ride with me, my warrior."

And over the undulating dunes, by the shore of the crashing luminescent sea, they flew, chill white spray thrown up by the luma's flashing hoofs, sparkling their hair and faces. Her feet were bare, digging into the creature's flanks, spurring it on.

"Kiri," he called. "What of the Council? What trick have you played on me?"

She shook her head, hair like a vast fan. "No trick. Only the truth." Her pale face turned to him. "If I had told you, you would not have believed me." The sea crashed around them as they sped into the yellow surf. He could hear the jangle of the bits, the creak of their saddles very clear on the cold air. "The Council is an elaborate myth. It is best for the people to believe that a body rules their lives and governs the city. But the truth is that no such Council could exist here and survive. Sha'angh'sei would not tolerate it."

"You talk as if the city were alive."

She nodded. "There is no other place in all the world like it. Yes, a Council of the factions makes

204

sense here only as thought. In reality, they would tear each other apart."

"Who sees the people who wait for audience in the walled city?"

"They see me, when they see anyone at all."

He stared at her, back erect, hair billowing, eyes like wells out of time.

"You? But why? Do you lead a faction within Sha'angh'sei?"

She laughed then, deep and long, a delightful sound, the wind carrying her melodious voice into the reaches of the night.

"No, my warrior, not a faction."

Surf sprayed along the lumas' flanks so that they gleamed in the phosphorescence. She dug her heels into her mount and she sped ahead, over the sighing dunes, their white crests shifting, and he took the water route, cutting across a crescent cove, the sea flaring outward like wings in his wake. The stars seemed very close at that moment.

He broke from the surf, his steed's coat fire red now, as deeply crimson as a hurled torch, hearing her startling cry, "Not a faction, oh no. Only one can rule. Into one's hands is delivered the ultimate power." Her face a platinum and onyx helm in the cold light. "It is I, Ronin. I am the Empress of Sha'angh'sei."

The night was an expert shroud. Somewhere, water dripped dolefully. The lamps were unlit and no one came to relight them. A strident argument raged from an open window on the second story overhead. There was a slap and a brief cry. Silence. He crouched in a doorway, cloaked in shadow, still and watchful. A dog howled and he heard the pad of its paws. The sharp odor of sweat as two women reeled by, laughing, their robes held together by unsteady hands; the momentary glow of white skin. Then the street was quite deserted.

The gates opened at their approach and he inhaled the humid perfume of the green velvet garden, black now in the night, for only after they had dismounted and their glistening luma were led away, snorting and prancing, was a tiny torch lit.

The lushness was overwhelming after the barren beauty of the white sand and black sky. He breathed the jasmine air, listened to the myriad rustling all around him.

Yellow insects dancing in the torchlight as she moved toward him. The silence was startling and he put a hand out to stop her. After a moment the nocturnal noises commenced again.

She took his hand, her face a pale oval, wreathed by the trembling forest of her hair, and they walked across the grass, through a maze of hedges reaching far above their heads, past whispering firs, scented and jeweled with dew, to the other side of the garden. She dropped the torch and smothered the flame. They were in total darkness and the small sounds were suddenly amplified as vision went to nil. His pupils expanded. They stood before a blank stone building. A recessed door stood ajar and she bade him enter. He turned on the threshold.

"Kiri, why did Tuolin suggest I seek out the Council?"

She shrugged. "Perhaps he wished to give you hope."

"But there is no Council."

"I hardly think that Tuolin would know that."

"Are you sure?"

"Reasonably. Why?"

"I—do not know. For a moment I thought—"

"Yes?"

"Why should he leave so unexpectedly?"

"Soldiers are governed by their own time. He left because he was summoned early."

"Of course, You must be right."

He turned. They were in a black corridor.

"Walk straight ahead," she said from behind him. "There are no turnings."

Still he kept his eyes moving.

"The woman you brought in is much better. She is up and wanting to help the girls. Her recovery has been remarkably swift."

"What has she told you?"

"Nothing."

"Nothing at all?"

"She is mute."

"I would like to see her."

"Certainly. Matsu has told her about you. She wants to thank—"

He staggered and almost fell, the breath lost inside of him, sucked away. Before him was light, an abrupt end to the blackness, and what he saw was an immense hall built all of streaked marble, yellow and pink and black, the arched, gilt roof supported by twelve pillars, six on each side. The muraled walls were dusky in the light from golden braziers hung at intervals, watery and flowing in their depiction of strange, beautiful women and men, golden-skinned, sapphire-haired, tall and lithe. He blinked and forced his lungs to work.

"What is it?" Her hands on his shoulders.

"I have seen this place before." Voice thick and furry.

"Oh, but that is impossible. You—"

"I have been here before, Kiri—"

"Ronin—"

"Will be here again, I know that now. Believe me, I know this place. In the City of Ten Thousand Paths, in the house of dor-Sefrith, the great magus of Amano-mori—"

He had waited long enough. He went cautiously

across the street, from shadow to shadow, and when he stood beneath the stone jar his sword was out.

He went in quickly and silently, leading with his right shoulder to present the smallest target. The stench of the shop's supplies of potions and powders was heavily in the air and he knew even before he looked that the bottles and jars and phials were lying smashed on the floor, their mysterious contents spilled darkly, lying in small mounds and thick streaks, mingled in arcane combinations, drifting on the night wind.

He found the apothecary against the side of the counter in back, spread-eagled, the blade of an ax protruding like an obscene growth from the frail chest. Ronin tried to pull him down but the blade had gone entirely through him, impaling him to the wood. Ronin pulled at the haft and it came away, the body sliding limply down into the dry rivers of powders littering the floor.

Ronin stared at where the old man had hung. Along the wood were two dark streaks in the shape of an inverted V, as if he had been trying to write some message in his own blood as it gushed from him, life ebbing away.

The last hope gone now, the scroll useless and nothing to stop The Dolman, the death of man assured, and his blade was a silver arc and he felt the bite and heard the scream at the same instant. He hacked through both legs and an ax fell heavily to the floor. Creakings as of weight on the floor boards and there was movement all around him. He whirled and thrust obliquely, short and chopping, the blade biting deeply, then, reversing the momentum of his thrust, used the opposite edge to slice into another man's neck. Hot blood spurted at his face and he moved away from the bodies dancing frenziedly as they died.

They rushed him now, lunging for his sword arm,

and he swung, fingers dismembered, hands split like butchered meat, but there were far too many, they were taking no chances, and at length they had it and pulled him down to the airless floor. Forearms along his windpipe. He struggled but his hands and legs were pinioned and, lungs laboring, finding no oxygen, he began to tumble down an endless escarpment of sand into a black land where sickle-bladed axes grew like uncut wheat from crimson corpses.

"We are not greedy souls."

Tourmaline hung in the smoke.

"We are what we must be."

Red green brown, its facets winked dully in the pearled glow.

"What history decreed we become."

The blue haze, frozen, rose and fell like the swell and suck of the sea.

"Pawns."

There was a raucous burst of laughter bubbling like the release of water under pressure.

"Oh my. Oh my." Voice deep and heavy.

Tourmaline dancing in multicolored splendor, a miniature sun upon the convex surface.

"Yes. We are the result of an unforgiving past. Hurled this way and that by the necessities of our land. Did we arise before the need for us had arisen? Could we?"

Tourmaline sun shaking against its quivering sky.

He had fat cheeks and heavy jowls which wobbled when he laughed. Wide flat nose, cheekbones lost in flesh guarding long almond eyes of cobalt blue. No neck, his billiard head stuck to his massive shoulders and bare chest, deep green robe open to the waist. His mouth was small and delicate.

"We were formed from the minds of our gods, in

centuries too distant to calculate, for the protection of our people, to guard the wealth of the land."

He was sitting in a wicker chair, its high back curving up and out like the questing necks of some monstrous and headless creatures, mindless twins.

"To destroy the Reds!"

A massive arm lifted, fell to the wicker with a sharp snap.

"To undermine the power of the rikkagin. To take vengeance on all who come within our precincts seeking only wealth. Thieves and worse. Murderers."

The cobalt eyes shifted their focus.

"Our price is high, yes; and it is met every hour of every day and night within the borders of Sha'-angh'sei. We are paid to protect those who live like frightened ants within the walled city. Yet the walled city is ours if we so wished. The fat hongs deliver up to us the tariffs we request. The rikkagin, who grow rich on the war to the north, pay us taels of silver on the last day of each month——" The eyes flashed. "How I hate them! How I work to defeat them. It is not enough to take their money, no, not nearly. Infiltrate, am I not correct?"

There was a noise. The eyes peered down in front of him.

"Has he heard, do you think?"

He made a motion with his hand, a flicker of movement, and Ronin was drenched with sea water, chill and fecund with microscopic life. The salt burned in his wounds but it cleared his head. He groaned again.

"We wish you to be fully conscious." said the immense man.

Ronin broke his bleary gaze from the tourmaline around the man's neck. He was in a room whose walls were constructed of bamboo, coated in a clear lacquer so that they gleamed in the low lamplight. There were no windows but overhead a skylight was open to the clear night.

"You have caused us many deaths, brought grief to many women and their families." He sighed. "We are the Ching Pang. The Greens." His hand reached into his robe. Something sparkled in the air and dropped in front of Ronin. "There."

It was the silver necklace he had taken off the dead man in the alley and which T'ung had taken from him at the gate of the walled city. He stared at the tiny silver blossom, wiping the salt water from his eyes, and for an instant he fancied he heard the tolling of far-off bells, the muted call of a horn, seeing again the lazy fish in the perfect garden of that mysterious temple, lost now within the maze of Sha'angh'sei. Eternity.

"Tell us who you are. Who sent you to Sha'angh'sei?"

Ronin coughed, put his hand up to his throat. He swallowed experimentally.

"Not the Reds, surely. They know less of the sakura than we do."

"I know nothing of this necklace."

"That is a lie. You attacked Ching Pang in the alley, trying to save your friend."

"Who?"

"The man in black." The voice was patient, an uncle speaking to a mischievous child.

"I saw someone being attacked by many men. I went to help him." The immense man laughed.

"I have no doubt. Stupid to expose yourself to us so openly. You underestimate us. Why were you sent here?"

"I came to Sha'angh'sei to seek the answer to a riddle."

"Where did you come from?"

"The north."

"Liar. There are savages only to the north."

"I am not of this land."

"And the sakura."

"I do not know what you want."

The immense man looked with pity upon Ronin and then lifted his eyes.

"T'ung, it is time for you to do what you must do."

"Shall I kill him first?"

"No, but be content, that will come later."

"I want him."

"Yes, of course you do. But first you will take him with you."

"But—I—"

"Let him witness it."

They moved stealthily through the twisting, refuse-strewn alleys of the city, deep in shadows where no night lanterns shone, where the sweet smoke drifted through the air and the rattle of gaming dice was an intermittent atonal tattoo.

He went with four of them. T'ung and two other Greens garbed in deep blue, ax blades sheathed in black fabric so as not to reflect. They had with them a man with lusterless skin and bright burning eyes, whose body trembled with fear and who ceaselessly implored them to spare him. His hands were bound to a short bamboo pole behind him.

T'ung, ever by Ronin's side, had whispered to him, "If you attempt to cry out, I will stuff a rag in your mouth. This is Du-Sing's order. I would slit your belly now, if I could. But I am a patient man. My time will come when we return."

The shadows were endless as they moved silently through the replicating alleys in the night. A dog barked throatily. There was the sound of someone urinating against a wall close by, curiously distinct. They heard distant laughter, the thrumming of nocturnal hoofs, a tense and enervating noise. They walked through the litter of the tiny animals who screeched briefly at the disturbance.

"Where are we bound?" said Ronin, careful to keep his voice down.

T'ung smashed him just above his ear.

He called softly to the Green leading the way and they turned to the right, into a dimly lit street, residential, a fairly wealthy area.

They approached a house and one of the Greens produced a bowl of rice from beneath his cloak. The man's eyes bulged at the sight and the other Green was obliged to hold him.

Carefully, ritually, the first Green set the bowl of rice onto the street directly in front of the steps leading up to the front door. Then he rose, produced a pair of sticks, bent again, setting them beside the bowl. He turned and, bowing to T'ung, went and stood beside Ronin.

Swiftly T'ung moved to the side of the squirming man, slammed his fists into the hinges of his jaws so that they gaped open in reflex. His left hand moved into the mouth, the fingers expertly grasping the slippery tongue while the right hand flashed upward. The glint of naked metal. The man was about to gag and the blade had already slashed through his tongue. Blood spurted, black in the dimness of the street, and the man's head whipped about. Terrible guttural sounds issued from him like an animal pathetically attempting to mimic human speech.

Again the dagger rose and flashed forward and the man's head recoiled horribly and the mouth redoubled its efforts to scream. The Green gripped the dripping hair and the blade came up for the third ghastly time. Then the Green let go of the head and it bounced back and forth as if on a spring. The maimed face came up and stared sightlessly at Ronin, two black holes, wet and shiny, running with blood and ribbons of viscera.

T'ung nodded and the Green unsheathed his ax, arcing it down, severing the tendons at the backs of the man's knees, so that the body folded in on itself and he was forced to kneel in the dust of the street. He fell over into his own blood.

T'ung bent and arranged the tongue and eyeballs on their bed of rice as if they were savory delicacies to be consumed by the most discerning of gourmets. When he had finished, the Green placed the body of the man next to the bowl and sticks.

The Green who stood beside Ronin handed T'ung an immaculate yellow silk cloth as he came up. T'ung wiped his hands.

"He knew many things," he said to Ronin when he was quite close. He handed the cloth back. "But he said them to the wrong people."

He shoved Ronin and they all vanished into the alley from which they had moments before emerged and were swallowed up by the Sha'angh'sei night.

"You see how unfortunate it is," said Du-Sing. "We who are the protectors of Sha'angh'sei must rule it by fear. It is an imperative of this city, a given rule, if you will, which we view simply as another fact of our existence. There are no two ways about it. Fear cuts through all boundaries. If you say to a kubaru, 'Tell us what we wish to know or we shall be forced to cut off your foot,' why then he will respond because, without his foot, he cannot work the poppy fields and thus feed his family. Similarly, if you say to rikkagin, 'Tell us or we shall cut off your sword hand,' what do you imagine his answer will be?" He laughed, his fat face jiggling.

Then Du-Sing's face took on a sorrowful edge. "It is the hongs and the rikkagin and the Canton priests

214

spewing their soulless filth who rob the people of Sha'angh'sei. Yet it is the Ching Pang which gains the reputation of thieves, murderers, and evil men." His fat hands clapped together. "Nothing could be further from the truth!"

"Is that justification for what T'ung and these others just did?" asked Ronin.

"Justification?" cried Du-Sing. "We require no justification here. We do what must be done. No one else will do it. And this city must survive. Through us it does." He settled himself more comfortably in his wicker chair. "You were shown that as a moral lesson. You are drawing breath now under our sufferance." He drew out the silver necklace. "Where is yours?" he snapped suddenly.

"I have only seen that one," replied Ronin.

"Did you bury it, perhaps?"

"I have only seen that one."

"Is your mission in Sha'angh'sei the same as the other's?"

"I never heard of this city until I was fished out of the water."

"Is that where you met the man?"

"I never saw him before—"

"There are many ways to induce the truth from you and T'ung knows them all. I need not remind you how eager he is to have you all to himself."

"The truth has already been spoken."

"Spoken like a true hero," said Du-Sing sarcastically. "Are you so stupid as to believe that we lack the skills to break you?"

"No. You will eventually find a way and then I shall be forced to tell you a lie so that you will kill me."

"The truth is all that we require."

Ronin laughed shortly. "That and my life. I am not

215

a kubaru or a fat hong whom your threats can affect. I am not of this city. I do not hold you or the Ching Pang in reverential awe as all do in Sah'angh'sei. You are nothing to me." He stared at the deep blue eyes, which had not blinked for the longest time. "And besides, this is all academic. Tomorrow's handwriting is already on the wall. All your carefully built networks of power will be for nought if The Dolman cannot be stopped."

T'ung stirred behind him. "Such foolishness is—"

A flicker of Du-Sing's heavy hand stopped him. The blue eyes blinked and within the instant Ronin thought he could detect a hint of some emotion quite foreign to Du-Sing flickering uncertainly in those depths.

"He knows of the Bujun," said T'ung. "I know it. He can tell us—"

"Silence!" roared Du-Sing. "Fool! Do you wish your tongue ripped from your mouth?" He made a great effort to calm himself. "Have Chei send in four men," he said after a time.

T'ung went to the door and spoke softly to a Green standing just outside. When he returned, Du-Sing looked up at him and said: "Now give him his sword."

Ripple like liquid silver. One, then two in the lamplight. Cold and hard and honed. Whistle of curved blades swinging through the air, the hot pungency of sweat and animal fear. Ripple along the periphery of his vision. Light squirting across the double edges of his long blade causing his heart to soar, the adrenalin pumping again, the brain thinking in rapid-fire bursts. Double. Thrust and reverse.

They did not understand, their style was different and adaptation takes time. He did not give it to them. A blade scythed upward at him and he deflected it out and away, reversing simultaneously, his own blade biting into the flesh of the Green behind him on the vicious downswipe. The man cried out as the blood spurted from his side. He stumbled and fell.

Ronin whirled as he felt an ax nick his shoulder, ripping into his robe. His sword thrust forward, scraping along the curving blade, and blue sparks flew. He parried two more blows before lunging in under an oblique swipe, thrusting with the point, spitting a Green through the mid-section. The man went to his knees as Ronin withdrew, his shaking hands clutching at the ooze, trying vainly to stem the flow. The stench of death thickened the air.

He was out of position now and the second man slammed his blade against Ronin's sword and it all but flew from his hands. The ax came at him again and he went to his knees in parrying the jarring blow. His sword flashed again and again but he could not regain his feet, so profuse were the slashes raining upon him. He waited patiently for an opening and when it came, an instant when his opponent reached back to deliver the killing blow which would break through Ronin's defense he used his blade vertically, driving upward with all his strength. He caught the man under the chin, the tip biting deep. He jammed it in, through the throat and into the brain. The body jerked, arms flying out wildly as if the man were attempting to fly. The mouth gaped open and bits of pink and gray spattered out. The corpse convulsed as if trying to throw off a tremendous weight and the ax skittered along the floor.

Ronin ripped his sword through the head and dropped, rolling across the room until his back was against a lacquered bamboo wall. The fourth man moved toward him but T'ung caught him by the arm and, staring at Ronin, said, "He is mine. Stay away."

T'ung advanced on Ronin then, crouching, his gleaming ax blade swinging. He came in low, aiming

217

for the knees, wanting to cripple first and then kill, and Ronin got his own blade down barely in time. As it was, the sickle came away with skin and a film of blood.

T'ung feinted right, came in on the left. The blow was deceptively sluggish and he got in behind Ronin's guard, the crescent of sharp metal rushing toward the collarbone. Ronin was in no position to block the attack so he swatted at the ax with his gauntleted hand.

The blade made contact and T'ung's eyes widened as, instead of slicing through flesh into bone, it was deflected harmlessly.

Ronin saw the look and immediately dropped his sword, lunging for T'ung with the gauntlet. Light spun off the scales as his hand went in. He slammed the right arm to get the ax out of the way and his fist hammered at T'ung's windpipe. The eyes bulged, the tongue came out in reflex and the ax dropped.

T'ung tried to get his hands inside Ronin's arms so that he would have the leverage but Ronin would not let him. The gauntlet, balled into a fist, slammed into T'ung's face and his cheekbone shattered. He screamed and his head twisted. His hands scrabbled along the floor for his ax. The remaining Green moved to give it to him but stopped at a motion from Du-Sing. Again Ronin smote him, visions of the dark alley and the pleading and teeth cracked under the force of the blow, the lower jaw smashed and hanging, eyeless sockets like the gates of hell and a mouth that could not speak, and he drove in again with a kind of black joy and the nose a pulpy mass spread over the crimson face.

Then he was rolling off and grasping the hilt of his sword all in one motion, moving in on the last Green, the balanced weight in his right hand like holding lightning.

And now he moved in, the blade a humming instrument of destruction, hacking at his opponent with the blood singing in his ears and his vision pulsing with the power welling up, shooting through his arms, his skin gleaming with sweat and sea salt, rippling as if a serpent reared beneath his skin.

Terrified, the Green retreated, and then he stumbled, his ax coming up centimeters to the right of where it should have been, and Ronin's blurred blade, pulsing platinum along its length, screamed downward and clove his head in two. The body leapt into the humid air like a speared fish and he whirled, the blur a halo of death surrounding him.

One step, two, the corpse jerked as if it were still alive and as it crumpled to the slick floor Ronin scooped up the fallen silver necklace. He raced for the door and, picking up momentum, crashed into the Green just outside, sending him flying.

Chei came through the door, ax over his head.

Du-Sing made a brief gesture. "Leave him." And then, after a moment, "Close the door and come here."

Chei went through the carnage, stepping carefully across the outflung corpses, thinking of the dangerous man. Crimson dripped along the shining bamboo, beading like bright tears of pain.

Du-Sing rubbed at his eyes with his thick hand, waiting for Chei's return.

"Summon a runner," he said slowly, "and an escort of three Ching Pang. Our best. You will go with them." He stared at the man in front of him. "I wish you to take a message to Lui Wu."

"But, Du-Sing, you cannot mean that you will now—"

"Yes. That is precisely what I mean to do. I am contacting the taipan of the Hung Pang."

"The Reds," breathed Chei, and there was only

wonderment on his face as he gazed upon the cold blue eyes of Du-Sing.

He was not running from the Greens. It was not in his nature and, too, he felt that somehow they were not a danger to him now. Not after what he had seen in Du-Sing's eyes. The man knew of The Dolman, or at least that the war to the north was no longer what it had been for so many centuries.

Nonetheless, he ran through the torpid Sha'angh'sei night, down back streets filled with slumbering families and roaming yellow dogs, skin ribboned with jutting ribs, through the wider thoroughfares where nocturnal revelers staggered and moaned and vomited, sodden with drink and lust and the smoke of the city's notorious pleasure houses, coughing and shaking as with a fever, kissing, pressed together against filthy brick and wood walls, fighting with bleeding fists and crusty knives, locked within the penultimate stages of arguments whose beginnings had already been forgotten. A woman screamed somewhere in the jasmine night, a piercing shriek abruptly cut off, and at last he knew that it did not matter where the sound came from.

And he ran on, his lungs on fire, his legs pumping on their own, desperation sweeping over him as he headed toward Okan Road. His mind was filled with a succession of minute details, words and events and hints which he had absorbed but which had been floating in the back of his mind. Separately, they were meaningless, yet as pieces of a whole they held a terrifying imperative. Oh, Kiri, like a song in his dazzled brain, as he slipped through the crowded labyrinth of streets.

And at last Sha'angh'sei came alive for him, a glowing throbbing entity with a corporeal existence of its own. As he rushed through its sinuous entrails, filled with naked thighs and almond eyes, thrusting breasts and canted hips passing him by, pouting lips, drowsing children and petty thieves sharing the same oblique bars of shadows, comfortable in the blackness, he felt its presence like a lover's body, hot and moist, exciting and frightening, possessive and insatiable, and the mingling of triumph and terror was overwhelming within him.

The Okan Road was perfectly silent in the unlight of predawn, the tall trees still and calm, the night sounds of the city seemingly far away, as if they belonged to another time, some dimly perceived future perhaps, voices chiming in the slow changing of the centuries.

Up the gracefully curving stairway he flew, reaching the top and pounding on the massive yellow doors. When they opened, he clutched at the wide-eyed woman, panting, "Kiri, where is she?"

She recognized him of course and stayed the guards who would otherwise have attempted to restrain him, taking him to the room of tawny light and then leaving him hurriedly.

He prowled among the settees and tables, searching anxiously for some wine, but as usual it had all been put away. He turned as the woman came down the staircase.

"She will be with you."

Relief flooded him and he allowed himself to relax somewhat and he opened up his breathing to oxygenate his system.

Then she was on the stairs, slender and lithe, black hair falling around her, and for a moment she seemed to be someone else. Then he gazed into her violet eyes, platinum flecks swimming in their depths.

"What has happened to you?" She came down the

221

stairs quickly, with an economy of movement. "Are you hurt?"

He glanced down at his torn and bloody robe.

"Hurt? No, I do not think so." He looked up. "Do you know Du-Sing?"

She stared at him. "Where have you heard that name?"

"Greens were waiting for me at the apothecary's. They took me to him."

"Yet you are not dead." She looked surprised. "He thought you had information. But what kind—"

Ronin sighed. "In the alley that evening, when I fought the Greens, remember, I told you—"

She waved a hand, flowing lavender along her nails. "Yes, go on."

"I took a silver chain from around the dead man's neck. It was an impulse only. That was the basis of my altercation with the Greens at the walled city."

"You showed it to them."

"Like a fool. Trying to buy my way into seeing the Council."

"It would be funny if it was not so serious."

"Yes, well—"

"What is the chain's importance?"

"It holds a silver flower. The 'sakura,' Du-Sing called it."

"I—"

He held up a hand. "I will show it to you when there is more time. Right now I must see the woman I brought to you. Moeru."

"But it is so late. I do not want to wake her."

"Kiri—"

She smiled. "All right, but then you must tell me what Du-Sing wanted. And about the man in the alley—"

"Come on," he said.

She led the way upstairs into one of the rooms

222

along the dim corridor. They went in and she lit the lamp on the wooden table beside the wide bed.

She was quite beautiful, he saw now. Stripped of the filth and mud and pain, dusky face in repose, with days and nights of food and rest behind her, Moeru was lovely. Her long oval eyes and wide mouth gave her face the openness of innocence, a child asleep in a distant land.

Kiri bent over her. Her eyes came open and she stared at Ronin. He saw the wild open sea.

"This is the man who saved you, Moeru. Matsu told you about him."

The woman nodded and reached out a slim hand. They had cut and polished her ragged nails and they had already begun to grow shiny and translucent with clear lacquer. She touched his hand, stroked the back of it. He watched her mouth, but the coral lips did not move. Mute from birth, he thought.

"Moeru, I must ask you to do something for me. It is very important. Will you do it?"

She nodded.

"Pull down the bedcovers," he said.

Kiri watched him silently.

Moeru did as she was told. She was naked. Skin like burnished gold. Perhaps a trace of olive. Her body was as beautiful as her face, firm and rounded and sensual.

"Has the bandage been changed?"

"You asked Matsu that it not be," Kiri said.

"Moeru, I will take the bandage off now."

The long blue-green eyes regarded him placidly. She opened her legs.

Ronin reached between them, fingers on her warm thigh. A muscle jumped under her skin at the contact. He pulled carefully at the dirty fabric, a bulge against her inner thigh. He looked at her legs. Apart, they formed the configuration of an inverted V. He lifted

223

the bandage from her thigh. Beneath it, nestled within the cloth, was the man-shaped root.

Moeru stroked her thigh where the bandage had come off, then covered herself.

"She had no wound under the poultice, Ronin," said Kiri.

"Yes, I know. The old apothecary used that as a ruse to hide this." He showed her the root.

"What is it?"

"The root of all good," he said with a laugh. "Or of all evil."

The scream came then, filled with terror and something more, and he bolted out the door with Kiri just behind him. Down the hall he ran, his ears questing ahead for sounds of scuffling. Then he smelled the stench and felt even through the closed door the unutterable cold.

He stopped.

"No," moaned Kiri. "Oh no."

And he did not understand until he had flung the door open and was already within the room. Then the enormity of his error hit him and cursed aloud and, brandishing his sword, slammed the door shut behind him. Kiri pounded on it from the other side. He ignored her, concentrating on the thing in front of him.

It was over three meters in height with thick powerful legs, short, twisted, hoofed. Its upper limbs were much longer, with six-fingered hands tipped by curved talons.

Its head was monstrous. Baleful alien eyes, the orange pupils no more than vertical slits below which protruded obscenely a short curving beak opening and closing spastically. The creature pulsed unsteadily, its outline ebbing and flowing. A tail whipped behind it.

It turned to look at him and a short eerie cry broke from its beak. It threw the remains of what must once

224

have been a man at him, a broken pink and white husk.

Ronin moved easily out of the way but it had Matsu and his stomach contracted again because he should have known. He had been with Matsu, not Kiri, that night when the Makkon came to Tenchō and killed Sa. *Thee,* The Dolman had called in his mind. *Thee.* Thus had he raced to return to Tenchō, less concerned with Du-Sing and the Greens than he was with the revelation that the Makkon had been searching for him that night and that it would surely return soon. He had thought only of Kiri, with whom he had been so much lately, and now he saw the look in Matsu's eyes and his heart cried out in sudden pain.

His lips moved, calling softly her name.

The Makkon cried out again and its taloned fist slammed into her hip and she screamed in pain as her pelvis cracked and white bone pushed itself through her soft flesh.

"Matsu."

Ronin rushed the Makkon now, nauseated by its awful stench, his unprotected face already beginning to numb from its unearthly chill. He yelled reflexively as the pain raced through him, his blade sliding off its scaly hide.

The hideous beak opened and a peculiar sound filled the room, a dreadful laughter, and the thing brushed Ronin aside with a lightning motion, moving toward the open window and the werelight of pre-dawn.

The whistle came then, high-pitched and piercing, echoing in his mind, and the Makkon fell silent. The sound came again, insistent now. The Makkon screamed in fury, wrenched at Matsu's arm, ripping it from its socket, and as Ronin advanced, still dazed from the mighty blow, the thing reached up and slowly, deliberately, tore her throat out, all the pale flesh of her body running red now, and the Makkon threw her at him finally as it went swiftly out the window.

Ronin staggered as she came into his arms. Too late, he thought numbly, why did I not think of the gauntlet? He stared down at her crimson corpse, oblivious to the renewed pounding at the door, did not even turn around when it splintered and flew open.

He knelt in the center of the room, a cold wind blowing over him, cradling all that was left of Matsu. Only when a shadow dropped across his face did he look up to behold Kiri in breastplate of deep yellow lacquered leather, high polished boots, and light leather leggings.

She went straight to the window and looked out. She gasped as she saw through the dawn's deep haze the hideous orange beacons, pulsing, the snapping beak with its thick gray tongue.

The Makkon screamed again.

And Ronin, clutching the chill frame to him as if he could prevent the life from leaking from her, thought of the night he had held her close, feeling the delicious warmth seep into his body, listening to her speak as he watched the slow wheel of the stars in the glowing heavens. Again and again, bound upon a tortuous circlet. Are my feelings so well hidden? Ah, Chill take me.

Surely, he thought, I am a doomed man.

FOUR

·Hart of Darkness·

"Strange," she said, reining in her mount.

To their right the sky was pearled lavender, the sun still but a ghost ascending behind the morning's thick haze. To the north and west it was not yet light.

Their luma snorted and stamped at the earth, eager to be galloping before the wind again. Sha'angh'sei was a sprawl at their backs, a dirty smudge stretching, entangled, to the sea.

They were on a hill burned brown by the sun which overlooked the wide snaking river whose mouth Ronin had glimpsed when first he sailed into port aboard Rikkagin T'ien's ship. It was deep, turbulent in spots, quiet and sluggish in others. It ran out from the edge of the city at seaside almost due north. The Makkon was following its path and they it.

"What is it?" asked Ronin.

She turned to look at him, her long hair trailing across her face.

"The autumn wind is blowing," she said.

He felt the strong gusts, chill and damp, plucking at their cloaks, shivering the lines of tall slender pines.

"What of it?"

There was a curious cast to her face caused perhaps by the oblique light.

"It is," she said softly, "the season of high summer."

"You are going after it and I am coming with you."

He was about to say no but he saw across her visage the play of stormy emotions. She was beyond weeping, her face a white mask of hatred.

"I want to tell you something—" His chest hurt as if he had been struck down.

"There is no need." The sound of bitter tears, the clash of gleaming metal.

"I do not understand. You cannot know—"

"I can and I do." She turned to the window, the budding light strange and spectral still. "Matsu was more than sister to me. More than daughter."

"What then?"

"If I told you, you would think me mad."

They sped through the new day, the light quickening around them like molten metal, the winds of autumn whipping at their cloaks. Kiri's unbound hair swept behind her like the tail of some mythical creature, half animal, half human.

Over the bleak countyside they raced, past the long level fields of marshy plants in precise rows down which myriad kubaru women and men in wide-brimmed straw hats, skirts gathered and tied about their waists, waded, bent almost double as they plucked the raw rice. Along the shooting waters of the river as it sliced ever northward toward the death and destruction of the war, its banks wide and brown with mud and silt, precious minerals thrown up to nourish the far-flung fields.

After the Makkon they flew and Ronin, glancing at Kiri, the noble profile with its firm nose and high cheekbones, failed to notice the movement behind them, as a pursuing luma kept pace with them.

By midday the land had swallowed them and all vestiges of civilization, all habitation and settlement, seemed a thing of the past. The remnants of the alluvial delta which was the source of much of

Sha'angh'sei's material wealth had long since dropped away. The terrain became increasingly dry and rocky, undulating in ever higher waves, like a storm-tossed ocean.

There was little vegetation now. Brown and green plants, scraggy and deformed, grew here and there among the chunky rocks, hanging on tenaciously for whatever nourishment they could find. The earth was drier and coarser and ran before them in a gentle incline, rising higher the farther they got from the sea.

Once, to the east, they spied a long line of soldiers marching northward, a supply train of horses to the rear, horsemen to the front, kicking up long plumes of dust. They spurred their mounts onward and soon left the column far behind.

Sun still shone to the south but overhead and to the north billowing gray clouds were roiling.

"Tell me now what Du-Sing wished from you."

Ronin shrugged. "He wanted something that I could not give him. I know nothing of the sakura."

"And what of the man in the alley?"

"He had been struck by Greens, perhaps four of them, maybe more. I went to his aid."

"What did he look like?"

His head came around and he thought, Ah.

"Now why would you ask that?"

"It is a natural question."

He shook his head. "Not really."

She smiled. "All right. I have a reason. Will you tell me now?"

He contemplated her for a moment, watching her hair brush her cheeks. It reminded him of Matsu. Her hair would—

"He—did not look like the Sha'angh'sei people and he did not look like my people. But it was difficult to see because of the light—"

"His skin was yellow?"

229

"Yes."

"And his face?"

"Black eyes. High cheekbones."

"Let me see the chain." She took it, saw the silver blossom.

"Bujun." Her breath an explosive sound.

"The Green, T'ung, mentioned that word and would have gone on but Du-Sing cut him off."

"Yes, I imagine he would." She gave the necklace back to him. "The Bujun are the lost race of man, purportedly the greatest warriors and the elite magi during the ages when sorcerous elements formed the primal elements on the world. The sakura is their symbol. It is a flower which is said to grow only on their isle."

"What happened to them?"

"No one knows if they actually exist. The stories of the Bujun dropped away sometime during the sorcerous wars. Perhaps Ama-no-mori was destroyed—"

Ronin started.

"Their island is called Ama-no-mori?"

"The floating kingdom, yes."

"Kiri, the scroll I possess is written in the hand of dor-Sefrith, the most powerful magus of Ama-no-mori."

"Who told you this?"

"A Magic Man from the Freehold. He had been studying ancient codices which told of the scroll. It was confirmed later by a man I met in the City of Ten Thousand Paths, Bonneduce the Last. Dor-Sefrith is Bujun, there is no doubt."

"Then the man in the alley was Bujun also. They still live!" Her violet eyes flashed. "No wonder Du-Sing was so anxious to learn of your involvement. The presence of a Bujun in Sha'angh'sei indicates that their interest in the continent of man will cause the

230

balance of power to change. He wishes the Ching Pang to stay ahead of the Hung Pang."

Ronin nodded.

"Yes, at first. Now I believe he has other concerns; the same as ours."

"What do you mean?"

"Du-Sing could have had me killed at any time, yet he did not. All right, it is obvious that he wanted information from me. But he is a shrewd man and at some point he realized that I knew nothing of the sakura—"

"Why should he believe that?"

"I do not think that he had a choice and he knew it. I told him the truth and he was aware the I would not break. I told him then about the coming of The Dolman. And he knew, Kiri!" He slapped the pomel of his saddle. "The fox knew! You know better than any save Du-Sing himself how extensive his network is. Every caste in Sha'angh'sei is involved with the Ching Pang. He has ten thousand eyes and ears within the city and without. He knows that the war in the north is no longer against the Reds; he understands the rikkagin's anxiety. They fight that which is non-human. You have already seen the Makkon and what it can do to human life. The traditional lines of enmity which have guided the fates of the Greens and the Reds, and thus Sha'angh'sei itself, have broken at last. The forces of The Dolman have come to the continent of man."

They had been traveling along a high plateau and this gave now onto a gorge of red rock and dry dust, their luma leaving a vapor trail drifting high above them as they descended. On the plateau behind them came the sky-blue luma, carrying its slim passenger.

They were well into the gorge now. Far to the right, atop a low bluff beyond the perimeter of the red defile, a last row of green pine trees swayed in the gathering wind. Above them, a flock of gray and brown birds flying high moved swiftly southward before the oncoming clouds. Ronin thought that he could hear them calling to each other in shrill cries of longing, but perhaps it was merely the wind shivering the lonely pines. The desolation of this land lent their presence the symbolic strength of eternal guards at the outpost of man.

They wended their way through the gorge, around huge boulders and stratified shelves of crimson shale until, at length, they found the way rising again onto another plateau.

They reined in and Ronin dismounted, stroking his steed's long neck as he went around it to look at the tracks. It danced impatiently as he knelt, fingers moving in the dust. Unmistakable. The hoofprints of any lesser creature would have been at least partially obliterated by the wind-swept dust. But the signs of the Makkon's passage could not be so easily obscured. At least if it wished to leave a deliberate trail. *Thee.* An echo in his mind. *Thee.*

"Are we gaining?"

He shrugged. "If it wants us to, then we will."

He leaped upon his luma and they took off over the plateau, riding easily, giving their mounts their heads so that they galloped full out. The creatures seemed indefatigable, happiest when they pushed themselves to their limit.

"I would choose the place of battle this time," he called to her over the rushing of the wind and the hard jangle of their riding gear.

"That may not be possible."

"I know that better than anyone."

They were aware that the sun was about to set only when the light abruptly began to fade. It had been diffuse for most of the day, gray and vitiated by the thick tumultuous cloud layers that now enveloped all the sky for as far in every direction as they could see.

The land was colorless and shadowless and they had had for some time the peculiar and disquieting sensation of traveling across an endless dreamscape, that they moved not in kilometers but rather in spirit farther and farther from the familiar world of man into the realm of another kind of life that was both more and less than they.

It was dark in the north already when they reached the far edge of the plateau and so rode downward into a vast valley completely engulfed in shadow. They had descended perhaps halfway when Kiri gasped and strained forward in her saddle. She pointed wordlessly ahead.

Below, rushing toward them as they sped over the rubble-strewn slope, was a field of waving flowers, as white as bleached bones. Then the sweet smell flooded over them like a sticky cataract and they were within the meadow.

"Poppies!" Kiri breathed.

The luma shook their heads and called to each other and they lifted high their legs, careful now because they could not see the earth.

It was a sea through which they plunged, rustling with an infectious insistence, white crests and blue troughs caused by the rippling of the blossoms as the wind swept across their illimitable faces.

At that moment the sun broke through a rent in the clouds at the edge of the sky to the west and the sea was stained a lurid purple. That same singular light illuminated before them a hulking shape, rising up as if from the floor of the ocean, a fearsome, apparition with lambent orange eyes.

Its outline pulsed as it waded heavily toward them, its long arms swinging, the talons cutting dark swaths in the purple sea. The luma screamed in fear and reared, kicking out their forelegs. Their eyes rolled in their sockets and Kiri yelled to him, "Dismount! Dismount before it throws you!"

Into the waving poppies they dropped, up around their waists, Kiri's curving sword already out. He waved her back.

"Your blade will hurt it no more than did mine."

She did not glance at him.

"I must kill it." Voice like frost as she advanced on the Makkon.

Ronin grabbed at her, held her tightly, his face very near hers. She struggled in his embrace.

"Hear me, Kiri. I know how you feel. The Makkon slew my friend. I have fought it before. Mere metal and muscle are useless against it. It is not of this world and therefore not bound by its laws." Still she stared over his shoulder at the shambling monstrosity coming toward them. "Too many have already lost their lives. G'fand, Sa, then Matsu. You will not be the next."

Her violet eyes were glowing coals in the dusk as she looked at him at last.

"This is not a time for reason; that has fled for all time." With an effort she broke away from him but he still stood between her and the Makkon. "I am already half dead," she cried wildly. "Oblivion will be heaven if I can take that foul thing with me!"

She came at him and he hit her then, swiftly and compactly and without warning, striking her along the jaw. Just a ripple of movement. He caught her as she fell, thinking, At least you will not die, and gently laid her down in the purple poppies. They danced, whispering, above her still form.

"You cannot kill it," he said sadly. "And you also mean something to me."

The long sword was a heavy weight around his waist, threatening to pull him to the ocean's floor, and he turned, watching the stumbling rush of the Makkon as he unbuckled the belt. The sword fell beside Kiri.

The creature screamed as it recognized him and he heard the luma away behind him calling nervously to each other as he went out to meet it, out from the shallows into the depths of the sighing sea, the strange blossoms caressing his legs, the rich sweet aroma mingled now with the choking stench of the thing.

He came in under the swift sweep of its arms, his gauntleted hand held before him like a shield. He leapt at the last instant so that his balled fist smashed into its cruelly curved beak. The Makkon howled and he thought that his eardrums had burst. They were hot and blood began to leak from them because of the vibrations but he had opened the beak and was fighting now for leverage in order to force the gauntlet down its throat.

The howling increased in intensity and he was forced to close his eyes to the terrible slitted orbs which hung before his face like hateful crescent moons in an inimical alien sky.

But now as he struggled for purchase on the scaly hide, needles of pain shot through him like shards of broken glass and tears welled up in his eyes, coursing down his cheeks. The cold was so profound that his legs were already numb as they attempted to climb the alien musculature. He began to shake with the pain and his resolve weakened. The beak ground down against the gauntlet and unless he kept up the thrusting pressure it would slip out and he would be as good as dead. Slowly and purposefully it had stood there and torn out her throat, ripe flesh that he had kissed and stroked ruptured now and gouting red and bits of it flying in his face, the taste of her blood, salt and sticky with spume like sea water, and what are we anyway but salt and phosphorus and water like the ocean? And the hate burned at his core and its heat glowed and grew as he banked the fire with the images, forcing himself to remember the details, her blood in his mouth in an abrupt spray, and he yelled silently, bringing the killing power together within him, and he reached up with his arm, though the pain still shook him and water was in his eyes, forcing the gauntlet farther inside.

Then the Makkon's arms came up across his back, the talons seeking his flesh, trying to pry him from its maw. There was no longer air in his lungs and he subsisted from heartbeat to heartbeat, time taken, molded like putty in some monstrous claw, perverted and realigned so that it no longer bore any resemblance to the concept which ruled his world. His heart pounded and he was Outside, his stomach churning in nausea, his back aflame with pain, his legs hanging uselessly, a cripple, and still he persisted, though the numbness now lapped at his brain, an unstoppable crimson tide, and still he strove, long after his last inhalation, his lungs deflating, pulse surging vainly—And he took the last step, all thoughts but one gone, out into the deep.

From his hip, up through his massive shoulders and along his arm, as unyielding now as a forged metal blade, pushing solely by instinct, reasoning at an end, berserk at last, reduced to pure matter, elevated to pure matter. *Survival!* It bellowed through his brain like a firestorm, battering behind his blind eyes, and a warm rain now washing the lining of his body, emanating from his core, the central vortex of which he mercifully had no understanding, and blue lightning ringing the sky above him, gyring across the opening heavens, something feeding him now and, though he was past knowing it, the shaking fist enclosed within the sanctity of the Makkon gauntlet, scales bright with alien saliva, finally slipped past the spasmodically working tongue, breaching the roof of the creature's mouth, driving with inhuman power upward into its eye cavity.

The vibrations became intolerable and he burst apart then into ten thousand fragments, his hot red flesh drifting upon a cool wind which gusted upward in a tenacious spiral, the serpentine breaching the roiling lavender clouds, away, away . . .

First it was the sweetness and then the darkness.

Night had fallen.

He attempted to rise but he seemed incapable of any movement. All about him the susurrations of the poppies. Above him the nodding bell petals.

He rested, concentrating on his breathing, his mind turning over with curiosity each of his senses. Sight, sound, taste, smell, touch: life.

At length able to move his fingers, then his hand, finally his arm. He attempted to sit up. No movement. He explored, found that he could not feel his feet. It was his back then, where the Makkon had enwrapped him.

He called to Kiri but his voice was a quiet croak in the restless meadow. His throat was dry. He heard movement, above and behind him, and he called out again as loudly as he was able and there was a snort, hesitant, questioning. The sounds of the poppies parting, stalks whooshing, and he longed to look but could not.

A long head and wet muzzle were abruptly over him. His luma. Its blue eyes looked at him with intelligence and he whispered to it softly, wordlessly, a crooning singsong as he had heard its attendant talking to it in Kiri's jeweled garden. The luma moved closer, extending its muzzle. He heard its hoofs very close and felt the columns of its strong forelegs almost touching his head. It opened its wide mouth and licked at his face and then lower so that he could drink its saliva. Then it rested its head against his while he spoke to it again, stroking the side of its head, reassuring it.

After a while he slept and the luma stood over him, watchful in the night, its wide nostrils flared for first scent, its triangular ears twitching to pick up any movement. Several times it called to the mare who stood some meters away, over Kiri's sleeping form.

The luma guarded them through the night. But no one came.

And only Ronin heard, deep within his being, below the dreams that played across his mind, the confused jumble of echoing voices, calling, calling in some desperation now, *Have you found him? You must find him. Yes, I will. But if he does not have it? We are truly lost then. Even if I find him, the Kai-feng still comes. There is little time then, even for us—*

Abruptly, borne on some desolate wind, the voices drop away from him.

The blue morning light woke him. Above him stood the roan luma, its coat a glowing red in the sun's first oblique rays. It shook its head and stamped the poppies beside him. The exhalations from its nostrils were white clouds in the chill air.

Ronin reached up, grabbing for the swinging stirrup, pulled himself hand over hand until he stood on his feet, testing his legs and back. The numbness was gone but his co-ordination was off and he leaned on the luma for a moment, gathering his strength. He walked with its help across the white and blue field to where the golden luma stood over Kiri.

She was still asleep deep within the rustling sea. A large purple bruise swelled along the left side of her forehead.

She awoke as he bent over her and he stepped quickly back, half expecting her to unsheathe her blade and cross swords with him. She was, after all, the Empress of Sha'angh'sei and he had struck her. But she was quite calm.

She broke out food from her saddlebags, feeding the luma before she would eat herself. She offered some to Ronin.

"Against your strong advice, I rushed the Makkon," she said ruefully. "You did not hit me that hard. When I looked it already had you and I struck at it with my sword." She gave him a small smile then. "I did not believe you, I suppose. I thought, well, you are a warrior and—the rikkagin do not approve of women warriors; they are frightened, I think."

Coming against him in the metaled ellipse just below the crust of the surface, his equal perhaps as warrior, who knows, no one ever will now.

"Now you know I told you the truth."

"Oh, but yes!" She reached up and gingerly touched the bruise. "It slapped me, just a backhand swipe of its claw. I have never felt such power. I was flung a good distance away. That is all I remember."

Ronin chewed on his food. "I wounded it," he said.

"But how?"

He lifted the gauntlet so that the strange scales caught the light of dawn.

"With this! Its own hide." He laughed then. "Thank you, Bonneduce the Last, wherever you may now be. A better gift you could not have left me."

He went to pick up his sword and as he buckled the belt around his waist she said, "What now? Where has it gone?"

"Impossible to say. Too much time has already passed for us to attempt to continue to pursue it. Do you know of Kamado?"

"Of course."

"Can you guide us there?"

239

"It lies north, along the river. I do not think that we shall have a problem finding it."

They rode hard due north, keeping the snaking river on their left, and it was not long before they encountered soldiers streaming northward in long lines, columns bristling with weaponry and machines of war.

They joined this caravan for the last part of their journey, riding swiftly by the soldiers' sides.

Flags fluttered in the wind, the men in leather jerkins and metal helms, armed with long curving swords and bright, finely tipped lances. There were archers, their immense longbows strung vertically on their backs, and cavalry, acting as outriders and scouts, protecting the column's flanks. Metal clanged and jangled and the wooden carts, laden with food and spare arms, creaked under their heavy loads.

They moved up gradually until they reached the horsemen of the rikkagin's retinue who directed them to their commander. He was a sharp-faced man with a long queue and many scars along his desiccated cheeks.

"Are you bound for Kamado?" asked Ronin.

"All are bound for Kamado these days," said the rikkagin darkly. "Or away from it."

"Do you know the Rikkagin T'ien?"

"By name only. There are many rikkagin."

"I have heard that he is at Kamado."

The rikkagin nodded. "Yes. That is my understanding also. You may ride along with my men, if you wish."

"Thank you."

They rode in silence for a time, listening to the wind and the creaking of leather, the clop-clop of hoofs in the dust, the clash of metal.

"You have been to Kamado before?" asked Kiri.

The rikkagin turned his bleak gaze upon her.

"Too often, lady. We were not due back there for

another fortnight but the enemy grows stronger each day and we must return now. From whence they come, I cannot say. Nor can anyone else, though we have made strenuous efforts to find out."

"You have learned nothing?" said Kiri.

"Nothing at all," answered the rikkagin. "For none of our scouts have returned."

They caught sight of Kamado just past midday, its dun-colored walls, thick and high and crenellated, dominating the huge hill on which it had been built long ago. The wide river crashed along the left of the fortress and, to the north, it was possible to make out the verdant splash of a forest.

It was truly cold now and the sky had been lowering as they moved farther north. A fine rain had sprung up a short time before but it was freezing, turned to sleet by the unnatural weather, and it hammered now against the soldier's helms, caked the mounts' hides.

They had broken the crest of a rise and, across the last gentle valley the yellow outline of the great fort had come into sight, rising like a spectral city in the wilderness of the bleak landscape.

The stone walls rose upward, an extension of the dusty hill, wider at the bottom. It was roughly circular, with newer extensions to the east and west, rectangular bulges which gave it a peculiar look.

Massive metal-bound doors faced them, guarded by wide outcroppings of the walls along which soldiers constantly patrolled. To the west, the hill dropped away, sweeping down to the water. A wooden bridge with two stone pillars spanned the river at that point. On the far shore, a multitude of tents and pavilions could be seen among which strode many soldiers, some leading horses. Cooking fires were already being started in several places.

The rikkagin halted the column and sent a rider ahead to inform the citadel of their arrival. The man spurred his mount up the slope of the hill, through the thickening sleet, calling out to the guards on the ramparts.

After a brief time he turned in his saddle and signaled the rikkagin who, spurring his horse forward, ordered the column to move out.

With an enormous clash of arms and booted feet, the soldiers marched to the war, trudging in a tired procession through the huge gates of burnished bronze, dwarfed by the towering walls, into the dark and dismal depths of Kamado, the stone citadel.

It was a city unto itself, constructed expressly for the agonies of war; not petty raids or vengeful strikes but centuries of sustained conflict. There was no way of determining this by observing it from outside, where all that was visible were the awesome stone fortifications four and a half meters thick so that men could walk atop the walls, safe behind the stone crenellations. And perhaps this was artfulness also, for it gave no hint at all of the citadel's interior.

Kamado was so vast and so complex in construction that, seated atop his luma just inside the southern postern, Ronin could not discern the far northern limits of the fortress.

Long two-story buildings formed the immediate southern area of the citadel. The walls facing outward were windowless and constructed of stone so that they could not burn should any invader choose to rain liquid fire into Kamado's streets. They were blank, featureless, save for the stains and scars of the years.

However, their appearance changed as one went between them, down the angustate streets. Their inward faces were of wood, with wide beams carved in the shapes of the ancient gods of war, fierce women in

242

high curving helms, attended by dwarfs with curling beards and rings in their noses, from whom the warriors of yore sought advice and favors to assure victory.

Certainly, from this evidence alone, Kamado predated the building of Sha'angh'sei which, Ronin had been told, had sprung up largely because of the rikkagin from other lands. Who then had constructed this fantastic monument to battle? Surely not the Sha'angh'sei people.

All about them as their luma danced gingerly down the dirt streets, the corps of the conflict were to be seen preparing themselves for battle. Grinding wheels sharpened axes and scimitar-bladed swords in a shimmering cascade of cold blue sparks, archers stringing their bows, fletchers gluing feathers to thin wooden shafts that would soon, in their diligent hands, become arrows. Soldiers doubling as stable hands fed and watered horses, wiping at their lathered flanks. Men trotted by them, relief for the soldiers manning the battlements. Up narrow stone stairways they clambered, reaching at last the topmost ramparts.

All about them too were the wounded, a pain-filled world of blood and bandages, of the one-armed and the one-legged, of the eyeless and the scarred. They lay, backs against the wooden pillars or curled in the dust in front of their lost gods of war, who looked down upon them, arrogant and uncaring. Perhaps their rikkagin had not gone before these deities with sufficient humility, perhaps their sacrifices were not great enough, or, more likely, the time of their power had long since been swept from the face of the world. Alone and forgotten, they yet looked out mutely on a domain no longer theirs.

Ronin stopped before one group of wounded men and asked for directions to Rikkagin T'ien's quarters.

They moved on, through inner gates and circular

courtyards, along straight avenues and around stone buildings, and at length dismounted before a wooden-fronted barracks. They turned, hearing voices and the heavy tramp of boots.

He saw Tuolin first, his blond hair and height unmistakable in the crowd of soldiers.

"All right, bring him out here."

A group of soldiers with drawn swords emerged from the barracks. Ronin strained to see whom they held prisoner. Slowly, he drifted toward the men, circling to get a better angle. He stopped short.

The man the soldiers escorted, hands bound behind his back, was Rikkagin T'ien. Light gleamed along his hairless head. He stared straight ahead.

At Tuolin's command, T'ien and his guards halted.

"You are Ching Pang, do you deny this?"

"No." Eyes straight ahead.

"You are a spy."

"I am Ching Pang, that is all."

"All?" echoed Tuolin sardonically. "The Ching Pang wish us destroyed."

"We wish only for the freedom of the Sha'angh'sei people."

"And what would they do with this freedom?" Tuolin said contemptuously. "Return to the mud and bamboo hovels of their ancestors?"

"Our ancestors were great once. Greater than your people ever dreamed of becoming."

Tuolin turned abruptly away and, as if that were a signal, the soldiers surrounding T'ien slashed at him simultaneously and in an instant he was but so much dead meat.

"I do not understand this," Ronin said to Kiri. "Rikkagin T'ien a Green?"

"What are you talking about?" She glanced at him. "The Rikkagin T'ien comes toward us now."

"That is Tuolin."

244

"Yes," she nodded. "And Rikkagin T'ien." She noted the look of puzzlement on his face. "All rikkagin take a second name at the end of their training."

"Then who was the man Tuolin just had executed?"

"Lei'in, the rikkagin's chief adviser." She seemed amused. "And a Ching Pang; Tuolin must be furious."

Ronin was about to tell her of the ruse T'ien had used on him but thought better of it. He wanted to think it through himself now. He recalled the events aboard the rikkagin's vessel. He had not been disarmed when he was brought aboard; he had been kept at ease. When they judged him well enough, he had been interviewed by Lei'in masquerading as the rikkagin. He had been tested. Only then had he been allowed abovedecks into Tuolin's presence. Yes, it made perfect sense now; war breeds its own form of paranoia. It all fitted now, the assassination attempt on the ship, his night out with Tuolin.

The big blond man had seen them now and he seemed unsure whether to scowl or smile, finally opted for a neutral look.

"Did you find the Council of assistance?" he asked Ronin.

"I—never got to see them." Ronin remembered Kiri's warning that Tuolin did not know.

"What a pity," he said without much conviction. He turned to Kiri. "I almost did not recognize you." He glanced down at the sword scabbarded at her left hip. "Can you actually use that or is it for show?"

"What do you think?" Kiri said.

"I think I prefer to see you at Tenchō," Tuolin said quite calmly. "I distrust women on the battlefield."

"Oh, why is that?" She was struggling to control her anger.

"They never seem to know which way to go."

"I do not understand you at all."

245

He shrugged. "There is nothing to understand. Fighting should be left to those who can do it best. End of discussion."

He turned his attention back to Ronin as if she did not exist. "Why are you here?" He began to walk toward the barracks and they went with him.

"That depends."

"Oh, on what?"

"On whether you think you can trust me yet."

Tuolin threw his head back and laughed.

"Yes, I see." He wiped at his eyes. "I think we can safely say that your time of trial is at an end."

They went up the wooden steps and into the interior. It was dim and cool. The low ceilings were beamed and dark with smoke residue. The furniture was sparse and utilitarian. In the main room of the first story a fire burned on a large stone hearth.

Tuolin led them through this space, filled with soldiers, into a smaller back room, windowless, with a desk of scarred wood, several hard chairs, and a low cabinet against the back wall. At some time previous, the doors had been removed. The rikkagin sat down behind the desk and reached into the cabinet. He offered them cold wine, which they drank.

Ronin wondered briefly about the rikkagin's changed attitude toward Kiri, then put it out of his mind.

"Sa was killed, then Matsu, by a creature whom I had fought in my own land. It came north out of Sha'angh'sei. It was waiting for me in the poppy fields half a day's ride south of here." He paused. "You do not seem surprised."

"My friend, many things have transpired since first we met. I have seen many sights, battled foes I could not have dreamed of in my worst nightmares." He gestured at the walls. "We fight non-men." He sighed.

"Not many here remember the things spawned by the sorcerous wars."

"I do not think that these creatures are connected with that time."

Tuolin drained his cup and poured himself more wine without offering them more. He waved the cup. "No matter. These men are not cowards; for most, fighting is all they know. But they are used to foes who bleed when they are cut; give them an enemy that they can see and kill. But this——" The wine sloshed over the cup's rim and onto the desk. He ignored it. "We are losing this battle."

Ronin leaned forward. "Tuolin, this creature, the Makkon, is an emissary of The Dolman. Do you remember? I told you——" The rikkagin waved his cup at him. "There are four Makkon and it is imperative that I kill at least one before they can all gather."

"Why?"

"Because when the four come together they will summon The Dolman and then, I fear, it will be too late for all of us."

"You have already fought one of these—Makkon?"

"Yes, more than once. But this last time I was able to injure it. With this——" He held up the scaled gauntlet. "Tuolin, it cannot be harmed with ordinary weapons. But this is made of its own hide. I hurt it but it almost killed me."

The rikkagin ran a hand over his eyes and Ronin became aware of the new lines of fatigue etched into his face.

"The Makkon is likely here then."

"I must find it," said Ronin.

"All right." Tuolin pulled at the ivory bar which pierced one ear lobe. "We must cross to the field encampment. There we will be most likely to find news of your Makkon.

"I am pleased that you believe me."

247

The big man sighed. "I have spent too much time with the dead and dying not to," he said wearily.

The dusty streets of Kamado were filled with the din of hoarse shouting, the clang of iron against heated iron, the snort and stamp of war horses, the moans of the injured, the tramp of booted feet.

They went out through the southern postern, escorted by soldiers as far as the bridge.

Dark thunderheads were piling up in the northwest, writhing their way rapidly southward. The wind had died and the air was leaden and chill. The moist land steamed whitely.

They moved as swiftly as they could across the wooden planks, hands gripping the rope sides. Ronin peered down into the frothy depths, catching an occasional glimpse of glistening black rocks and sleek leaping fish.

To the south, the land was brown and barren, as if blasted by intense heat. Off to their right, almost due north, lay the encampment with its rows of tents and bright pavilions, lines of tethered horses and bright flickering fires, like silent insects, around which the shadows of the soldiers darted.

The encampment was on the near edge of an undulating meadow of high green grass perhaps a third of a kilometer wide, beyond which began the first low bushes and wide trees of the forest Ronin had seen as they approached the fortress. Now, as they neared the far shore, he could see that the forest was immensely thick, the tree trunks so tall and the numerous branches so heavily foliaged that it appeared to be a solid wall of green.

Soldiers met them as they stepped off the bridge. Tuolin ordered them to take them to Rikkagin Wo's pavilion. They went into the high grass. Fireflies swept the twilight with minute arcs of cool light. The meadow rustled in the wind and cicadas chirruped. Everything was steeped in deep blue except the far-off forest, cloaked in black shadows, pooling and impenetrable.

The pavilion was striped bright yellow and blue, its canvas walls quiescent now as what little breeze there was died. Lamps were being lit throughout the encampment. Wood smoke and charcoaled meat were the dominant scents which came to them.

Within, it was warm and bright from a multitude of lamps. Shadows danced along the insubstantial walls as soldiers went to and fro, preparing for battle. An almost constant stream of runners came and went, depositing and receiving coded messages on slips of rice paper.

Tuolin led them a seemingly circuitous path through the disciplined confusion toward a tall man who broke abruptly into their field of vision. He had dark hair which he wore long and loose and a thin pinched mouth. His chin thrust forward. He turned and gazed at Tuolin as they approached.

"Ah, T'ien, has Hui arrived with his troops?"

"Yes, just before sunset."

"Good. We need every man."

Rikkagin Wo took a slip of paper from a runner, went a few paces away, nearer a light and farther from them. He read the message, went to his desk, and wrote several characters with his quill. He gave the slip back to the runner, who left.

He turned back to Tuolin. "We lost another patrol this afternoon."

"Where?"

"Due north. In the forest."

"How many?"

"Thirteen. Only one came back." Wo looked disgusted. "And he is no good to us. Raving like a lunatic."

"What did he say?"

Wo took another message. He did not look up. "I cannot remember. Ask Le'ehu, if you wish. I would not bother myself."

Tuolin, with Ronin's urgings, sought out a heavy squat individual with his black hair in a queue, fat cheeks and long glittering eyes.

"Le'ehu drew them to the side, against the canvas, where few passed close to them.

"He is gone now, the last soldier." He paused, his eyes on Ronin and Kiri.

Tuolin patted his arm. "Go on, these two will not pass on what you say."

"All right, it is just that"—he rubbed at his upper lip, which had begun to sweat—"I killed him, you know, in the end." The glittery eyes glanced quickly around. "I mean he was dying anyway and he pleaded with me. He could not bear to live another moment, after what he had seen—"

"What attacked the patrol?" asked Ronin.

Le'ehu looked startled. "How—how did you know? How did he know, T'ien?"

"Know what?" asked Tuolin.

"He knew a 'what' attacked the patrol."

"Did the man describe it?" asked the blond man patiently.

"Yes, curse him. I will not sleep this night. It was huge with great claws and a nightmare face. It ripped out their throats, he said."

"The Makkon," Ronin said and Tuolin nodded.

"In the forest?"

"Yes." The man tried to swallow. "Over the meadow's ridge, perhaps a kilometer into that cursed place—"

They were silent, waiting for him to continue. Le'ehu stared over their shoulders at the fluttering shadows along the far side of the pavilion.

"What else?" Tuolin said very gently.

"It was not of that creature that he talked before he died." The words came out of him reluctantly now, as if by saying this aloud he might conjure up terrifying creatures. "Something came in that thing's wake."

"Another one?" asked Ronin.

Le'ehu's head snapped around. "Another——? Oh no. No, it was, I do not know, something else. There was whirling fog, he said, and blood raining in the melee. He caught a glimpse only——"

"And," prompted Tuolin.

Le'ehu swallowed again.

"Rikkagin—he said it was the Hart——"

"Oh, come on," Tuolin snorted.

"Rikkagin, he bade me kill him," the squat man said miserably. "I do not think that otherwise——"

"The Hart is but legend, Le'ehu, a foul——"

"What legend?" asked Ronin.

"The tale is told," said Tuolin, "of the Hart. He is half man and half beast."

"That is all?"

Tuolin stared at Le'ehu, who winced at his words. "Some say that he is evil incarnate. And others suggest that he was once a whole man, transmogrified, forced now to serve a sorcerous liege, fighting those who are really his kin."

"Whatever is truth," said the squat man, "that soldier believed that he saw it"—he turned his head——"out there. In the forest."

Ronin turned to Tuolin.

"I care not for legends. The Makkon is my only concern. At first light I must go into the wood and destroy it——"

Le'ehu's eyes bulged. "Surely you must be mad. The Hart——"

"Be silent," snapped Tuolin. "We are confronted with enough real monstrosities without you fabricating nightmares." He swung his gaze toward Ronin and his tone softened. "You cannot mean to go alone. I will accompany you."

Ronin shook his head.

"You will not be able to help. I require two men who know this area. When I find it I will send them away."

The big man put a hand on his shoulder.

"My friend, I have done many things for you. Fished you out of the sea when you were half dead, introduced you to Tenchō. It is time now to repay me. I want to see this Makkon for myself." His grip tightened. "I must know the enemy, can you understand that?"

Ronin searched the cerulean eyes and nodded. "Yes, that is something that I can accept."

Le'ehu stared from one to the other, backing off.

"You are both mad! You—"

A stifled yell. The clash of metal against metal.

They all turned at the sounds. Boots pounded outside and there came now confused shouts.

"Quickly," Tuolin said. "Outside."

The heavy darkness of the massive forest seemed to have pervaded the meadow. The fireflies were gone. Above the waving grass now rolled an oncoming tide of black shadows.

They came swiftly and silently, without the telltale gleam of metal. Somehow they had pierced the perimeter of the encampment without an alarm being sounded.

They were like tree trunks, dark, with wide shoulders and thick legs. Their long beards and wiry hair were greased and plaited. Their faces were moon-shaped and perfectly flat as if evolution had decreed to their ancestors that the protrusions of nose and cheeks and forehead were superfluous. They seemed more animated creatures from the wall paintings in

Kiri's palace than true men. Yet they were real enough, brandishing wide scimitars of an unreflective metal that was almost black with bell-shaped fist guards.

Behind them loomed other shadows, coalescing slowly in the dark, impossibly tall and bony, their skin pallid gray, their faces desiccated and fleshless, their skulls gleaming in their nakedness. These creatures strode behind their fellow warriors, swinging heavy short chains ending in fanged iron spheres. Ronin caught the sound of their brief hissing arcs in the close air.

Tuolin unsheathed his sword as did Ronin and Kiri. All about them were confusion and disarray as soldiers scrambled for their weapons. Fires guttered and flickered out as if by a strong wind, although the air was calm.

Mist rolled in, sweeping through the meadow and into the encampment, and there was a choking stench as the enemy advanced, the first wave already past the hapless outer patrols. The scimitars swung darkly in whooshing arcs, cleaving a hideous harvest in this sorcerous high summer.

Still within the long grass, the gaunt warriors whirled their chains, the deadly globes hissing in the night like locusts, crushing flesh and bone indiscriminately, and the groans of the dying mingled with the wet slap and crunch of the reaving.

Ronin leapt forward with a cry and his blade swept to and fro in mighty two-handed slashes, ripping into the torsos of those wide men closest to him. They squealed and backed into each other, bewildered, and he stepped into their midst, using oblique blows now, slicing into the juncture of neck and collarbone of one warrior, withdrawing his sword and, in the same motion, decapitating another.

Beside him came Tuolin and Kiri, hacking at the

253

warriors as if they were wild foliage. He concentrated, moving slowly forward, his blade singing its fiery song of death, gleaming, running with blood. He hammered at them without letup, his heart thudding in his chest, his arms electric with the power of the destruction he was reaping, no longer conscious of the peripheral sights and sounds of the night; he was intent, content as he hammered at them, severing bodies which convulsed and spurted their liquids hotly about his swaying form. His muscles rippled and glistened with a fine film of sweat, beaded with sprays of his enemies' blood and entrails, and he grinned in savage delight. He clove a warrior from shoulder to ribcage on a forward swing, slashed into the mid-section of another on his backward arc.

Near him, Kiri was nearly disemboweled as she watched horrified and fascinated. She parried at the last instant and turned her face away from him, working at her own task.

At their backs, they heard Rikkagin Wo's voice lifted in sharp command. Men ran everywhere, attempting to form themselves into defense lines, but it seemed useless; the warriors moved inexorably forward. The mist rolled past them and over the soldiers, burning their calves with cold. And more of the gaunt warriors appeared as their shorter compatriots fell beneath the swords of the soldiers. These were destroying the rikkagin's men with terrifying expertise. They carried round iron shields, in addition to their weapons, which seemed much too heavy for any man to wield effectively yet these warded off most of the soldiers' blows while, with their other hands, the fanged spheres described their tight orbits, exploding with terrible impact.

Ronin felt himself ingulfed in a dark tide, no longer an individual, another piece of floating flotsam carried along by the undertow. He fought and the warriors fell before his blurred blade like wheat before a scythe but always there were others to take the place of the fallen, as if in each individual's death two more were created.

Onward he waded, the footing unsure and gluey with the innards of the fallen as he made his laborious way out into the meadow to meet the gaunt death-head warriors. Tuolin and Kiri were just behind him. The rikkagin's great blade lifted and fell and in his left hand was the emerald-hilted dirk with which he slashed and parried. For her part, the Empress was using her sword with consummate skill. Her breast-plate was shiny, sodden with blood and splattered gore, her black hair had slipped its bonds and now whirled about her, a dark mantle.

With an enormous swipe that ripped apart a barrel chest, Ronin went through the outer fringes of the wide warriors and for the first time in many moments there was space around him. The still air was alive with the harsh whisper of the globes. The last of the soldiers went down, his head smashed open like a ripe fruit, and he peered into the roiling night at the grinning faces, as white now in the guttering firelight as the pallid poppies. Their sunken eyes were featureless holes with no discernible trace of iris or pupil; their heads turned on their spindly spines as they looked about them.

Ronin lifted his blade and went in quickly, driving it down in a blur, through the collarbone of one of the warriors. The neck was severed and the head flew from the bony shoulders. There was no blood but a shower of gray dust which plumed momentarily, spitting shards of vertebrae from its periphery. The decapitated torso came at him, its arm still lifted, the fanged globe whirring, and he was obliged to duck the blow that came. A hissing passed over him as he crouched and the creature, shuddering now, stumbled on its nerveless legs and collapsed.

At that moment he felt a titanic wrench and his blade went spinning to the sodden ground. He lurched forward and almost fell on top of the gaunt corpse. He turned, saw another deathhead warrior whipping back the globe that had slammed into his sword. It advanced upon him, the deadly sphere a menacing blur.

The creature leaned back and the globe came at him with such speed that its fangs grazed his cheek even as he jerked away. He risked a glance downward, saw that he was too far from his sword to risk lunging for it and the gaunt warrior was circling so that he was now between Ronin and the weapon.

Ronin turned his body sideways, waited for the next swing, counting to himself so that the timing would be perfect. The globe glistened as it came at him and he was away, counting again to be certain of the rhythm. He timed his dive to coincide with the peak of its arc away from him to give himself the maximum amount of time.

He hit the ground and rolled onto the warrior he had just slain, his fingers scrabbling along the moist earth for the chain and globe. The long grass made it difficult to locate but his peripheral vision had picked up where it had fallen when the warrior fell and now he had it and he was rolling. He regained his feet and went down immediately to avoid the globe.

Whir. The other's weapon was circling again and he swung his own globe, gaining momentum, but the fangs loomed at him without warning and he had time but to throw up his globe reflexively. The chains clashed, momentum taking the globes and whipping them around as the chain entwined.

The gaunt warrior pulled viciously and Ronin, caught off balance, was jerked forward, slamming into his adversary. The skeletal figure bent and the head darted toward him, the mouth opening impossibly wide. Filed yellow teeth, long and ragged, snapped hideously at his face and he writhed away just in time. The clashing jaws pursued him as he attempted to disengage himself. But to break free now was to lose his only weapon. Snap, snap. The neck, long and willowy, brought the fangs at him again and again.

Still holding onto the chain, Ronin brought his left hand up and, balling the Makkon gauntlet into a fist, he smashed upward into the working mouth. Shards of fractured teeth rained upon them both and Ronin punched once more and the thing let go his weapon, bringing his shield up with both hands.

Ronin whirled the spiked globe and aimed it. The bony skull caved in, the entire left side crushed, and the thing went down on its bony knees. Ronin hit it again and the warrior keeled over as its knees splintered and the bones in its legs cracked.

Ronin ran for his sword then, dropping the chain and globe and, grasping it, turned back into the fray. The soldiers were dying under the assault of the deathhead warriors.

He heard Tuolin's shout and, looking around, he located the tall rikkagin. He moved off in this direction, dodging hissing spheres. He saw Kiri fighting at Tuolin's side.

"We cannot hold against them, Ronin," he panted as he hacked at a skeletal figure. "The encampment is routed, I fear. We must find Wo and marshal the remaining men in a retreat to Kamado."

Ronin looked about them. The gaunt warriors were advancing steadily and were now within the perimeter of the pavilions. The moans of the dying were in his ears as he retreated with Tuolin and Kiri back to the pavilions, slashing at their foes with each step. Firelight blazed up briefly and he saw a tent bursting into flames. There were screams from soldiers trapped inside.

The night was streaked with yellow and orange and heat danced in waves, alternating with the chill. The earth steamed whitely until they could no longer see their boots. Kiri slipped and fell over a body, her head cracked against a skull, and when she lifted her face, her forehead was black and shiny with blood. Ronin lifted her, her hand grasping his arm, and they went on, through the narrow dark lanes between the canvas walls, ducking flames, hacking at the wide warriors who blocked their way. The ground was muddy with viscous liquids and soft things squished under the soles of their boots. More pavilions began to smoke and crackle with flame.

Just ahead of them, the green canvas wall of a pavilion bulged and ripped open, three men tumbling through, slashing at each other. A wide warrior hit the ground at a bad angle and his neck snapped. At the same instant a deathhead warrior swung his globe, smashing the breastbone of the soldier, who moaned and folded in upon himself.

Ronin's blade struck off the head of the gaunt warrior and the skeleton body crashed backward into the pavilion's interior.

They went on, Tuolin leading them now, searching through the frenzy for the yellow and blue pavilion, picking their way through the grisly litter stewn across the earth like stinking loam.

It was already in flames when they reached it, sheets of orange sparks cracking open the night. They swept aside the burning walls and went in, finding Rikkagin Wo armless, his shoulder sockets crimson. White bones protruded pinkly. One side of his head was a pool of blood and pulpy matter. His face was untouched.

Tuolin took them out of the burning pavilion. A

shower of bright sparks fell along their shoulders. Outside, the night had heated up. Flames crackled everywhere. They ran into a pack of the wide warriors and slew them. They backed away from Ronin and he went after them, back into the torched pavilions, and Tuolin was obliged to take him by the shoulder and turn him around. More of the deathhead warriors were arriving.

"We have lost the field this night, Ronin," he said. "We must return to the fortress."

They went out of the encampment, the earth once again firm beneath their feet, along the black and deserted road leading to the bridge. Blood rolled off them like black rain. They were numb and sick at heart. Onto the bridge, the screams and crunchings following them like living creatures. No other sound could be heard. No insect trilled; no bird called to its mate.

A wind had sprung up from the northwest, chilling, plucking at their sodden cloaks, twanging the ropes on the bridge. Below them, the water whooshed by, pale, ribboning in the gloom, swirling against the black rocks.

It was quieter now and the night lit up as they passed a stand of tall firs and the illumination of the flames reached them again. And Ronin was singing all at once at the shadows looming grayly between them and the sanctuary of Kamado. They had been waiting for retreating soldiers, standing in the shadows midway across the bridge. Only the flickering firelight had betrayed them and the night was abruptly filled again with the hiss and whir of the fanged globes. One gaunt warrior swung into Tuolin's side before he had a chance to react. Ronin heard his sharp exhalation like a dull explosion as he swung in a short oblique arc, severing the chain. The rikkagin clutched at his bleeding side, leaning on the guide ropes along the bridge's edge. His legs began to buckle and blood oozed through his fingers.

Kiri moved in front of the big man, slashing within the guard of a warrior, her blade sinking into its narrow chest. Its head weaved on its long neck and it threw its shield at her. It slammed into her shoulder as she attempted to twist away, caroming over the side of the bridge, its flight a dull booming in their ears. She staggered and her guard came down and the wounded warrior launched his globe.

Two of the warriors pressed Ronin back, attempting to split him off from the other two, but he counterattacked, his blade blurring whitely, lashing out at the two globes filling the air around him like flying creatures.

Tuolin was panting, his face a pale mask of pain. He tried to lift his blade. Sweat broke out on his face with the effort.

Near him, Kiri pressed her attack, rolling to avoid the warrior's blow, leaping up and slamming her boots into its stomach. She swung at him, two-handed, her feet wide apart and planted firmly, swinging up, from the hip, the power traveling into her shoulders, along her arms, the momentum flashing the blade in the night. It clove into the warrior's skull, down from the cranium into the blackness of its eye, crashing at length into the roof of its mouth. The skull flew apart like a shell, the bone fragments whirring and pattering around her. The body folded and went down heavily.

She turned then, eyes flashing, and in one long beautiful sweep of her sword cut through the torso of one of Ronin's foes. The head swiveled even as she began to withdraw the blade and the gnashing mouth reached for her. Startled, she stepped back and almost fell off the slickened verge of the bridge. The teeth clashed together as the torso fell at her feet.

Ronin swept aside the whistling sphere, timing it

perfectly so that he deflected its flight back into the warrior's face. As it jerked desperately away from the oncoming globe, its head whipped directly into the path of Ronin's extended blade, flying apart in a gray flurry of bone and dust.

Another deathhead came at Kiri and she calmly cut its legs under it. Ronin saw her wince with the blow. With a second swipe, she sent the collapsing body over the brink, a bony blur cartwheeling out of sight. But she was spent now, the blow from the heavy iron shield taking its toll, and she stood, gasping, leaning on her sword while her thighs trembled with fatigue.

Ronin heard a grunt and swung around. The last of the gaunt warriors had taken his severed chain and had wrapped it around Tuolin's neck, the silvered links biting into his flesh. The inconstant light of the flames played over their struggling bodies, the one wiry and stooped now, yellow as old bone, the other twisting in pain, dark with running blood. The rikkagin's eyes bulged and his empty hands scrabbled uselessly at the metal links tightening about his throat. Blood pooled at his feet.

Ronin leapt at the thing, grasping its wide shoulders, attempting to wrest it away from Tuolin. The head swiveled and the jaws gaped, snapping at him. He raised his sword but he lacked the room to use it and he could not step away and attack the warrior for fear of cutting the big man.

The creature's head snaked forward while he was thus debating and caught the blade in its mouth, the teeth gripping it so that Ronin could not pull it away. Still the warrior heaved on the chain and Tuolin sagged, choking on his own exhalations as his lungs vainly strove for air. His knees buckled and the death-head warrior pulled mightily on the chain, the grinding sound of the links tightening unnaturally loud in the night.

Only Ronin's left hand was free, his right was trapped on the hilt of his blade and he dared not let go. He brought the hand up, using the thumb at his opponent's neck, pressing in through the small space under his horizontal sword. Just above the base of the neck, he located the triangular soft spot and lunged inward, puncturing the throat. Fetid gas swirled at him and he gasped, turning his head away, ripping upward along the stalklike neck with his thumb. The long teeth rattled against the smooth metal of his blade and the grip of the powerful jaws loosened as the thing tried to regain its breath. He drove inward then, using the full weight of his body through his right hand, and the keen edge of his blade swept before him, unstoppable, shearing through the warrior's skull.

Ronin slammed the corpse aside, working frantically on the chain still tightly bound around Tuolin's throat. The bony hands refused to relinquish their hold on the links, though the body was half slumped over the side of the bridge. And Ronin pried at the fingers, staring into the rikkagin's pinched face. His skin had a blue tinge around the eyes.

Kiri was there, then, using a small curved knife to slash at the clenched bones, shearing through the knuckles until one by one they came apart. With a harsh grate, the links slid back slowly as Ronin forced the chain from around the big man's neck. He caught him as he fell.

It had begun to snow, the large white flakes sheeting down obliquely, dusting the corpses on the bridge, their faces white masks already, sparkling in the flickering glow from the encampment. They hissed in the flames and Kiri shuddered, thinking of the spinning fanged globes.

She turned, holding her left arm to her side, tucked

262

in, using her hipbone as support for the weight to ease the pain in her shoulder.

Ronin sheathed his sword and scooped Tuolin into his arms.

"Now, Kiri," he called, pushing her before him. They sprinted across the remaining expanse of the bridge and onto the high road stretching uphill to Kamado.

They were met by soldiers who escorted them to the towering walls, calling to the guards at the postern. The metal-bound gates creaked open just enough for them to slip through. Then they swung shut with an echoing clang.

There was an immediate tumult around them. Ronin delivered up the rikkagin into the hands of his men, his neck torn and black with terrible marks, his shirt and leggings dripping blood; they bore him away to his barracks. Ronin followed, his arm around Kiri as she struggled against unconsciousness. He declined the soldiers' aid but when he stumbled they took her from him and two of them lifted her up the barracks steps and through the entrance. Ronin sank down on the steep steps, too weary to go any farther.

After a time a man came out of the barracks and sat down beside him.

"He almost died."

He was tall and wide-shouldered, with graying hair and a full but close-cut beard. His nose was long and curving; his eyes were black.

"T'ien's own physician is inside if you need attention."

"I am tired," said Ronin. "That is all."

"Perhaps he had better see you anyway."

He called for the physician, who came out and grunted when he saw Ronin. He was the one from aboard Tuolin's ship. While he worked, the other said, "Good for us that he did not die, eh?" Then, more softly, "What is your name?"

"Ronin."

"I am Rikkagin Aerant."

"Ronin leaned his head against the wooden banister. The ancient gods of war, carved into the columns, looked blankly out at the darkness.

"You saved his life."

"What?" There was a stinging along his shoulders.

"Tuolin told me that you saved—"

"Do you always call him by his other name?"

"We are brothers."

Ronin turned his head. "You hardly look it." The physician finished tying the bandages. He went back inside.

"We had different fathers."

"I see." He thought of nothing.

"I can help you."

Ronin ran a hand over his face. "How?"

"Tell me what happened."

Rikkagin Aerant nodded his head as Ronin related the events in the encampment.

"Best that Wo is dead, truly. His mind was closed to this war; he was so used to fighting Reds and the northern tribes that he could not see that the war had changed."

"How could he explain the warriors who do not bleed?"

Rikkagin Aerant shrugged. "The military mind can rationalize any situation. He lacked imagination." He brushed at his leggings. "Pity. He was a fine leader."

"He was unprepared for that attack."

"Yes. I would dearly like to know how they got through the perimeter so easily."

"Tuolin told you—"

His face was bright in the torchlight. "Yes. I have seen this thing which you have fought."

264

"You told Wo?"

Rikkagin Aerant laughed shortly. "I told no one but Tuolin and even he——" His eyes were like cool crystal, they were open and keenly intelligent. "You know, even brothers do not love each other all the time."

"He wanted to go with me."

"He will not have that now." Several sentries ran by, their boots echoing against the wooden walls. The snow had ceased for the moment, but the sky was low and the air felt heavy and damp. "It is best that way."

"Do you wish to go?"

Rikkagin Aerant turned his head away. A dog barked along the next block of barracks. "I do not know. But it does not matter. I am needed here. I will send you two Reds. They were born in this region."

"All right."

He stood up, his eyes dark and unreadable as he stared down at Ronin.

"Perhaps you will return."

He went off down the muddy street.

Snow fell quietly along the rampants, dampening the scrape of the guard's high boots against the stone. It pattered about him, obscurring the last dying embers sparking in the ashes of the encampment, a wan carpet humped along the earth, hiding the bodies of the fallen combatants.

It was still in Kamado save for the crunch of an occasional group of soldiers on patrol. Soft voices floated up to him for a moment then were gone in the hissing of the snow. He pulled his cloak closer about his shoulders. The pain there was lessening. He willed his mind to be blank, not wanting to anticipate.

He saw Kiri walking along the ramparts, searching for him. He called wordlessly to her.

"How is your shoulder?" he asked.

"Better." She sat beside him. "The bone was knocked out of the socket. He is very good." She meant the physician.

He nodded into the night.

She put a hand along his arm, ran it upward. "There is a room in the barracks."

"I do not think so."

"I will return to Sha'angh'sei at dawn. I must talk to Du-Sing. The Greens and Reds must unite now."

"Yes."

"And you must go into the forest at first light." Her breath ran in warm white puffs against the side of his face. "Why not?"

He looked into her face. "You have changed."

He did not know what he expected to see there but he was surprised. She looked humiliated, her cheeks flushing pink.

"Of course. Matsu is dead. I am half a person now, not fit to be with." She got up and went away from him, along the white escarpment of the high rampart, disappearing down the steep stairs.

Dawn was a blood-red smear, burning coldly through a long rent in the massed gray clouds, pink-edged and pearled now in the east where the bloated oblate disk of the sun rose with agonizing deliberation.

He watched the light come into the world, atop the southern rampart where he had stayed all the long night. The snow had stopped falling just before first light and this day seemed somehow more natural than the last.

Ronin stood up, breathing deeply the chill air, and stretched his cramped muscles. He peered southward along the barren trail, completely white now. Higher up the snow was pink. He could pick out no imprints and the sparse foliage and his angle of elevation made

266

it clear to him that the way was clear back to Sha'-angh'sei.

He went down to the barracks. Two short men with long queues and black almond eyes waited patiently for him. A soldier came down the steps with a steaming cup of tea. He took it gratefully and sipped it, savoring its warmth and spice. He declined the bowl of rice.

Kiri was already at the stables. She saddled her luma silently, running her hand constantly down its flanks. His luma snorted and beat its hoofs against the earth as he came in. Straw floated through the air.

She mounted the animal and it pranced in its desire to be away. She pulled hard on the reins to keep it in check. It called to the roan, a plaintive farewell touched with the exultation of the wind and the road, and Kiri pulled again on the reins.

She took the luma out from the stable, Ronin at her side. They went along the quiet streets, the mount's clop-clop muffled by the carpet of snow. The luma's head bobbed as it sniffed the cold air, plumes of smoke shooting from its wide nostrils. Its ears twitched and Kiri spoke to it softly, a singsong litany.

At the southern postern she drew up and he pulled her down to him, kissing her cheek.

"Kill it," she said in his ear with a sob. "Kill it before I return."

And she dug her boot heels into the luma's flanks, rattling the reins, and it leaped through the parted gates, a saffron streak, out from the citadel, onto the long white road home.

The silence was like a clap of thunder, lapping at his eardrums with an unnatural proximity. Deep in the forest, the snowfall was but a light dusting because of the canopy of thick branches overhead. He was stuck by their austere beauty, frosted white across their interlacing upper surfaces, the spreading undersides a deep green shading into black among the blue shadows.

The quietude was extraordinary. If he ceased to move, he could hear the hissing of his own breath and, somewhat farther away, the inhalations and exhalations of the two Reds.

With a shivery rustle, a miniature snowslide fell from a branch and Ronin instinctively looked up. The wide green bough with its sweet-smelling needles bobbed and a flash of deep scarlet flew off in a flutter.

They were in a minute clearing but even so the sky was entirely obscured. Within the tall stands of pines, beds of fragrant brown needles cushioned the forest floor. The frozen earth was hard near the ancient twisting oaks with their entwining networks of branches and the profusion of oval leaves.

They moved deeper into the forest, Ronin carefully imitating the Red's slow, deliberate movements, creating a minimum of disturbance. The way was so entangled that more often than not they were forced to go single file, turning their bodies sideways in order to move through the narrow gap between the trees.

He became aware that they were on an incline and, as the way became steeper, granite outcroppings began to appear. Soon they crested the rise and the forest floor fell away from them. Off to their left, they could make out the clatter of a stream. Black birds flew among the laden branches, calling in shrill staccato cries, sending occasional showers of powdery snow onto the earth about them. There was little underbrush, only green moss and a grayish-blue lichen which clung to the rock faces.

They saw no tracks that morning and Yuan, one of the Reds, sent his companion off on a tangent.

"Perhaps we will have better luck this way," he said to Ronin.

They went ever north, the forest unchanging in its denseness. Once Yuan halted and pointed to their right. Ronin saw a red fox, long tail sweeping the ground as it ran from them.

Just past noon the Red signaled to him and, crouching, he moved from tree to tree as silently as he was able until he was next to the kneeling man.

Yuan whispered in his ear and Ronin looked through a stand of thick oak. There was movement and he inched closer, changing his angle of vision. On the other side of the trees were perhaps a dozen of the gaunt deathhead warriors, shields on arms, fanged globes swaying at their hips as they marched. Beside them strode a score or more men with straight black hair combed back into a queue. They had black almond eyes. They were armed with the single-edged curving swords and short-hafted axes identical to Yuan's. Another man came into view and he started. Eyes like stones magnified in still water, long drooping mustache. He would not forget that face. Po, the embittered trader who had walked out of Llowan's dinner party.

Ronin touched Yuan on the shoulder and they moved back from the oaks.

"Who are the men with the tall ones?" Ronin asked softly.

"Reds."

"Why are they with the enemy?"

"They hate the Greens. That is an old hate. The tall ones promise them power in Sha'angh'sei where the Greens are supreme in exchange for their aid here in the north."

"They would battle their own kind; join forces with those that are not men?"

"Power is strange, is it not?" said Yuan.

"Yet they will die along with us, if this enemy is victorious."

The other stared at him. "Do you think that you could convince them of this?"

Ronin thought of Po's outburst. He shook his head.

The afternoon waned as they searched vainly for any trace of the Makkon. Near dusk they gave it up and Yuan led them back to the clearing where they had arranged to rendezvous with the other Red.

"We can only trust that Li had better luck," said Yuan.

The clearing was darkling when they arrived, the snow blue, the shadows bluer still. Across the small open space a tree loomed in the dusk, lumped and misshapen. Yuan went and stood in front of the tree. Ronin went slowly after him, his eyes raking the shadows.

At perhaps the height of five meters from the forest's floor a branch had been torn from the tree, leaving a long ragged stump like a spear. Upon this makeshift stake Li had been impaled through back and breastbone, as if he had been hurled there by a titanic force.

Without a word Yuan unsheathed his sword and swung it over his head, shearing through the branch behind Li. He fell heavily to the ground, his legs crumpled under him, his eyes open, staring wildly. The snow was dark where he half sat, back against the old tree trunk.

The ground was too hard to bury him so they moved north, making camp shortly. Yuan gathered dry wood and set about making a smokeless fire.

Ronin took the first watch. The pale firelight danced against the blue expanse of snow and black trees. Shadows ran to and fro. Just outside the ring of light, he heard the small skitterings and soft susurrations of the nocturnal animals.

If he leaned to his right he could just make out the crescent moon and its attendant star, bits of glittering platinum, cool and remote, through a tiny gap in the forest's canopy.

Something howled, a snow wolf perhaps, and the forest chitterings ceased momentarily. But the sound did not come again and gradually the tiny myriad sounds sprang up once more. An owl hooted and, unseen, a bird flapped its wings above his head.

Near the end of his watch it began to snow, a fine dusting filtering down upon him and Yuan through the maze of branches, leaves, and needles.

He woke the Red, who stretched, yawned, and went to put more wood on the dying fire.

Ronin fell asleep instantly, a long dreamless flight until the blackness gave way to a flickering crimson and it seemed to him that the sky dripped blood. He heard low voices, far away yet so close that the individual words seemed to reverberate upon his eardrums. *Not yet? There can be no more delay. You know as well as I what must transpire before I can find him. Yes. All right. I am already in place; the vessel is prepared. I will get him there, be assured of that. I am assured of nothing now; time flows past too quickly: the Kai-feng comes. But we are Outside. Yes, but we must depend on those who are not; our time is ending.* He fell away from it and opened his eyes. He heard the soughing of the branches in the wind, a whippoorwill's mournful call. He turned his head. The fire crackled, the embers glowing orange and white. Yuan sat, arms around his knees to keep out the cold, staring out into the forest's shadows.

Ronin closed his eyes and went back to sleep.

The chill blue light of dawn woke him. He remembered the voices and for an instant, disoriented, thought that two men had been by the fireside.

The fire was out, the ashes gray and cold. Yuan sat in the same position, staring into the trees. Ronin crossed to him, reached out a hand, and paused. He

271

crouched down. The Red was dead. There was a black hole through his heart. Something had gone swiftly through him from chest to back. He might have been gored by a wild animal. He had not moved during the night.

Ronin went away from the campsite, swiftly and without a sound, moving north, farther into the forest. His spine tingled.

Snow began to fall again, harder now, deadening sound and limiting what visibility there was in that maze.

A wind arose, plucking at his cloak and swirling the snow into his face. He thought then that he heard a horn sound, plaintive and far off.

Mist steamed from the forest's floor, pearled and thick. Now all sound, all sense of direction was blotted out. His boots were silent along the ground but he heard the hammering of his heart. Oblique bars of gray light slanted down, illuminating the translucence of the mist, and abruptly he was lost in wilderness of smoke and vague shadows.

The minute sounds of the forest were gone now and with them the small comfort of being with other living creatures. He felt cut off, as if he no longer trod the world of man.

The snow fell silently, mingling with the syrupy mist. He went cautiously forward with one hand held before him like a blind man to guide him around the tree trunks which loomed in his path, visible only at the last moment.

His sense of time slipped away. He no longer knew whether he had been marching for hours or days whether the sun shone above the roof of his world or whether it had set.

He opened his mouth, letting the snow melt and slake his thirst. With that, he was suddenly aware of his hunger. He began to search the forest for game but he saw nothing. No animal, no fruit-bearing bush or tree. His hunger grew, gnawing at him. He pushed on.

At length he stumbled over an exposed root and he knew numbly that he must rest. Exhausted, he sat with his back against the trunk of an old pine. Its scent was all around him. The brown needles were soft beneath him. His head nodded on his chest but the hunger would not let him sleep.

It seemed darker now, the diffuse light flickering at the periphery of his vision. He became aware of a bulge under his belt. Half asleep, he fumbled with his fingers, found something. It was spongy. Food. He looked down at it but the uncertain light made it impossible to see. He took a bite, then another, chewing thoughtfully. It tasted slightly bitter. It was only when he had finished that the mist seemed to clear from his mind and he knew that he had eaten the strange man-shaped root from the apothecary's in Sha'angh'sei. An immense urn, fish swimming lazily, gossamer fins waving in the current, the feel of the curving side—Eternity. He shrugged. He felt a renewed strength already. All he needed was—

At that moment he thought he heard a distant call, like a shout of triumph, and he stood up, about to move in that direction, when he heard a more immediate sound behind him. He turned.

The mist was thicker now, the pearl gray glistening in rainbows at the edges of his vision.

He faced a shadow, distinct from those of the trees, within a line of vast ancient oaks, within the deep blue of their shade. He took a step forward, sure now that the Makkon had found him. His hand went to the hilt of his sword by force of habit. It would do him no good against the creature.

The figure stepped out from the shadows, a minute snowfall fluttering about its shoulders as a branch was disturbed by the movement of its head. Shivering, the branch turned from white to deep green.

The sound of Ronin's sword unsheathing was an unnaturally sharp rasp, its volume shattering, for he looked upon a visage so strange as to drive all thought of the Makkon from his mind.

Ronin stared at the Hart.

He was over four meters tall, with wide shoulders and long, slender arms, thick-thighed legs. He was dressed in leggings of the deepest black, a peculiar, dense shade that was difficult to focus on. He wore a mail shirt lacquered the same color, dull and unreflective. A cloak swirled out behind him to the forest's floor. He had a massive black metal belt strapped across his waist and from it hung two scabbarded swords, one so long that it almost scraped the earth, the other shorter than the traditional Sha'angh'sei weapon. Ronin stared at these for long moments, wondering why they were so familiar. He was certain that he had never seen their like before and still—

His eyes were drawn irresistibly to the head yet with a reluctance that he found confusing. He was not afraid of death but he was terrified now. There was shivering inside himself, not at all a physical thing, as if someone was plucking the cords of his nerves at the core of his being and there was a terrible laughter from somewhere within him, a chill and ghastly rending. His stomach contracted.

The immense head emerged into the uncertain illumination of the mist. Shadows fluttered behind it. It was dominated by a long muzzle with wide wet flaring nostrils and, below them, a huge mouth with large square-cut teeth. The swiveling ears were triangular, furry and, beside them, growing out from the canted forehead, were two enormous antlers, curved and treed.

The entire head was covered in deep black fur, rich

274

and glossy. His gaze moved along the pelt until he looked into the Hart's eyes. They were not round like an animal's but rather oval, the intelligent eyes of man. They were piercing, pigmented with a cold color that had no analogue on this world.

The Hart opened his lips and something screamed through Ronin's brain so that his knees buckled and he dropped his blade, falling before the creature. There was maniacal laughter and beyond that a horrified voice was screaming *Get up! Get up and slay the beast, for beast is all it is!* But his arms would not respond and his fingers were numb as they clutched the soft pine needles of the forest's floor. *Destroy him before he destroys you!* He tried to vomit but nothing would come up. His head bent to the snow, the cold like flame against his forehead as the Hart moved farther out from the cerulean shadows. His high boots crunched the snow, echoing among the trees. The wind rose steadily, howling through the maze of branches like a hateful child. Ronin felt rooted to the earth, another tree in the forest, gravity sucking at him.

One strange horny hand moving to his side, the Hart withdrew the long sword, its blade a deep black onyx, translucent, forged by ancient anvil. There was a sighing as the leaves trembled, whispering his name: *Setsoru.*

The Hart came to rest before Ronin's kneeling form and, reaching down with his free hand, he gripped the hair, pulling the head back so that he stared into Ronin's face. The immense sword was held high, flashing through the mist which curled about them. And then the Hart looked down. He stared into Ronin's colorless eyes. The animal lips pulled back in a snarl and his own eyes rolled in their sockets. The antlers shook the snow from the branches overhead.

Hatred and fear swam in his visage and the onyx blade trembled.

No! the Hart screamed. The wind howled. There was a voice in Ronin's mind; his ears heard only the gathering wind.

And in that instant of hesitation, when both figures, locked together, seemed incapable of movement or cohesive thought, there came a fierce growl and a frantic blur of lithe motion. From out of the swirling mist streaked a shape, huge jaws agape and slathering forepaws extended. Their curving talons raked at the Hart's throat. Still distracted, his face a hate-filled mask, he could do little more than throw up his free arm to ward off the unexpected attack. But the creature held on tenaciously, the jaws snapping, the claws raking at the exposed pelt again and again. The body thrashed powerfully.

The Hart's mouth opened and from it emerged a terrifying scream of rage and confusion which echoed in Ronin's mind like a crack of thunder. He gave one last swipe at the creature with the hilt of his sword and, with amazing swiftness, he bounded into the maze of pines and oak, vanishing instantly.

The attacker was still now, sitting calmly in a bed of pine needles near Ronin's prostrate form, licking quietly at its forepaws.

You have found him then.

As you knew I would. The attacker's head lifted. He was perhaps two meters long, a four-legged animal with a tough scaly hide along his muscular body and powerful legs. He had a furred head with a long wicked-looking snout filled with sharp teeth. His eyes were red and quite intelligent. His wire-thin tail whipped back and forth, rustling the needles.

Hynd, did you . . . ?

Yes. The intelligent eyes looked at Ronin. *The luma is waiting at the edge of the forest.*

Excellent. Is she still there?

Yes. She will come. Is that good?

It is what must be. The disembodied voice some-how conveyed a shrug. *The Makkon is being other-wise occupied but I do not know for how long.*

I understand.

The creature stuck his snout down and began to push at Ronin's head, directing the cool snow onto his face.

He awoke, blinking, seeing before the green and white trees or the glint of his fallen sword the friendly face of Hynd. Hynd, the cruel-visaged but wondrous companion to Bonneduce the Last, the mysterious small man whom he had encountered in the City of Ten Thousand Paths, who had made him a gift of the Makkon gauntlet.

He sat up, still half dazed. The pearled mist was re-ceding. Golden sunlight streamed down in fluttering bars through the forest's canopy. He rose and, sheath-ing his blade, allowed Hynd to lead him through the tangle of trees. The forest's floor became less rocky and softer as the ancient oaks gave gradual way to stands of willowy pine and blue spruce. Unerringly, Hynd led him to the eastern fringes of the forest. They broke through the last stand of trees, pushing aside the smaller ground foliage which formed the verge, and Ronin saw his luma, its coat glowing crimson in the light. He saw the sky, a rich blue, evening already in the east.

Beside his luma stood another, smaller, its coat sky blue. Astride this sat Moeru. He went to her, Hynd loping easily at his side. She smiled and touched his face with her small pale hand. Her long black hair whipped about her, covering one eye. Just like—

"Moeru, how did you get here?"

She looked down at him, drew in the dust coating her saddle two dots, moving, one behind: riders.

He gripped the quilting of her riding jacket.

"Why did you follow us?"

She laid a finger along his collarbone, tracing down the contours of his chest. Her clear nail scraped against the fabric.

Abruptly, he felt a wave of dizziness and he leaned his head against the cool leather of her saddle. The riders disappeared. He felt her hand on his neck, stroking. His head cleared. She wiped the dirt from his forehead, licking her fingers.

Ronin felt a pulling at his pants leg and he looked down. Hynd growled. He knelt, stroking the strange plated hide.

"It was you I heard searching for me?"

Hynd coughed softly. He swung his snout at Ronin's luma.

"Where do you take me, then?" It was a rhetorical question.

He stood up, went to his steed. He paused with one foot in the stirrup. "What of the Makkon, Hynd? I must slay it or we are all doomed."

The creature growled again, low in his throat.

"I must follow you, I know." He glanced down at Hynd. "And how did you find me, I wonder?" There was no answer.

He swung up across the saddle and gathered in the reins. The luma snorted and reared, calling, and Hynd loped up an incline heading east. Ronin pulled on the reins and his luma wheeled. He dug his heels into its flanks and took off, Moeru beside him, into the darkling east, away from the forest of bowing pines.

The land gradually fell away from them as dusk gave way to night. They galloped along a winding path, the terrain now filled with outcrops of rock against which dense scrub foliage flourished in wild abandon. Yellow blossoms studded the earth in great patches.

Abruptly, they were struggling up a steep incline and he soon realized that they were winding their way up the slopes of a mountain. The flowers disappeared as the way became increasingly precipitous. Here and there the black outline of a stately pine broke the skyline, but the farther they climbed the sparser the trees became until all flora was gone.

The night sky was filled with dense turbulent clouds with vaguely phosphorescent undersides sliding through disturbing hues. Ronin watched them pile and shape themselves as he felt the luma's powerful musculature working under him in fluid cadence and coordination.

Through the chill darkness they swept, the animals tirelessly galloping at full speed. The luma rejoiced in their kinetic flight, perhaps drawing energy from the journey itself, for it seemed to Ronin that the farther they went the stronger the mounts became. They were guided by Hynd's bounding body, calling to him or to each other.

It began to snow in cold driving bursts, the wind like a cruel knife, ripping at body and face, shoving them, moaning through the boulder-strewn mountain pass along which they continued to climb. The air became frigid and the snow turned to hail, pattering onto them, bouncing off the granite, the frozen earth, matting the luma's coats, ringing like metal off Hynd's armor plate.

Once Ronin glanced behind him. The plain from which they had ascended was still visible and he saw the spread of fat flames streaking the velvet of the night and he heard deep rumblings that were impossible to fathom. And it seemed to him that he saw the dark shadows of moving men, marching to a deep drumbeat, and the arcane structures of a full array of the machines of war, inventions to kill and maim, mutilate and cripple. It was raining fire, the continent of man shaking with the movements of war. Breath left him and, his eyes half closed, he dug his boot heels into his steed's flanks, following the lithe form of Hynd as he loped easily ahead. Then immense projecting rocks blotted out both sight and sound as they raced around a turning, adrift among the restless sleeting clouds.

His eyes flew open at the sound of a high shriek beside him. He drew up, calling to Hynd, who was already doubling back. He peered into the gloom, saw Moeru on the ground pinned beneath her luma.

He dismounted and went to her. The luma cried out and he saw that its left foreleg was broken. He bent down and carefully pulled her free; she seemed unhurt. He withdrew his blade and swiftly cut the luma's throat.

Sheathing his sword, he mounted his roan and, leaning over, drew Moeru's slim form up behind him. She wrapped her arms around him. He felt her warmth, the press of her breasts, the quickness of pulse at the back of his neck, the rhythm of her breathing.

All through the night they climbed the mountain and, as the coming sun commenced to stain the eastern horizon, they reached the summit. Ronin reined in for a moment to take in the mounting light. The mountain's eastern slopes were spread out before them, leading far below onto a plateau of geometric fields and meadows, dotted with the deep green of several forests, which descended gradually to the sea, sparking and glistening as the red sun inched over the horizon. It lacquered the sea crimson, flat and shining like burnished metal.

Then they were making their zigzag way down the mountainside and by dusk they were on the verge of the plateau. They raced across the undulating carpet of grass. There was no trace of snow here and the sky was clear, a deep blue, dark already near the eastern horizon where the sun was first to come and first to leave.

Hynd led them a winding path as the grasslands gave way to cultivated fields, sodden and deserted rice paddies on the edges of which stood ramshackle wooden houses on stilts, roofed with paper, tiny lanterns hanging from their front doors like glossy insect eyes in the gathering darkness.

Several times Hynd guided them into the shallows of the dripping paddies, the water sloshing around them until they stood perfectly still, Ronin stroking his luma's neck so that it would not call out, as distant rumblings became the urgent thunder of many horses' hoofs, scattering clods of dirt and grass as they passed in long lines.

At length the rice fields ceased and they flew past groves of trees hissing in the night. They were on dry land again, picking up speed, Hynd's instincts superb.

And now they ran with the wind, due east, the land flat with only low brush to break the monotony. Hynd bounded forward as if sensing that the end of their journey was near. The luma snorted and took off after him and Ronin, drunk with the speed and the repetitive rhythmic movement of the long ride, still not recovered from his singular encounter in the forest, held on now, allowing his mount to take him, no longer contemplating the journey's end, Moeru's cheek a gentle weight on his shoulder, no longer caring whither he went, wishing only for it to end now or for it never to end, numb, spent.

Thus, led by the strange hybrid that was part crocodile, part rodent, and something far more, riding a sweat-streaked crimson steed, with a woman he barely knew clinging to his back, he rode into the small port town of Khiyan, exhausted and bleary-eyed, half starved, his lips puffy from thirst and his face black with travel, past startled early risers, for it was just before dawn. They pounded down the slick cobbled streets, past wooden houses with slanting roofs and stone chimneys from which thin trails of smoke were already rising into the cool salt air of morning.

Gulls wheeled in the sky, skimming low off the water, crying into the sunrise. And at last Hynd led them onto the waterfront, to a tavern with a swinging wooden sign hanging above its open double doors, its black lettering too worn by wind and rain to make out. The crescent webbing of fishing nets was strung along one wall.

At the side of the door stood a short man with white hair held back from his face by a worn leather band, a grizzled beard, and deep green eyes set wide apart on his lined tanned face. He was dressed plainly in a creased leather jerkin over which was hung a chain mail vest. He wore brown leggings and low boots of a soft leather. He came away from the door to greet them when they drew up. He had a discernible limp when he walked.

"Ah, Ronin," said Bonneduce the Last. "How good it is to see you again."

"The continent of man is under siege from all sides now."

"But Kamado is the main thrust."

"Yes. I believe that the Kai-feng will be won or lost there."

"I have heard that word before—"

"It is the last battle of mankind."

"But the key is the Makkon. To destroy one is to stop The Dolman from appearing on the world." He gulped down a piece of meat, poured more wine for

Moeru. "Why then did you have Hynd take me away from it?"

"Because," Bonneduce the Last said slowly, "you cannot yet defeat the Makkon. If it had got to you in the forest, it would surely have destroyed you."

"How do you know?"

"How did I know that it would slay G'fand in the City of Ten Thousand Paths? The Bones."

"You knew, yet you let us go?"

"You would not have let me stop you."

They sat in the dim interior of the tavern, near the front windows and the open doors which faced the wide wharves of Khiyan. Tall ships with square-rigged sails as white as snow lay at anchor, their fittings creaking. Longboats laden with men and stores made their way across the short expanse of water from dockside to the lee of the ships. Two fishermen passed by the doorway, began to take down the nets from the side of the tavern. There was laughter. The owner of the tavern went out from behind his bar and stood talking to the fishermen.

Within the tavern, the stone hearth along one wall was spitting flames upward into the lower reaches of the blackened chimney but it was still too early for the place to have become smoky. The wood rafters were dark with an accumulation of charcoal and cooking fat.

Bonneduce the Last had granted Ronin three hours of sleep in a small room on the second floor with leaded windows overlooking the docks and a high goose-down bed onto which he fell without a sound and not even the harsh cries of the sailors along the short embankment outside disturbed his slumber. The little man had shown Moeru to the adjoining room. She was up before Ronin, gently shaking his shoulder to wake him when she heard Bonneduce the Last's limping step on the stairway.

"Where are they?" Ronin asked suddenly.

Bonneduce the Last reached into his leather jerkin with a thin smile and produced the seven geometric shapes, carved, so the little man had told him, of the teeth of the legendary giant crocodile. Strange glyphs were etched into every face. The Bones.

"What do they tell you?"

"The Kai-feng has commenced, Ronin. All are now committed to playing out their parts in the last struggle. Even Hynd and I."

"Even?"

The little man's face darkened. "By this battle will mankind stand or fall. A new age is dawning, Ronin, and no one can say what it will bring."

"Not even the Bones." It was not a question.

"No man, no being, may know the balance of power now." Hynd stirred at his feet. His forepaws twitched. Ronin glaced down at him. Perhaps he dreamed, as Ronin had, of grasslands flying by under his feet, racing with the Hart, transmogrified, his great treed antlers now a gleaming helm. "Thus, with all the glistening lines to the future severed, are the blind forces arrayed. Thus is the struggle for power made complex, thus is the winning worth the suffering: thus"—he reached down and stroked Hynd's plated back—"I know no more of this battle's ending than do you."

Thoughts of the Kai-feng and the Hart, inexplicably intertwined, filled Ronin's mind. Then he put these questions aside, raised his gauntleted fist.

"I have cause to thank you. Your gift has aided me often."

Bonneduce the Last smiled. "I am pleased then."

From somewhere, Ronin thought he heard a sonorous ticking like that he had heard in the little man's house in the City of Ten Thousand Paths. He poured more wine.

"You must tell me how Hynd found me."

"Yes, of course. I thought you knew. It was the root."

"You mean eating it?"

Bonneduce the Last nodded. "Once you had possession of it, it was only a matter of time before you ate it—"

"But how could you know—"

"Circumstances." He rubbed at his short leg. "In any event, our connection is now stronger and that is important—"

"But—"

"You did not question the Makkon gauntlet," Bonneduce the Last said carefully. "Do not question this. It was the penultimate step in the ending of the Old Cycle." He held up a hand as Ronin was about to voice another query. "There is no time now. Three of the Makkon are already come to the continent of man and the fourth is very near."

"What of the scroll?"

"I was just about to tell you," the little man said sharply. "You must sail," he said, "for Ama-no-mori."

There was silence for a time. Across the room the flames licked along the huge logs in the hearth and, with a soft crash, the bottom one split, eaten through. Sparks sailed upward. Outside, along the docks, the calls and songs of the sailors outfitting their ships for their sea runs seemed dim and remote. The sunlight streamed down in molten bars, warm as honey, far away.

Ronin stared at the seamed face.

"You know where the isle lies?"

The little man nodded. "I have plotted your course. The knowledge you seek, the knowledge which mankind needs, no longer exists on the continent of man."

"The Bujun—" said Ronin.

"Yes."

The air was warm and gentle as the air of summer should be. The aged sun seemed to burn stronger here. Yet it was not possible to forget the strife destroying the continent of man beyond the blue hazy slopes of the mountain in the west.

Ronin's face was grim as he strode along the foreshore and out onto the docks. Bonneduce the Last and Hynd loped along. He held Moeru by the hand.

The little man pointed and, shading his eyes from the sun, Ronin followed his hand outward and saw the two-masted vessel lying off the shore. Its square sails were unfurling and men climbed its rigging, preparing to weigh anchor.

"The *Kioku*," said Bonneduce the Last. "Your ship."

"Mine?" Ronin stared.

"You are its captain. The crew is already picked and on board." He put his hand on Ronin's shoulder. "You sail on the tide. Now."

Along the quay, a longboat had heaved to and its crew waited patiently as it rocked in the gentle swells. Ronin let go of Moeru's hand.

"Take care of her."

But Bonneduce the Last shook his head.

"She sails with you, Ronin."

He looked from the little man to the woman beside him. Perhaps it was the light, but he thought that her eyes were different, not at all like the eyes of the people of Sha'angh'sei. Within them, some far-off, storm-tossed sea.

"Yes. Perhaps it is better this way."

Bonneduce the Last glanced out to sea.

"It is the only way."

They climbed down to the longboat and sat in the midship seats, facing the bow.

"I wish you could come," Ronin called out.

The little man's hand scratched at the fur along Hynd's neck.

"We have much to do and other places to go. I trust your journey will be successful."

"Will I see you again?" Ronin called. But the long-boat had already pulled away from the dock and the wind swept the little man's reply away into the dazzling sunlight. And they moved out from the shores of the continent of man.

The *Kioku* weighed anchor as soon as the longboat had delivered up its passengers and had been hoisted aboard. The white sails billowing in the freshening wind, the ship headed into the morning sun.

Ronin stood on the high poop deck at *Kioku's* stern watching the creaming water wash along the sleek flanks of his ship as it headed out into the deep, toward Ama-no-mori, toward an uncertain and enigmatic future. *Thus, with all the glistening lines to the future severed, are the blind forces arrayed.* Even the Bones useless now. Moeru stood by his side as the last gulls wheeled about the masts of the ship before sheering off and returning landward.

And so entranced was he by the enormous vista of the swelling open seas, by the anticipation of at last seeing the mysterious fabled isle of Ama-no-mori, the end to his long and arduous journey, that he failed to recognize or even notice the visage of his first mate, now hideously disfigured and scarred about his twisted mouth, which had no lips, no jaw. Had he taken more care he would have seen within that bizarre mask of pale white flesh the writhing of controlled loathing burning like cold flames in the black eyes so well known to him. But his mind, filled with new and arcane visions, was very far indeed from the unguided ship arcing away from him on the vast uncharted ice

sea so long ago; far from the Saardin he thou
who now stared balefully up at him from the
gleaming foredeck, contemplating his terrible
nizing revenge.